"You will not use this as an excuse to take this land. Your quarrel is with me and me alone."

Ivar's insolent gaze raked her form, burning through Thyre's clothes. Against her will, the memory of what it was like to lie wrapped in his arms welled up inside her. Angrily she damped it down, but not before a knowing gleam appeared in his eyes.

"I did not hear you complaining last night. What passed between us was your suggestion."

"That was different. It ended this morning."

"We are far from finished, you and I."

The back of her neck prickled a warning. She took a half step backward, but his hand shot out, clamping around her waist and pulling her forward. His thigh hit her hip. Ruthlessly he lowered his mouth. His tongue delicately traced the outline of her mouth. Her hands came up and buried themselves in his hair, wanting the warmth to continue.

Abruptly he let her go and ran a finger down the side of her face and neck....

"Mine."

The Viking
Harlequin® Historical

Author Note

This is my third story about the jaarls who raided Lindisfarne and what happened to them afterward. It is a linked book, rather than a continuation of the story. All you need to know is that the book is set at the beginning of the Viking era and the hero is a Viking warrior. The countries or areas of Ranrike and Viken did exist, but the exact nature of their relationship is lost to the mists of time. Because a number of you have written wanting to know, several characters from previous books do make appearances, and it was great fun to be able to revisit the world I created in the other two books. Hopefully you will enjoy reading about Thyre and Ivar.

I am very excited that *The Viking's Captive Princess* is appearing during Harlequin's sixtieth anniversary year. Over the years Harlequin books have been there for me in times of trouble or when I simply needed to escape from the pressures of everyday life. In fact, one of the reasons I started writing romance was because I wanted to write books that offered a ray of sunshine and a chance to escape—just like the Harlequin novels I have read ever since I was a preteen. Long may Harlequin's tradition of offering excellence in romance fiction continue!

As ever, I love getting reader letters either via post to Harlequin Books, my Web site, www.michellestyles.co.uk, or my blog, www.michellestyles.blogspot.com.

THE
VIKING'S
CAPTIVE PRINCESS

MICHELLE STYLES

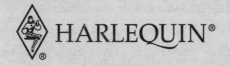

HARLEQUIN®

TORONTO • NEW YORK • LONDON
AMSTERDAM • PARIS • SYDNEY • HAMBURG
STOCKHOLM • ATHENS • TOKYO • MILAN • MADRID
PRAGUE • WARSAW • BUDAPEST • AUCKLAND

Recycling programs
for this product may
not exist in your area.

ISBN-13: 978-0-373-29574-6

THE VIKING'S CAPTIVE PRINCESS

Copyright © 2009 by Michelle Styles.

www.eHarlequin.com

Printed in U.S.A.

Praise for Michelle Styles

VIKING WARRIOR, UNWILLING WIFE

"A family in conflict, an ambitious hero bent on vengeance and a bold woman hiding a secret quest for salvation combine for a heady, tension-filled, passionate sequel to *Taken by the Viking*."
—*RT Book Reviews*

TAKEN BY THE VIKING

"Styles' descriptive writing and jump-off-the-pages characters shine in this awesome story."
—*RT Book Reviews*

Chapter One

'Thor's Hammer, Uncle Ivar, you were right! They are waiting for us. Sitting there. Bold as you like!'

Ivar Gunnarson, jaarl of Viken, glanced towards where his nephew pointed. In the shadow of a rocky island Ranriken dragon boats lurked. Ivar tightened his grip on the steering oar, moving the oar fractionally to the right, and the *Sea Witch* responded instantly to his command.

'The Ranrike honour us. Five boats against a single boat. It will make for an interesting race.'

All movement had stopped on the boat and the men had turned towards Ivar, their expressions a mixture of fear mingled with anticipation as their calloused hands lightly rested on the oars. Ivar knew he would prove worthy of their trust. He would see them safely home. Ivar put his trust in things—the strength of his sword arm, the tautness of his sail, the trueness of his aim—rather than the mumblings of priests or the wearing of amulets. Deeds, not words.

'But, Uncle Ivar,' Asger said, 'why are they waiting for

us now? Why didn't they attack us when we were going out to Birka?'

'They were no danger to us on the way out to Birka, young Asger. Listen to your uncle,' Erik the Black shouted from where he sat. 'The Ranriken king wanted us to do the hard work. He desires the spices and silks we are bringing home to Viken, but fears the open sea. Your uncle predicted this for months before the voyage began. Despite all those who proclaimed a supernatural cause for our boats not returning, your uncle said there was another cause. Trust him. He knows the sea and its ways.'

Other oarsmen echoed Erik's words and Asger's worried frown disappeared.

'And now the race with the Ranrike begins.' Ivar adjusted his grip on the handle of the steering oar as he considered the silks, amber and other precious cargo that filled his hold. More than a king's ransom if he could make it to the markets of Kaupang. 'Here is where you learn what it is to be a true Viken warrior and a member of the *felag*, Asger.'

'How can we hope to succeed against the boats and the storm?' Asger wiped his hand across his mouth, his face becoming pinched as he glanced towards the clouds skittering across the sky.

'We go forward, outrun them. The *Sea Witch* is the fastest of the Viken ships under sail. She will do anything I ask her.'

'Anything? Even with those storm crows hanging in the air?' Asger asked, pointing to the gigantic flock of black-winged birds beginning to circle the boat. 'You know what they say about them and this passage. The crows are Ran's messengers, telling her where to cast her net for men's souls, Uncle Ivar.'

'Crows are birds. They enjoy the wind. It gives them a chance to spread their wings,' Ivar said.

'Oh, I had not thought about them enjoying the wind.'

Ivar concentrated on the waves hitting the boat. Some day when the time for voyages had ended and he could again think about getting a wife, he would like to have a child like Asger. In time, the lad would make an able warrior.

The wind stirred the sea into a froth of white-capped waves and the sound of the crows screamed in his ears. Ivar kept his hand steady on the steering oar. The *Sea Witch* could hold her own in any contest with the weather. The keel and the rigging had been made to his design; if they held throughout the voyage to Northumbria two years ago, they would hold now.

'Erik the Black, did you put new rope on the right rigging?'

The seafarer looked up from where he sat at his oar and scratched the side of his nose. 'I did. Exactly how you instructed, Ivar.'

'The Ranrike expect us to make for the nearest inlet. Once there, all they have to do is wait and lurk, putting the stopper in the jug and stealing all our hard-won cargo.' Ivar paused, allowing the men to absorb his words. Then he raised his fist. 'I refuse to have that happen. We will outrun this storm and their boats. We will make it back to Kaupang.'

'Put the sails to the test!' the crew cried.

'You read my mind.' Ivar leant forwards as the wind whipped his dark blonde hair. With impatient fingers, he pushed it back from his face. 'Erik the Black has said he followed my instructions. The rigging will hold. We raise the sail on my command.'

'Viken! Viken!'

The Ranrike began their move, gliding forwards. The shouts of the oarsmen echoed across the strait. Within a few breaths, the only avenue of escape would close, but the timing had to be precise. The Ranrike could not be allowed a chance to regroup.

'The mast creaks in the wind, Ivar!' Erik the Black shouted. 'We need to lower the sail soon or risk breaking it.'

'Keep those ropes taut!' Ivar eyed the storm clouds in the sky as the *Sea Witch* strained against his steering oar, ready to fly over the waves to safety. 'And I want double-quick time when the sail comes down.'

'At your command.'

The entire crew's eyes were on him, hands poised on oars, trusting him and his judgement. He held up his hand, waiting as the water slapped against the side of the boat, enjoying the heady feeling of pitting his wits against the world. The storm crows wheeled around the ship one more time. 'Now!'

The chequered red-and-white sail unfurled, hung for a heartbeat flapping in the wind as the men struggled with the ropes. The shouts from the other boats drowned out the cawing of the crows. Ivar saw the swords glinting, held aloft, poised to strike. One Ranriken boat began to lower its boarding plank, anticipating the moment. Ivar reached forwards, grabbed the end of the rope and tightened it with a few expert twists.

The sail filled and strained against the ropes. The *Sea Witch* picked up speed, sliding between the two lead Ranrike boats close enough for Ivar to see the astonished expression on the men's faces as their prey escaped. Ivar saluted the chief Ranrike jaarl, Sigmund Sigmundson, a man who bowed and scraped when they had appeared before King Mysing, the Ranriken king on their way to Birka. Men, not curses, guarded these straits. And men could be defeated.

Ivar turned his face into the wind. All he had to do was

steer the boat towards Kaupang and Viken. The coming storm would test him and the men, but they would succeed because of the strength of the keel, the sturdiness of the sail and, above all, the skill with which he navigated.

'Ivar,' Erik the Black shouted, 'one of the Ranrike boats. It is giving chase.'

A wave washed over the prow of the boat, soaking him and his men to the skin. 'The fun truly begins!' Ivar called. 'May the best boat win!'

Thyre, Sainsfrida's daughter, picked her way amongst the sticks and boards that littered the shore of the hidden Ranriken bay, which was exactly halfway between the Ranriken capital city of Ranhiem and the Viken city of Kaupang.

She lifted the skirt of her apron dress so that it remained free of the seaweed and watery pools. The devastation from last night's storm was far greater than she had first thought.

'At least one ship perished in the storm, Dagmar, maybe more. This wood came from somewhere.'

'Do you think so? I thought the gods just made it appear,' her half-sister said, her pretty face frowning. She stood just beyond the high-tide mark, keeping her elaborately pleated apron dress pristine. 'I wish my Sven was here. He would use the wood to build us a proper house. And he would know exactly which ship they had come from as well. He is like that, Sven. Useful. Knowledgeable. My father should have valued his opinion more and then Sven might have stayed, instead of going off to the high pastures to see about felling the king's trees.'

Thyre carefully composed her features. Dagmar had been infatuated with Sven ever since she had first laid eyes on him earlier this summer. The bold forester had captured her half-sister's heart with his ready wit, dancing eyes and dazzling smile, despite his lack of money and status. For once, Dagmar had ignored Thyre's hints and warnings about how a jaarl's daughter would never be allowed to marry a forester and had kept on finding excuses to meet him. But Thyre knew her stepfather, Ragnfast the Steadfast, had plans for his only child, plans that did not include marrying her off to a man who had few prospects beyond caring for the king's trees.

'Your father might think differently. After all, the ships have washed up on *his* land.'

'Far will give my Sven the lumber, once Sven asks for my hand in marriage.' Dagmar shook her ash-blonde locks, which were a complete contrast to Thyre's own black-as-night hair. Her daytime and night-time daughters, their mother used to say. 'He will have to. A married woman needs her own hall. And it makes perfect sense to use this wood.'

Thyre raised an eyebrow. She could think of a dozen better uses for the wood than saving it for some dream hall. 'Sven might wish to choose his own wood. There is a certain something about felling trees of your choosing to make a hall.'

'Hmm, perhaps you are right...' Dagmar tapped her finger against her overly generous mouth. 'Far will keep it for his own use. He never listens to Sven's ideas about how the farm could be improved.'

Thyre made a show of brushing sand from the piece of wood. She had already heard several of Sven's ideas for improvement and had thought little of them. Thankfully, just as Ragnfast had heeded her mother's counsel until her mother's death eight years ago, Ragnfast always consulted her and followed her advice. And the estate prospered.

'I know what your father is like.' Thyre gave a laugh. 'He will think the timber a gift from the gods. The lower barn has a gaping hole in its roof. It needs to be fixed before the cows come back from pasture. Your father made the appropriate sacrifice for this only last week and will not want to go against the gods' generous response.'

'Do you know where the ships have come from?' Dagmar asked, prodding a piece of timber with a delicate foot. 'Is it one of ours…a Ranrike? You know I can't read runes. The scratching jumps about so and never seems to mean the same thing.'

'If you would pay attention, Dagmar, you could learn. I did. Mother tried to teach you before she died, and I have offered to continue her teaching.'

Dagmar batted her lashes. 'I would rather be spinning or weaving. There is something so satisfying about creating cloth.'

'But the daughter of a princess should know how to read runes.' Thyre pointed to the markings on the board. Some day, she would win the argument and Dagmar would learn to read. 'See, this bit says Ran and the other bit says hammer. You can do it if you try.'

Dagmar shook her head. 'It is all far too boring and the runes jump about so. Besides, I will have my older sister to read the runes for me. You will always be here on the steading. I do not know how Far would manage without you and your advice.'

'Yes, you are right. I have no plans to go anywhere.' Thyre gave a tight smile. Dagmar might have dreams of marrying her Sven, but Thyre also had dreams of her own. Some day she hoped to meet a man worthy of her love— one who would respect her counsel as well as love her, one who would want her for herself rather than anything she could bring to the marriage. 'If you ever change your mind, I will be happy to teach you.'

Sometimes Thyre walked out to the headland and looked out at the strait, wondering what lay beyond. It was not as if she hated her life here, but she did wonder what else there might be. Ragnfast and her mother had promised to take her to the Ranrike capital when she was grown. But her mother had died during the winter of her eighth year and Ragnfast had been loathe to leave the farm unattended.

'Who does the ship belong to, Thyre? You must know from the runes.'

Thyre forced her mind back from the horizon and concentrated.

'It is one of ours, a Ranriken, but it has not been in the water long. The etchings are too fresh. The shipwreck must have happened last night during the storm.' Thyre tapped a finger against her lips as a thousand unanswered questions crowded into her brain. Why had the ship been out on the strait? It was most likely one of Sigmund Sigmundson's. The jaarl had promised to protect the seas from marauding Viken intent on plundering Ranrike. Had they perished, keeping this bay safe? 'We need to inform Ragnfast immediately.'

Dagmar nodded, accepting Thyre's verdict. 'That is unusual. Normally our ships are all safely at harbour when the storm breaks. The Ranrike understand the enormity of Ran's wrath. How very foolish of the captain. If my Sven had been there, he would have told the captain to stay in his bay.'

'It happens.' Thyre put the board down. 'Ran will have had her net out and will have collected the drowned men.'

'Drowned men? Dead men!' Dagmar screwed her face up and Thyre winced. 'I had not thought of the dead.'

'I had, and somewhere wives and children will be waiting.'

'We should go back and tell Far now. He will want to gather the wood and dispose of the bodies.' Dagmar's nose wrinkled and she lifted the hem of her skirt, carefully stepping around the piles of seaweed and smashed boards. 'It is a pity there is no cargo. I could have done with a new dress.'

'Always the practical one, Dagmar.' Thyre shook her head in dismay. Dagmar never seemed to consider the future beyond its impact on her, whereas Thyre found herself always asking questions and pondering the reasons why a thing happened.

Dagmar clutched Thyre's arm, preventing her from going further along the shore. 'There is a ship on the horizon. Is it one of ours?'

Thyre shielded her eyes against the glare of the sun, impatiently pushing a lock of crow's wing black hair back from her eyes. She should know the answer without even seeing the ship's prow. 'The sail is unusual. Chequered, red and white. Viken, not Ranriken.'

'How many are there? Is it a raid?' Dagmar's voice dropped to a soft whisper as if she feared the unknown boat might hear them. 'Do we light the beacon?'

'Not yet, Dagmar. Let Ragnfast be the one to make that decision.' Silently, Thyre vowed to help him make the right choice.

'I'm frightened, Thyre.'

Thyre patted Dagmar's arm. Both of them knew the tales of the Viken raids. The most recent had been the daring raid on the fabulously wealthy monastery in the British Isles. The men who had participated were now fêted as heroes in the north countries, but they were also feared. Who knew where their ambition lay? Before her marriage to Ragnfast, their mother had been a hostage of the Viken king. Thyre had been the result of her mother's time in Kaupang and the reason for her mother's subsequent banishment to this far-flung estate.

'There is only one boat that I can see but there are still things that need to be hidden, even if the Viken are only here for a short time.'

'But the Viken rarely come here. This inlet is not on any trading route.' Colour drained from Dagmar's face. 'They can't wish to…'

Thyre grabbed her half-sister's shoulders and gave her a slight shake. Now was not the time for self-indulgent panic. 'Dagmar, you must pay attention. It is important. We have no idea of the ship's intentions, but we have to assume they will be seeking to raid. If we act properly, we may only lose a few sheep or pigs.'

'You always know what to do, Thyre.' Dagmar gulped air. 'It is good to be prepared.'

Thyre's mind raced. She knew every detail of the plans to survive a raid—where the gold would be hidden, and the grain, where the women would go and hide. The plans had been in place since before her mother died of a fever. A cool head and an even manner solved more problems than a quick temper. Thyre shook her head slightly. The Viken would not find them an easy target, not while she had breath in her body.

'My mind is a blank. What do I do next?' Dagmar's eyes were wide. 'I just wish Sven was here. He knows all about interpreting omens and what they mean.'

Thyre made a non-committal noise. The other night, the full moon had risen blood red, a potent portent of change and destruction for the Ranrike royal house. According to Ragnfast, the last time such a thing had happened, her mother had died. This time he had immediately ordered several sacrifices so that the farm could remain unharmed, but it appeared the gods were deaf. The Viken had arrived.

'Will you tell my father without me?' Dagmar put her hands under her apron. 'You know how he hates bad news. He will take it better from you. You will give him good counsel. I swear I do not know how you keep everything straight, but you do.'

Thyre drew in a deep breath. 'You need not worry, Dagmar, I will inform Ragnfast. He always listens to me in these matters.'

The anxious frown between Dagmar's two perfect eyebrows eased. 'You are good to me, Thyre. I don't know what I would do without you. You are always there to ease my fears.'

'You are my baby sister.' Thyre held out her hand, curling her long fingers around Dagmar's slender ones. Dagmar's hand tightened and she gave a trembling nod. A great fondness for Dagmar welled up inside Thyre. After their mother died, Ragnfast had raged for weeks on end. Thyre had feared for her safety, and she and Dagmar had clung to each other. They might not share as many secrets now, but Dagmar was Thyre's one true friend and her only beloved sister. 'Remember when we swore the blood oath?'

'You are right.' Dagmar's face cleared and she gave a brilliant smile. 'We spilled our blood together after Mor died. I had forgotten that we were once determined to be warriors.'

'But I remembered.'

'We greet the Viken with the respect any man should show his neighbour,' Ragnfast pronounced, using the words Thyre had agreed with him. The household stood on the shoreline waiting, watching the dragon boat draw slowly closer.

The shields still hung on the side of the Viken dragon boat, indicating that its occupants travelled in peace, for the moment. Peace was a fragile thing where Viken warriors were concerned. The tales the jaarl Sigmund Sigmundson had told about Viken treachery the last time he had visited made her blood run cold.

'The rules of hospitality are very clear in the north and we shall keep them, as we have always done.'

Thyre heaved a sigh of relief.

After his initial explosion of incredulity, Ragnfast had agreed to her plans. Now, all the gold and silver and the furs were hidden; the tapestries had been taken down and stored. The majority of the livestock remained on the summer pasture, so it was possible that the Viken would think theirs was a poor farm, rather than a prosperous estate. Thyre remembered the ruse working once before, when she was a little girl and Dagmar was little more than a babe in arms. Then the Viken had come and her mother had dealt with them, sending Dagmar and Thyre to the hiding place in the woods.

'But King Mysing decreed all Viken ships are fair plunder…or so the jaarl Sigmund proclaimed the last time he was here,' cried a voice at the back. 'What have the Viken ever done for us except burn our lands and take our wives?'

Thyre kept her back resolutely straight. She did not need to see Ragnfast's face to know how he'd react. He disliked the young jaarl and his ideas about how to solve the problem of the Viken plundering their coastline. He had rejected her first suggestion of lighting the bonfire to alert Sigmund to their potential danger.

'Sigmund and his cronies may have broken *frithe* with

the Viken King Thorkell, but *I* haven't,' Ragnfast thundered. 'I remember the days, the days of our old king, King Mysing's father, when Ranrike prospered and the markets overflowed with goods. Ships sailed to Ranhiem rather than to Birka or Kaupang. Now it is all bloodshed and plunder. My taste for bloodshed vanished a lifetime ago.'

'Dagmar, are the horns of drink filled properly?' Thyre asked, seeking to draw Ragnfast back to the present difficulty. Dagmar held up her horn of ale. Thyre was pleased that Ragnfast had agreed to her suggestion of ale rather than mead. It was only one ship, not a fleet. The Viken would understand. He was likely not high enough status to warrant a better drink. And this way he would think them a poor homestead rather than a prosperous estate. 'The other women and I can follow Dagmar after the Viken captain has the first drink.'

'It is a good idea, Thyre,' Ragnfast said. 'We do not have the men to provoke him. A soft word and a timely fluttered eyelash can do much, as your mother used to say.'

'Thyre, that is your second-best apron dress,' Dagmar whispered. 'And your face is far too solemn. What is there to worry about? Greeting warriors is supposed to be a happy occasion. We should honour them.'

'I have had more than enough swaggering boasts from Sigmund's warriors. I wonder if the Viken will be any different? All brawn and very little brain is my educated guess.' Thyre pasted her smile firmly in place. She remembered her mother's stories of her time as a hostage in the Viken court, about how fights broke out at the least provocation.

What excuse would the Viken use to destroy this farm? And what would they say if they knew who her natural father was, that her mother had disobeyed the time-honoured custom of children conceived in this way? She had not sent her newborn daughter to be killed by the Viken king and had instead prevailed on Ragnfast to accept her as a true Ranrike woman and member of his family.

'Thyre, I think I forgot to put the weaving frame away.' Dagmar's voice broke through her reverie. 'Do you think I should go back? That bit of cloth is nearly done and I was particularly proud of the raven pattern.'

'I already put it away.' Thyre struggled to keep the doors of her imagination closed. 'With so many warriors, it would have been in the way. You know how clumsy they are with their feet.'

'You are a love. You always know just what to do.' Dagmar patted Thyre's arm. 'Think positively. Who knows—you may find a mate amongst the Viken? They are supposed to be wealthy.'

Mate, not husband. The words were unmistakeable and ill-chosen. Thyre made her face into a bland mask. She was well aware of her limited options without Dagmar's thoughtless reminder. It was unlikely that any warrior would make an offer for her. She had no family, no land, nothing to make a true warrior desire her for a wife.

She gave a wry smile. Ragnfast had held true to his promise to her mother and let her manage the estate, but she also knew he would not provide a dowry. She refused to be just anyone's concubine. Royal blood ran in her veins. She deserved better. Her mother would have approved of her decision to stay unwed rather than to marry beneath her. In her dreams, Thyre longed to find the one man who would cherish her in the way her mother had been cherished by Ragnfast. Some day, she wanted to meet a man with whom she could exchange loving glances in the way Ragnfast and her mother had exchanged glances.

In the end her mother had discovered love with a man who treated her as an equal, rather than as an accessory, a pawn, or a stepping stone to the throne of Ranrike. In order to marry her mother, Ragnfast had taken an oath of loyalty to King Mysing, vowing never to claim the throne in his wife's name, or to permit any of his children to make a claim.

'I am not looking for anyone. I love it here. It is safe and secure. And if I did, he would have to be more intelligent than those Viken warriors. Can you see the biceps rippling on the leader? Definitely more brawn than brain.'

Dagmar put her hand on Thyre's sleeve and whispered in her ear. 'Love can just happen, as it did between Sven and me. One day, I glanced up and there he was, all silhouetted in gold, his cloak slightly drawn back, and I knew that he was the right man for me.'

'I am not you, Dagmar—in love one day and the next out of it.'

'You mean the warrior from Gotaland last summer who wanted to buy Far's lumber and thought to get a better price by seducing his daughter? That was nothing. A pure girlish fantasy. I have quite forgotten why I shed all those tears.' Dagmar sighed dramatically. 'I have sworn to be true to Sven. I want him to know that should I bear a child, it will be his.'

A warning twinge went through Thyre. Child? That was fantasy. They knew that Dagmar's monthly flow had come since Sven had left. Dagmar was given to dramatic statements, but there was something in her eyes. Exactly what had Dagmar sworn to Sven? Dagmar should know that she had no right to swear anything without her father's consent. It could only lead to heartache. Silently Thyre cursed Sven for being so selfish, and for Dagmar's fear in telling her father.

Once the Viken had departed, she would discover more about this oath. Unless it was made with Ragnfast's consent, it was empty words.

'The dragon boat has landed! The Viken have arrived!' The cry echoed up and down the beach.

Thyre pressed her lips together. Dagmar appeared normal enough, smoothing her skirt and biting her lips to make them appear ripe cherry red—all the actions she normally took. Thyre hoped her concerns about Dagmar were just wisps of doubt. Perhaps another warrior would capture her fancy, and her oath to Sven would become a distant and unwelcome memory.

Up close, the Viken dragon boat showed signs of battering from the storm—a broken oar, a battered prow and loose ropes—but nothing major. Not like the poor Ranriken ship whose remains were still scattered over the shore. Had it been hunting this Viken one? And if so, what had this Viken ship done? Which other farms had they attacked? Thyre shifted uneasily, weighing the possibilities, but knowing they had no choice but to offer hospitality.

The Viken warriors splashed ashore. The leader disembarked first, without a helmet or a shield. A gesture of peace, but also of arrogance, Thyre thought. He could have no idea of Ragnfast's strength, or the defences of the farm.

The Viken's golden-brown hair shone in the sunlight and, despite the jagged scar running down his right cheek, his face held a certain grace combined with raw power. He looked like a man unafraid to face the future.

His vivid blue gaze lingered on her for a heartbeat, tracing her form. She looked directly back at his face, rather than blushing and looking away as custom demanded. He gave a nod, and turned towards where Ragnfast stood, as if that brief instant had never been.

'We are grateful for the warm welcome after the rough seas of last night.' The warrior made an elaborate bow. Ragnfast's face reddened slightly and his chest puffed out at the courtesy. 'We are returning to Kaupang after a successful voyage to the markets of Birka. Last night's storm caused some damage to my trading vessel. It must be repaired before I continue on.' His steady gaze met Ragnfast's, and his words sounded more like a thinly disguised command than a polite request. He held out a stick covered in thick runes. 'We come in peace.'

'We have no quarrel with the Viken, nor do I seek reassurance from your king.' Ragnfast barely glanced at the stick before he handed it back. Thyre bit her lip and wished she dared grab it. She highly doubted the truth of the warrior's words. If they were peaceful, why had the Ranriken ship been wrecked? Sigmund had promised that Ranriken ships only defended. They never attacked the more skilful Viken ships.

'What is your name, Viken?' Thyre asked, making sure her voice was firm and clear.

'Ivar Gunnarson, jaarl of Viken, my lady.'

Thyre froze as the murmur rose behind her. Ivar Gunnarson. Ivar the scarred. Even here in the back waters of Ranrike, they had heard of him and his fellow Viken jaarls who had braved sea serpents to cross the Atlantic and had returned with a vast treasure from Lindisfarne. They were said to be some of the luckiest men alive, basking in Odin and Thor's favour, Ivar particularly. It was his prowess with the sail and ships that enabled the Viken to cross the sea. And he had fought the Ranrike before, killing Sigmund's brother. Now he was here, formidable and capable of wrecking the same destruction on her home as he and his companions had on Lindisfarne.

She stifled a gasp as Dagmar began to trip forwards, holding out her horn of ale. Her earlier plan to serve ale to show they were not a prosperous farm had been shoddy and wrong. She should have thought about the pitfalls and how easily a jaarl could take offence.

Sour ale was unlikely to bring about anything but war. It would give them the pretext for burning the farm to the ground. She had to act before the jaarl tasted it, realised the intended insult and destroyed them all.

Thyre raised her hand, signalling the danger to Dagmar, but Dagmar was oblivious to the potential disaster. Her smile became more flirtatious as she held out the horn to the Viken jaarl. Thyre forgot to breathe. Dagmar hadn't seen her warning.

Ivar Gunnarson took the horn from Dagmar's grasp and slowly lifted it to his lips.

Chapter Two

Thyre covered her mouth with her hand, unable to do anything but watch in horror.

Everything froze and time slowed.

Thyre wanted to run forwards, but her feet appeared rooted to the spot. A thousand images of burning and destruction rushed through her brain. And the worst was that she knew this mess was her fault. Would he draw his sword? She had to do something. There had to be a way of preventing bloodshed. But her mind refused to work, refused to find the necessary answer.

Just as the horn touched the Viken jaarl's lips, Ragnfast reached out and joggled the Viken's elbow, sending the contents spilling over the ground and the jaarl's leather boots.

'Clumsy woman,' Ragnfast swore, breaking the spell. 'She should take greater care.'

Thyre's lungs worked again. Ragnfast had realised the danger and had averted it. They might still be saved if everyone kept their head. She darted forwards and whispered in Dagmar's ear as Ragnfast began to call upon the gods to forgive this clumsy woman and her unintended insult. At Thyre's words, Dagmar stopped her furious exclamation and her mouth formed an O.

Thyre gave Dagmar's shoulder a pat. Her heart stopped racing. The jaarl appeared to accept the incident was an accident, but she would have to speak to Ragnfast about the enthusiasm of his denunciation.

'My daughter will be suitably punished,' Ragnfast said after he had finished calling on the entire legion of gods and goddesses to witness his shame.

'Woe is me, what shall I do?' Dagmar intoned, getting into the spirit of the thing.

'Her beauty more than makes up for any clumsiness.' The jaarl inclined his head, but his hand remained poised over his sword's hilt.

Thyre fought against the urge to roll her eyes. Dagmar's golden loveliness captivated every man she encountered. The gods had truly blessed Dagmar at her birth.

She glanced up and the jaarl's vivid blue gaze caught hers again. His lips curved upwards in an intimate smile as if he knew who was responsible for the mishap. Thyre blinked and the look vanished.

'Quickly now, daughter, go get some more *mead*,' Ragnfast said. 'Don't keep the jaarl waiting.'

'Mead?' Dagmar squeaked. 'But I thought—'

'I will get it, Ragnfast. I know where it has been put,' Thyre said firmly. 'The barrels were moved when I supervised the spring cleaning. I would not want to inadvertently give offence to the jaarl.'

Dagmar demurely lowered her lashes. 'Thyre knows where everything is and I get muddled so easily.'

'Very well, Thyre, but go quickly. The Viken need their proper refreshment.' Ragnfast waved his hand.

Thyre walked away from the Viken group, her stomach

Chapter Two

Thyre covered her mouth with her hand, unable to do anything but watch in horror.

Everything froze and time slowed.

Thyre wanted to run forwards, but her feet appeared rooted to the spot. A thousand images of burning and destruction rushed through her brain. And the worst was that she knew this mess was her fault. Would he draw his sword? She had to do something. There had to be a way of preventing bloodshed. But her mind refused to work, refused to find the necessary answer.

Just as the horn touched the Viken jaarl's lips, Ragnfast reached out and joggled the Viken's elbow, sending the contents spilling over the ground and the jaarl's leather boots.

'Clumsy woman,' Ragnfast swore, breaking the spell. 'She should take greater care.'

Thyre's lungs worked again. Ragnfast had realised the danger and had averted it. They might still be saved if everyone kept their head. She darted forwards and whispered in Dagmar's ear as Ragnfast began to call upon the gods to forgive this clumsy woman and her unintended

'And the other woman, is she your daughter as well?' Ivar pointedly looked towards the farmhouse. The woman's skirt was just visible as she entered the darkened door way. Brisk. Efficient. Had she been the one to decide on ale, to offer the insult? Or had she been the one to realise the danger? Or both?

'My stepdaughter. My late wife's child. I took her in after her mother's death. There was nowhere else for her to go.' The farmer ran a finger around the neck of his tunic and his eyes flicked everywhere except on Ivar's face.

Ivar tilted his head to one side, assessing the farmer. There was more to this tale. That woman wielded too much power to be there out of pity or duty. She held herself as if she was at court, rather than standing on a windswept beach. He normally preferred women who lowered their lashes demurely to women who tried to control one. Women like Thorkell's queen. But there was something in the way her eyes challenged him that made him think again.

'Indeed?' Ivar waited for the farmer to continue.

'The woman has very little to her name, but I hold true to my promise to her late mother.'

'It is well that you honour your debts. Her mother was a lucky woman to have such a husband. Not everyone would have been as generous.'

'Thyre's mother was truly an exceptional woman. It was a sad day for us all when she died. My world has never been the same.' The farmer shrugged and his eyes became shadowed as he toyed with his leather tunic. 'I do what I can for her daughter. But my farmstead is poor and we barely manage to eke a living from the soil.'

Ivar glanced up at the gabled longhouse with its weatherbeaten ravens. It was not as fine as Thorkell's palace, or knotting. Her legs wanted to collapse, but she forced them to move unhurriedly as if nothing was wrong. After all the omens she found it impossible to rid her mind of the thought, 'destruction was coming', just as it had once before to her mother. She clearly remembered her mother saying that she must wear her best dress and prettiest smile if ever the Viken came to call again and that it might save her. What had her mother thought when she had first met the Viken king? Had she been attracted to him straight away or had that come later?

Ivar watched the dark-haired woman stalk away, her hips slightly swaying as her skirts revealed shapely ankles and the hint of a well-shaped calf. Deep blue-violet eyes and black as midnight hair contrasted with the light blue-eyed blondeness of the rest of the farmstead. Her heart-shaped face with the dimple in the middle of her chin tugged intriguingly at his memory. There was something about the way she held her head. It reminded him of a woman, a woman who had once held the entire Viken court in the palm of her hand before vanishing into the mists.

The spilling of the ale had been no accident. It had happened on her initiative. He had seen the look pass between the woman and the farmer after he had announced his identity. This woman controlled the farm.

Who exactly was she? The farmer's wife? Concubine?

He nodded towards the retreating figure. 'Your daughter?'

'My daughter, the prettiest woman in Ranrike,' the farmer said, sweeping an overly obvious blonde forwards, the one to whom his name and reputation apparently had no meaning. The woman winced slightly as her eyes met his scar, but she rapidly recovered as she gave a bobbing curtsy.

even Vikar's estate in the north, but it exuded an air of shabby prosperity at the head of a good bay. Either this farmer was inept or someone was trying to mislead him. But who? Not the farmer. This was the mysterious dark-haired woman's doing. The farmer had emphasised certain words as if he were reciting a saga, glancing at her from time to time to seek confirmation that he had said the correct words.

Ivar lifted an eyebrow. He despised the game playing and manipulation that women so often resorted to, that his late wife had excelled at. Give him the straightforward struggle with the sea against the intrigue of court any day. He would discover the truth and act accordingly. But the farmer, and more importantly the stepdaughter, would be left in no doubt that the Viken possessed brains as well as strong sword arms.

'There is a tale that Bose the Dark tells. Perhaps it will help pass the time,' Asger said, stepping forwards from the line. Ivar frowned, but decided to allow the boy his chance. One day, he would have to meet and trade with men such as this farmer. 'About how the Swan Princess enchanted the Viken king and he captured her, only for her to fly away one dark night when there was no moon.'

'Why do you wish to speak of recent history?' The farmer's eyes shifted. 'You will remember the current Ranriken king is her brother. I understand that the Viken allowed her to return home when her brother came to the throne.'

'I thought the tale was an ancient one,' Asger replied, hanging his head.

'Forgive my nephew.' Ivar stepped between Asger and the farmer, reasserting his control of the situation. 'He is young and speaks with the curiosity of youth. He has no wish to insult your king or his sister. I, too, remember the last Ranriken Swan Princess and her great beauty.'

'You know that the Swan Princess died,' the farmer said. 'She returned home and sadly died, mourned by those who loved her.'

'The Viken King Thorkell wept when he heard.' Ivar forced his shoulders to relax. He had no time to think of shadows and mysteries; he had a ship and a crew to get home. 'Later, he made a better choice. Asa is truly the jewel of the court.'

The farmer's eyes shifted and there was growing unease in his stance. 'It is right and fitting to weep for such a lady. I, too, shed many tears at her funeral pyre.'

Ivar frowned. Had Asger inadvertently discovered a clue to this mystery? 'A simple farmer like you? Were you at Ranhiem when she died?'

'I once served with the Ranriken king, her brother,' the farmer said finally. 'Those were the days when I did not spend nearly as much time on my farm. But my mind turned against bloodshed and towards the love of my wife. It was she who chose to live here.'

'Forgive me, I thought you a farmer, but you are a jaarl?'

'A minor one. Ragnfast the Steadfast they called me. Through my sword arm I gained these lands, but my exploits are long forgotten except by a few.' Ragnfast made a sweeping bow. 'You are lucky. A day or two more and I would have been making my annual journey to the Storting and would have been unable to offer hospitality.'

'As you say…' Ivar murmured. A tiny nag tugged at his memory. He should know the name, but could not think of the reason. It would come to him. He deftly turned the conversation towards the *Sea Witch* and its repairs. The damage was minor, but he wanted to make sure the ship would survive if they encountered Sigmund's ships again.

Before he could get the reassurance, the dark-haired woman returned, bearing a horn overflowing with mead. Ivar stepped forwards before she could hand the horn to the jaarl's daughter. The woman's curves filled out the apron dress and her eyes were nearly level with his, shining with intelligence. There was little to indicate her parentage, but he assumed at least one of her parents was not from Ranrike. She might have the height, but she did not have the ash-blonde looks. Her face was far more exotic with its tilted-up eyes, dimple and cherry-red mouth. The old Ranriken queen had been called the Black Swan on account of her long neck and black hair. Perhaps this woman's parents had come from her entourage.

'Mine,' he said, reaching for the horn before she had a chance to protest and to continue with her game. She would learn not to underestimate his intelligence again.

His fingers touched the woman's own slender ones and a current like a full-moon tide coursed down his arm. It was raw and elemental. It jolted through him, insistent.

He drained the horn and pushed away the thoughts, concentrating on the drink. Mead. From the rich honey taste he could tell it was fine mead, the sort reserved for the most honoured guests. She had known about the ale and caused the accident. He looked forward to teaching her a lesson about warriors.

'Very fine.'

'The barrels had become mixed. I only realised the problem when the ale spilt on the ground,' she said in her low musical lilt.

Ivar allowed the polite lie, this time. She had realised before that. 'I trust it will not happen again.'

'I have solved the problem. Once solved, problems do not recur.'

He made an elaborate bow and started on the next part of the ritual, eager to see what her response would be this time. 'Thank you for the warm welcome, daughter of the house.'

'You should have waited and given honour to the true daughter of the house. I am merely a stepdaughter.'

'I doubt you are *merely* anything.'

'You seek to flatter.'

'A little,' Ivar admitted. 'There is nothing wrong with flattery.'

'I have little use for it,' she said, the throatiness of the Ranrike evident in her voice. 'I dislike game playing and banter.'

'Do you, indeed?' Ivar lifted his eyebrow. He looked forward to seeing her face when he revealed that he knew of the attempted insult. This woman appeared ready to give the trickster god Loki lessons in manipulation.

'Do you have no apology for my sister, Ivar Gunnarson? Or perhaps Viken are ignorant of the age-old custom of hospitality that the first drink should be offered by the senior woman of the house?'

'My thirst overcame me. No disrespect was intended towards your *younger* half-sister. It was most remiss of me, but then I have spent a great deal of my life at sea.'

Thyre lifted one delicate eyebrow. She tilted her head to one side and assessed the Viken with his strong shoulders tapering down to a narrow waist. He was arrogant and overly proud of his masculine appeal, but dangerous. He sought to bend the rules for his own ends. 'Pretty words did not change the deed. Or the presumption.'

'What can I do to make amends?' Ivar bowed low

again, keeping his gaze fixed firmly on her mouth. His voice slid like the finest fur over her skin. 'What is my lady's dearest desire?'

'My desires have nothing to do with you.' Thyre raised her chin and kept her gaze steady. He was a typical warrior, more intent on proving his prowess with his sword arm than observing the customs of civilisation.

'A man dying of thirst must drink or perish. Sometimes, he takes without asking. There again, is it wrong to wish to live?' He leant forwards and his hand skimmed her head kerchief. 'Forgive me, but I saw this trapped in your hair. Perhaps it is a sign from the gods that you are favoured.'

He held out a small crystal pendant. The sun caught it, sending its rainbow rays arching out over the sand.

Ragnfast gave a start and his eyes took on a speculative gleam.

'It is a pleasant bauble,' she said, making no move to take it. 'I am sure Dagmar will appreciate it.'

'If it will make amends, then she must have it. All the women shall have one.' He handed it to Dagmar, who blushed and curtsied, before signalling to one of his men who brought forwards more of the crystals, and distributed them to the other women. Thyre resolutely gave hers to Ragnfast. 'What else can I do to regain your favour?'

'Stay here as little time as possible. The storms can be bad this time of year.' Thyre forced her spine to stay as straight as a newly forged sword. A few well-chosen words and trinkets and the entire household were ready to bend over backwards in their welcome. 'Take advantage of the calm seas and go straight home.'

'The sea and I are old friends, as our countries once were.'

'Old friends can quarrel and become enemies.' Her hand plucked at a fold in her skirt. She needed to end this conversation now while she still had control of the situation. 'You can see the wreckage of another ship scattered on the shore. The sea can be unforgiving, particularly at this time of year.'

'The sea seeks to test those who sail on her. My ship passed the test.'

'Will it keep winning?'

'Yes. The *Sea Witch* can outsail any Ranrike ship.'

'The gods punish arrogance,' Thyre said with crushing firmness. 'Surely you have studied the sagas.'

'It is not arrogance speaking, but skill. There is a difference.'

Thyre held back a quick retort. Ragnfast should be saying these things and making this insufferable man understand that he needed to depart quickly, instead of simply standing there with a speculative expression on his face, his fingers stroking the crystal. 'Proud words for a man who presumes upon our hospitality.'

'One who requests what is due to him and who intends to honour his obligations.'

'There is nothing to interest you here.' She turned towards Ragnfast and cleared her throat. Now was the moment that Ragnfast was supposed to plead poverty. They had agreed on the wording. 'Is that not right, Ragnfast? We wish them to leave quickly. There is nothing for the Viken here. We live simply between the forest and the sea. We do not trade in ironstone.'

Ragnfast made a non-committal grunt, and gestured with his hand. 'The Viken are welcome to repair their ship, Thyre. Long ago, their king allowed me time to repair mine. He may have the same length of time—a day and a night—but no more. You will experience the same bountiful hospitality that I was offered.'

'Your stepfather has spoken, Thyre. Bountiful hospitality. We must abide by his wishes.' The Viken jaarl's eyes twinkled as he made another ironic bow.

'Ragnfast!' Thyre said in a furious undertone. 'You want a proper feast? I thought…'

'I cannot help but think that Ran sent him here for a purpose.' Ragnfast toyed with the crystal before placing it in his pouch. 'We shall slaughter some sheep for you, Viken, as you are clearly a favourite with the Aesir to give such crystals as welcoming gifts. You may use what you need from the estate. Do not let it be said that Ragnfast the Steadfast forgets his obligations.'

Thyre narrowed her eyes. What game was Ragnfast playing at now? If he allowed the Viken to go poking around in the outer buildings, they could discover the silver and gold she had carefully hidden. Buildings could be rebuilt given time, but the loss of the gold and silver would devastate everyone. Her hands curled into impotent fists. All Ragnfast could see was the promise of a departure gift.

'It is more than I expected.' Ivar Gunnarson inclined his head. 'Where can I find the timber and various implements that I will need to repair my ship?'

'I will help you.' Thyre said, giving Ragnfast a meaningful glance. 'The women have been doing cleaning, Ragnfast, and *everything* is not where it should be.'

Silently she prayed Ragnfast would heed her warning. He gave an elaborate shrug. 'My stepdaughter continually turns the estate upside down. In that she is like her mother.'

Ragnfast motioned for the others to go. The women made the customary gestures and departed. Thyre kept her back straight, waiting. She could do this. She could keep the Viken from guessing the true extent of their wealth. After all, she had put many warriors in their place before. They all seemed to think one ripple of their biceps and an indulgent smile was enough to drive a woman into their arms.

'What do you require, Ivar Gunnarson?' she asked.

'What do I require?' The Viken asked with a maddening lift of his brow, and his gaze lingered on the hollow of her throat. 'It depends on what you are offering.'

'Equipment to repair your ship and nothing more.' Thyre rolled her eyes towards the sky at the blatant attempt at flirtation.

He laughed and his hand brushed her elbow. 'Come with me and I shall show you.'

'Ships and I are strangers. I need a list. I would not want to be accused of giving you the wrong thing.' Thyre's lips became dry and she moved her arm away from the heat radiating from his hand.

He rattled off a long list of items. Thyre began to breathe easier. Everything was easy to obtain and she had clearly made her point. He would have to find another woman to romance. 'You shall have what you have asked for.'

'And if I need anything else? How shall I call you? Shall I ask for the dark-haired princess? Or maybe it is the dark-haired witch.'

'My name is Thyre and I am merely the stepdaughter,' Thyre said firmly.

'I will try to remember that. A stepdaughter and not a princess, although this certainly appears to be your kingdom.'

'It belongs to my stepfather.'

His eyes became cold and for a moment he seemed to search her soul. 'But you know where *everything* is kept, including the sour ale.'

Her hand flew to her mouth as the realisation hit—this warrior did possess a *brain*. He had seen through the ruse. The tiny pain in her head threatened to become a full-blown headache. He had warned her and not Ragnfast. It was she that he held accountable for the trick. 'You knew.'

'I will let it go this time, Thyre, but no more tricks or insults. My men are warriors, not farmers. They tend to act before considering the consequences.'

'I am well aware of who you are…now. You will be given the proper honour.'

Ivar watched the emotions play on her face. The woman understood what he was saying. Good. Perhaps they could avoid any unpleasant incidents and she would stop treating the Viken like they were ignorant or easily fooled. 'You should trust me, Thyre. All I want to do is get home. It is a simple enough desire.'

'We do not trust each other. It is how it has been since before I was born. Ranrike and Viken, there is too much between our two countries.'

'Will you be sitting at the high table during the feast?' Ivar tilted his head and examined the way a few tendrils of black hair escaped from her kerchief. 'Or will you find an excuse to be somewhere else? Why not take a chance and learn that the Viken are like other men?'

Her eyebrows drew together. 'I shall be there if my stepfather deems it necessary. Dagmar normally serves the important guests. It is a tradition.'

'Traditions can change. Countries do not always need to be at war.'

'Not this one.' She strode off, the skirt of her apron twitching and revealing her slender ankles.

'Is there some problem?' Erik the Black called. 'Your beautiful lady appears to have left in mid-conversation.'

'Nothing I can't handle.' Ivar watched her, struck again by the vague sense of recognition.

'She is a proud beauty, that one. She would be a right forest cat in bed.'

A primitive urge to strangle Erik filled Ivar. If he had noticed Thyre's appeal, others would have as well. 'She is not for you or the rest of the crew. You may inform the men.'

'But I take it the other women are…' Erik raised an eyebrow as a knowing smile spread across his face.

'If you must…as long as the women are willing and unclaimed. I will have no disputes over a skirt and a melting pair of eyes. We are here to repair the ship and to make sure the mast holds steady until we can get back to Kaupang. A night and a day.'

'Will it be enough?' Erik the Black asked. 'The mast has cracked. Definitely. I heard the split when we were buffeted by the last gust of wind.'

'Even though there is no sign of it yet, I trust you, Erik. We sail with our backs and our arms. We enjoy the feast and that is all.'

'As you say, hospitality is there for the taking.'

Ivar regarded Thyre's retreating back. Her head was proud and erect and her apron dress skimmed her curves. She moved with complete assurance. An appealing package, and one that held the possibility of being explored. She had flirted with him. For the first time in a long time, the beginnings of desire stirred within him. He would tame her. One single night—it could be done. 'But that one is mine. I will unlock her secrets. No man is to molest her.'

'Did anything untoward happen in the ceremony while I was away getting the mead, Dagmar?' Thyre asked before Dagmar even had a chance to sit down on the kitchen bench. 'Your father appeared distinctly uncomfortable when I returned with the horn of mead and he has gone to make another sacrifice to the gods. We had an agreement about what was to happen, and he broke it.'

'If Sven had been here, he would have made sure Far held firm. Why did Far offer so much hospitality? Why not fight? They are not that many.'

Thyre held her tongue. Dagmar's ideas about strategy were never particularly well thought out. This Viken warrior needed to be handled carefully.

'What else happened, Dagmar?' Thyre asked.

'There was some boring old story that one of the Viken tried to recite, but that was all.' Dagmar made a wry face. 'You know Far, he sees the boat and thinks of gold and spices. Far is too greedy and short sighted, Sven says.'

'And the leader, Ivar?' Thyre kept her gaze on the kitchen fire, aware that her cheeks suddenly burnt. 'How did he react?'

'He acted quickly to calm the situation and Far was mollified.' Dagmar wet her lips and smoothed her skirt. 'His scar bothers me. To twist his mouth like that. How do you think he acquired it? It looks far too jagged to be a sword mark. But if you don't see the scar, the rest of him is more than pleasant.'

Thyre stopped the words about Ivar Gunnarson's broad shoulders and bulging arm muscles just before they tumbled out. The last thing she wanted was Dagmar teasing her about a fancy for a Viken warrior after she'd proclaimed her loathing of them for so many years. 'As long as I see the back of him tomorrow, all will be well.'

'You are right, Thyre. His back is by far the best view.

A woman could feast on those shoulders.' Dagmar smacked her lips.

'Dagmar!' Thyre put her hands on her hips, but Dagmar looked unrepentant.

'I prefer a fine face and a gentle manner, so you may have no fears on that score. The Viken jaarl is all yours, if you want him.'

Thyre moved a bowl of cracked barley and took back charge of the conversation. 'We need to have some other plan, in case the Viken jaarl has another motive. In case he decides to stay beyond the day and a night that he agreed with Ragnfast. This Viken warrior possesses a brain.'

Dagmar raised an eyebrow. 'You and your plots. You should just allow things to happen.'

Thyre began to pace the floor, hating this feeling of helplessness. 'The bonfire could be lit. We could send a signal to Sigmund. He promised that if ever we needed help, he would send warriors.'

'Far would never allow it. It would give the jaarl Sigmund far too much power here. Besides, Sigmund would never reach here in time…and you know what Hilde said about how he hurt her and some of the other maids when he was last here.'

'The jaarl Sigmund deserves to know that his ship washed up on these shores. If the Viken outstays his welcome, then he should face Ranrike's mightiest jaarl.'

'But who will light the fire? Who will face my father's wrath?'

'I will. I will take the responsibility.' Thyre put back her shoulders. It had to be done and no one else could do it. 'I refuse to stand by and let the Viken win.'

'You do not even know if they will do anything. The

Viken might be honest. He certainly is generous. Or seeking some other excuse?' Dagmar held up her hand. 'I too heard what Sigmund said to Far the last time he was here, but Far refused to believe him. He might not like Vikens, but he respects them. And he has beaten them before. He brought our mother back to Ranrike.'

'That was a long time ago,' Thyre said, shifting uncomfortably. 'Ragnfast's courage was well known—steadfast in heart and with his arm. Mor never said anything against him, but I think she would have wanted to keep this farm safe, whatever the cost.'

'I miss her even though she has been dead for years and years. Sometimes, I can't really remember her face or her voice. But I do know you take after her far more than I do.'

Thyre reached out her hand and Dagmar's fingers instantly curled around it.

'All I know is that I have to try, Dagmar. I will go to the second bonfire and light that one. After the Viken have gone, I will confess to Ragnfast. He will understand my reasoning.' Thyre paused. 'It was what Mother would have done—confessed after the fact. It is what she would want us to do.'

'I hope you are right.'

'It has to be done. A day and a night are all we have left.' Thyre raised their clasped hands. 'We do this in the Swan Princess's memory. The Viken warriors will not abuse our hospitality. We will prevail and the estate will be safe.'

Chapter Three

'The bonfire is lit and I saw the answering fire on the other side of the valley,' Thyre announced to Dagmar on her return. It had taken less time than she had imagined to light the second beacon. Now her being was filled with a quiet exhilaration. How dare he make such statements about women? And look at her with such an arrogant stare? This Viken would learn that she was not to be trifled with. 'Has there been any trouble?'

'Nothing other than Hilde spilling the milk as she made eyes at one of the warriors.'

'Hilde always makes eyes at every warrior,' Thyre said with a laugh. 'She thinks the bigger the muscles, the more desirable they are.'

But rather than answering with another comment about Hilde, Dagmar gave a huge sigh and started to wring her hands.

'Out with it, Dagmar. What have the Viken done?'

'While I supervised the lighting of the fire in the bathing hut, I kept thinking about what you said earlier. About Mother and how she would want us to do something to protect the estate.' Dagmar gave a decided nod. 'Do you mind if I go and look for Sven?'

'He will not be back yet, Dagmar. He has been away only a few weeks. Is this truly necessary?' Thyre gestured towards where the table groaned with grain and vegetables. 'Much remains to be done. I need you here to help me with the cooking.'

'It seems like for ever since he left.' Dagmar gave a dramatic sigh. 'The feast is well in hand. It only looks like a lot of work, but the grain is mostly ground and the turnips are peeled. Then once the cooking starts you will say it is easier if you do it yourself. You always do and the feast always arrives on time. I am doing you a favour. Besides, if Sven has returned, he will be able to rally the foresters to Ragnfast's standard should the need arise. If you can do something brave by lighting the bonfire, I can do something as well.'

Thyre gritted her teeth. Ever since he had gone, Dagmar had made the daily trek up to the top of the hill to see if she could spy Sven's horse. After offering to go with her several times and Dagmar finding threadbare excuses why she did not want company, Thyre had stopped bothering. Ever since the advent of Sven, they had drifted apart a little. Dagmar was always keeping little things from her, inconsequential things, but it hurt all the same.

It would be easier in many ways if she just let Dagmar go. At least the sobbing into her pillow at night had stopped. Thyre wished that Dagmar had waited until she was safely married before falling in love. She could not see a happy outcome to this. Ragnfast would never accept the man. He wanted a man with a fortune and a strong sword arm to defend this estate for his daughter. But she would find a way through the tangle after the Viken left.

'You might be right. A few more men at the feast might help keep fights from starting. Be quick about it, then.'

'I will be.' Dagmar gave Thyre a quick kiss on her cheek.

'You will have to tell your father about Sven some time, Dagmar. He deserves to know. Would you like to practise saying the words with me?'

Dagmar's eyes slid away from Thyre. 'I will, but not now. Feasts bring out the worst in him. He starts sampling the ale far too early. Promise me that you won't say anything either. The last thing we want is for Far to lose his temper and start boasting about how he bested King Thorkell and therefore can beat any man. Remember how the last time he clutched his heart and turned beet red?'

Ice swept through Thyre. 'I promise to keep silent.'

'I will be back before the bread is finished. I promise you that. No one will even miss me.'

Thyre watched as Dagmar hurried purposefully from the kitchen. She shook her head, trying to clear it of foreboding. She had done the right thing by lighting the bonfire. She had done the only thing she could. The blood-red moon would be wrong this time. Change was not coming.

The late afternoon air was cool against Ivar's face after the heat of the bathing hut. The repairs to the ship had gone much as he had foreseen. The storm's damage was not as great as Erik the Black had feared. The mast appeared sound.

The gods favoured the brave. This bay was perfect for ship building with its stands of straight trees. He would have to open negotiations. Undoubtedly Thyre would find a reason to become involved. There was something about the way she challenged him with her eyes that said she knew more than she was letting on.

He regretted that she had not appeared at the bath hut.

Instead a gaggle of simpering and sighing maids had appeared to stoke the fire and make sure it was at the right temperature.

A movement in the shadows caused his muscles to coil. He relaxed slightly when he discerned Thyre's midnight-black hair. What game was she playing now, scanning the sky as she balanced a basket on her hip? Ivar moved stealthily nearer.

'Ah, here I discover you, Thyre,' he said smoothly when he had nearly reached her.

Rather than jumping, she calmly tilted her head to one side. Her tongue wet her lips, making them strawberry red. 'Were you searching for me?'

'I have been searching for you or someone like you…for what seems to be a long time.' Ivar smiled his most seductive smile. Thyre would provide a bit of sport for the evening, but then he would sail away. It was far better than allowing the thrill of the chase to fade and for recriminations to start. No, a single night of pleasure with her suited him.

He waited for the flirtatious sigh.

She lifted her eyebrow and her lips turned down slightly at the corners. 'Pretty words, Viken. Do I melt at your feet now or can it wait? The feast preoccupies my thoughts for now. Personally, melting has never held much appeal and I'd prefer to postpone the moment if at all possible.'

He drew his brows together, disconcerted. 'Pretty words for a beautiful woman, but they are sincere. I have been searching for you.'

'Your life must be very empty, then.' She tapped her boot against the earth, standing her ground as her hand on her hip emphasised the smallness of her waist.

Ivar schooled his features and waited. He had lost count of how many times he had played these sorts of games. She was tempted despite her protestations. He had forgotten how much fun it could be to spar with a woman, particularly a woman who had brains.

'You should find something more fulfilling to occupy your time than waiting for women,' she said.

'My life is full enough. All I need is the sea and a soft place to lay my head.' He took a step closer, laid a hand on her shoulder and noticed how her body leant slightly towards him, her breasts brushing his forearm. 'But right now it is missing something, something I desperately need, something I believe only you can give me.'

'Desperation can lead to mistakes.' Her voice had a catch in it. 'I have learnt to stop searching. You should be content with what you have.'

'I shall have to give you a reason to start searching again. Discovery can be rewarding.'

Their breath mingled. She would only have to sway slightly and their shoulders would touch. His hands would pull her to him and his mouth would encounter hers. Would it be soft or firm? Ivar wondered.

She moved imperceptibly towards him and he gave into impulse. His mouth touched hers—sweet and firm, inviting.

With an effort Ivar regained control and ended it after the briefest of tastes. She would be the one to beg for the next kiss.

'Please…' she whispered and her hands came up to rest on his chest.

'Please what?' he inquired softly, but he made no move to recapture her mouth. She had to make the request.

'Why are you searching? What are you searching for?'

Ivar stepped away and allowed the air to rush between them.

'At last the question I wanted. Fresh rope for my ship.

Two lines broke in the storm.' He held out his hands and a smile stretched across his face. 'What else would I be searching for?'

'Oh, that is…I mean, I had thought…' Thyre put her hand to her mouth. How had she, who prided herself on avoiding warriors' seduction, fallen so neatly into his trap? She had allowed him to kiss her. And if he had not stopped…the kiss would have gone on and deepened. She refused to think about what could have happened. Even now, her body longed for his touch. 'The rope is kept in the outer workshop. One of the thralls can get it for you. You should have said straight away. Then we would not have had to have this conversation.'

'Is this *conversation* distasteful?'

'Unasked for.' Thyre gave her most crushing nod.

'Any unasked thoughts are coming from you, Thyre, and not from me.' He paused, his eyes twinkling like the sea on a summer's day.

Thyre shifted uncomfortably. Had she been the one? Who had made the first move?

He leant forwards again and lowered his voice to a seductive caress. 'But you are welcome to share those thoughts with me. Never let it be said that I acted without considering a woman's wishes. Or forcing her.'

'No, that is to say…' Thyre stopped. Her hands touched her mother's amulet, which hung around her neck, and she regained control. She had more intelligence in her little finger than most warriors possessed in their whole bodies. She gave this warrior's intelligence far too much credit. He was a man like any other. 'It is best to be straightforward and honest.'

'I always am. I find it saves time.' He tilted his head to one side, assessing her. 'And you were prepared to offer something else? It is a pity that I was so forthcoming about my request.'

'I wasn't prepared to offer anything!'

'Who are you trying to convince? Me?' He reached out a finger and traced the outline of her lips in the air above them and instantly they ached as if he had kissed them again. 'Or you?'

Thyre held her body still, resisting the temptation to turn her face into his palm. Ivar made no move towards her. He simply stood close, waiting, without touching. Each heartbeat seemed to take an age. Thyre knew she should step away, but her feet refused to move.

'You were mistaken,' she said evenly. 'I have no need to convince anyone.'

His face sobered and he stared at her. 'How long has your stepfather been in this bay?'

Thyre blinked. Ice water crashed through her veins. He thought to confuse her and then to obtain information about the bay and its defences. She should have realised that the Viken jaarl would have a great deal of cunning.

'Since the king began his reign. He is very proud of his farm. Our goats and sheep are renowned for their wool and milk.' Thyre gave a careful laugh. She wanted to believe his story about only needing repairs. His ship certainly showed signs of damage, but was there another reason? Who had been chasing whom in that storm? Sigmund had sworn blind that his ships were only for defence, meaning Ivar must have been the attacker.

Had the news of Ragnfast's quarrel with Sigmund reached Viken ears?

The Viken were notorious in their dealings and she knew how they broke promises. And the worst thing was that she wanted to believe this man. Her blood ran cold when she thought about what he could do before help could arrive.

'The inlet is a perfect hideaway for ships, ships that could easily prey on undefended trading vessels,' he continued.

'Ragnfast does not possess that sort of fleet.'

'But others in Ranrike do. My king and many of the Viken think the strait is cursed.'

Thyre turned her lips up into a polite smile. Sigmund was doing the Ranrike people a great service. He protected them from raiders, even if Ragnfast refused to let him keep ships in this bay. He would answer the beacon in time. 'You would have to ask them. I am merely a woman. I have no interest in the sea and trade.'

'My queen proclaims no interest, but she knows everything that goes on.'

'I am not a queen,' Thyre replied quickly. 'I know little about what happens beyond the confines of this bay and am content to keep that way.'

'There is a great world out there, ready to be explored. Aren't you curious?'

Yes, yes, she wanted to scream. She did want to know what lay beyond the next horizon, but it was impossible. Too many people depended on her here. Her responsibilities to Ragnfast and this estate were far too important. Without her, everything might stop. She remembered the melancholy he had slipped into after her mother's death and how she'd had to make sure that the food was harvested and the animals were slaughtered. And once she had begun, Ragnfast had naturally listened to her counsel, just as he had listened to her mother's. Little by little she had brought the place back to life.

'I am content with my life.' She hated the way the white lies dripped from her mouth. 'I like the estate.

There is always something to be done—the weaving, the cooking. Last week, Beygul, the kitchen cat, went missing and I eventually discovered her, curled up beside an overturned pot of cream. You should have heard Dagmar scream.'

'You are trying to distract me with your talk of cats. You are not living. You are only existing.'

'There is more to life than visiting new places.'

'It is all I desire.' He leant forwards. 'But how does a mere farmer acquire such a bay?'

'Ragnfast is one of the leading Ranriken jaarls, not as great as Sigmund but he still does attend the annual Storting and his views are well respected.'

'Does he do much trading? The lack of boats is surprising. Forgive my curiosity, but the bay cries out to be used. You have stands of trees. He could build boats.'

'Ragnfast is no ship builder.'

'Nor does he keep his buildings in good repair. Your barn on the south side has a leaning wall. It needs support timbers. A simple repair job, which my men have carried out, but it will need to be properly fixed.'

Thyre stared in surprise at the Viken jaarl. He had sorted the problem that she had been attempting to get Ragnfast to do for the past six weeks. 'Ragnfast is loyal to the Ranriken king, if that is what you are asking. He says there is no need to change protectors. He quarrelled with the Viken when he was younger.'

'I have never asked him to. The Viken have no quarrel with those who do not attack our ships. We are grateful for your hospitality.'

'The Ranrike are a peaceful people. We give protection to trading ships, but we have always reserved the right to defend against those who would plunder.'

'The afternoon is young. There are so many more interesting topics that we can discuss besides the politics—' He broke off and his body became alert. His entire being seemed focused away from her. 'There appears to be a light on the hill.'

'You are seeing things.' Thyre hated the way her eyes went towards where the beacon was lit. From here, only the faintest trace of smoke curling in the sky could be seen. 'It is the sun on the rocks.'

His eyes grew hard. 'Are you certain? I would hate to be caught in a trap.'

'The Ranrike have no quarrel with you.'

'We returned from Birka and Permia. Ships were waiting and watching for us. One gave chase in the storm.'

'And I have seen the results dashed to pieces on the shore. The ship did not sail from here. Ragnfast has nothing to do with such behaviour.'

She waited with the breeze whipping her skirts and cooling her sweat-soaked back. Ivar had to believe her. His blue gaze bore into her and then suddenly his shoulders relaxed slightly.

'That is reassuring.' The Viken put his fingers under her elbow, held her for an instant. A warm surge went up her arm. 'Shall I see you at the feast?'

'The kitchen needs me.' Thyre cleared her throat. 'I supervise the production of the feast. Ragnfast is very particular about the manner in which the meat is prepared.'

'Then I shall have to hope to see you afterwards.' His voice dropped to a husky whisper, holding her in its embrace.

Thyre gave her most withering smile, the one which had discouraged all the other warriors. 'I sincerely doubt that.'

'As you wish, but the offer is there,' he murmured and

lifted her hand to his lips, burning his mark on her. 'I keep my promises.'

Thyre regarded her hand. There was no mark, but the skin pulsated with warmth. The sensation would pass in a moment if she kept her calm. 'I have made my choice and I never deviate from my course.'

'Did anyone miss me?' Dagmar asked, breezing into the kitchen as the sun was beginning to sink lower in the west, lighting the sky an intense orangey red. 'I should never have worn my new boots. I slipped twice and now my toes ache.'

'I missed you. And your father even came into the kitchen to enquire where you were.' Thyre pressed her lips together. She had wanted to talk to Dagmar about the Viken and to get her opinion. So far, Ivar appeared to have caused a dozen jobs to be carried out. And his honeyed tones had led Ragnfast to dream of riches. And there was that brief kiss to be considered. What did he really want? 'This feast means a lot to him.'

'He came in here? His head has really been turned with the tales of the wealth the Viken jaarls brought back from Lindisfarne. There is more to a man than his fortune.' Dagmar sat down and took her boot off. She wriggled her toes and started to massage the bottom of her foot. 'There, you see, I did hurt them. You have no idea of the pain I have gone through.'

Thyre bit back the words telling Dagmar that it had been her choice to go up to the lookout point rather than help with the feast. 'I did warn you about those boots. They look uncomfortable, no matter how bright and red they might be.'

Dagmar shifted uncomfortably as she reached down to give one of the sleeping cats a stroke. 'I met a forester.

Word has reached him. Sven should be here within days, a week at most. He has said that all the foresters will be sure to be at the feast tonight.'

'Back so soon?' Thyre commented, but privately she heaved a sigh of relief. Dagmar had been sensible. Having the foresters there would mean that the Viken would be less likely to start anything.

'His business was concluded more quickly than he thought.'

'Your forester knows a great deal about Sven and his plans.' Thyre tilted her head and tried to assess Dagmar. Dagmar was normally very truthful, but Thyre also knew how badly Dagmar wanted Sven to return. How much was wishful thinking? She shivered slightly, remembering the stories about Ragnfast's mother and how she had been touched by the gods.

'Sven set up a system of signals or something.' Dagmar waved an airy hand. 'I do not really understand it. But he has kept true to his promise. He alerted me. Now I can prepare. I will be a bride before summer ends.'

'You will have to be prepared to serve the ale,' a maid said, coming in and refilling her jug. 'Ragnfast is like a bear with a sore head. He keeps asking for Dagmar. And the Viken are calling for more ale, more meat.'

Thyre drew in her breath sharply, but the maid looked un-repentant, shifting the jug to the other hip and flouncing out.

Dagmar lifted her chin and her eyes swam with tears. 'I never shirk my work. It just took longer than I thought.'

'I will have a word with her,' Thyre said quietly.

'Thank you.' Dagmar reached out her hand and squeezed Thyre's fingers. 'Far knows there are more than enough women. He trusts your judgement. It is that maid,

Hilde, trying to make trouble. She wanted Sven and now she always tries to undermine me.'

'You can't go out like that.' Thyre brushed some of the brambles off Dagmar's skirt. 'You must wash your face and brush your clothes down. I will take the jug around until you are ready. The Viken will not notice the difference.'

'One might. The Viken jaarl's eyes seemed to follow you everywhere on the beach.'

'You are impossible, Dagmar.' Thyre kept her gaze on Beygul as the cat washed its back legs.

'You are so much fun to tease, Thyre. As if a warrior could ever get past your sharp tongue…you terrify them.' Dagmar tucked her head into her chin and batted her eyelashes. 'I promise to take over once I have changed…if your Viken jaarl will permit it.'

Thyre made an annoyed noise in the back of her throat. 'And do go quickly. I will expect a favour from you one day.'

Thyre picked up the remaining jug and ignored the temptation to smooth her skirt and pinch her cheeks after Dagmar had scurried from the room. She was doing this to help Dagmar, not because she wanted to see Ivar again.

The banqueting hall strained to hold all the Viken warriors. The central fire combined with the torches to bathe the room in a red glow, disguising the threadbare hangings and fading paint.

Thyre worked efficiently, pouring the ale with a steady hand. She managed to sidestep outstretched arms and ignored the playful remarks from various foresters. Several of the maids appeared less inclined to avoid the hands, giggling and boldly meeting the man's gaze as they perched first on this knee and then the next. One had an avaricious look in her eyes as she toyed with a Viken's golden torc. Thyre half-expected her to demand a morning gift before she had even bestowed a kiss. Thyre frowned and gestured towards the other tables. Instantly the woman leapt up and started scurrying about. The other maids quickly started putting more effort into their work as well. Thyre gave a nod as the banqueting hall began to hum with activity and purpose once again.

By the time she had returned to the kitchen, Dagmar had failed to reappear so Thyre refilled her jug with mead and started towards the high table. In the light breeze, the torches fluttered slightly, casting their shadows about. Her breath caught as the crowd parted suddenly, revealing the top table and Ivar. As Ragnfast was absent, Ivar sat in solitary splendour, much as a king might survey his court.

He had changed from his seafaring clothes to the ones he might wear at a market town. His fur-lined cape contrasted with the dark red wool and gold braid of his tunic. The leather trousers were moulded to his thighs and left little to the imagination. A pulsating warmth infused Thyre. His feet were encased in soft kid boots and at his throat he wore an intricate golden torc. Everything about him proclaimed that here was a successful trader, a man used to the trappings of power and wealth and not afraid to use them to his advantage.

Thyre bit her lip, gave her head a little shake and broke the spell. She concentrated on carrying the full jug of mead, rather than letting her attention wander again to the way his hair skimmed his shoulders.

'You left me until last, my disdainful lady.' The jaarl's voice rumbled in her ears. It was liquid and golden like the honey that first emerged from the comb. 'My horn awaits your nectar.'

'The mead needs to be served at the correct temperature,' Thyre replied, resisting the urge to tip the whole lot over his arrogant head. This time, he would not kiss her or trap her into some sort of flirtatious game. 'I had assumed that you would have been well looked after. My stepfather takes pride in producing a good feast, never allowing the horns to go empty.'

'He has been remiss.' His eyes danced as he held up his empty drinking horn. 'Perhaps the women feel that my men are in more need of nourishment than I. Perhaps they fear the Viken jaarl.'

'Your comfort is important as you are an honoured guest. Are you hungry?'

'It depends what is on offer. I can afford to be choosy.' His eyes deepened slightly.

'Then you are not starving.'

'I'm ravenous for the right morsel.' He took a long sip from his drinking horn. 'I have learnt the value of patience. Why rush when perfection may happen to pass?'

Thyre licked her dry lips and resisted the urge to smile triumphantly. She would best him at his own game. Leaning forwards, she lowered her voice to a throaty whisper as she filled the horn with the golden liquid. 'Patience is an admirable quality.'

'Ah, I wait for the right mead and you wait for…'

'My supper,' she said smoothly.

His direct gaze met hers and a half-smile crossed his lips. 'Very good. You are learning. Practice makes perfect. Shall we cross more than verbal swords?'

Thyre knew that she didn't want just one night. She wanted more—a life, watching her children grow up and a husband who respected her. The Viken wanted a flirtation. However, she could also not rid herself of the image

Dagmar had planted in her mind—the Viken's limbs entwined with hers, and his soft words rustling against her hair.

Thyre inclined her head. 'You are here and my stepfather has decreed we feast, so we feast and your horn is filled with ale. There is no time for anything else.'

'But I should like to learn more about you. What are you waiting for? What dreams haunt your beautiful eyes?'

Thyre resolutely kept her gaze away from his bow-shaped mouth. 'My opinion means very little except where the production of bread or cloth is concerned. My entire life is here at the farm. I have no wish to look beyond its horizons. Where is your horizon?'

'The ever-changing sea makes an admirable horizon.' His gaze narrowed and became focused on her eyes. 'Is there something? Is there something about my face that offends? You seem to be looking in the middle distance.'

'No, I am trying to make sure that two of your warriors do not come to blows over Hilde, one of the serving maids.' Thyre snapped her fingers over her head and gestured. Hilde screwed up her face, but obeyed Thyre's unspoken command. 'There, she has gone back to the kitchen and your men are friends again.'

'You avoided the question.'

Thyre regarded the savage markings on his face more closely. Without them, he would have been breathtaking. She knew Dagmar wanted physical perfection, but she saw the dignity in the scarring. Whatever he had been through must have caused considerable pain. It might even pain him still, but he did not hide away in solitude, he went out and met the world head on. 'Your scar adds to the character of your face.'

His eyes assessed her. 'Many find it hard to look on.'

'What caused the scarring? A sword fight?'

'An encounter in my youth with a wolf—I objected to becoming his next meal.'

'Did the wolf survive?'

'For many years his silver pelt has graced my bed.' He gave a lopsided smile. 'I made sure of that. He died with my sword in his neck.'

'Then the scars are honourable and should be worn with pride.' She paused, becoming serious. 'My mother taught me that it is how a man behaves, and not the way he looks, that matters. She had a disappointment early in her life and it was a lesson she learnt the hard way.'

The very air seemed to crackle between them.

He leant forwards and took the jug from her unresisting hand. 'Come sit beside me, princess. It has been a long time since a woman has kept me so entertained with just her words.'

'Why are you calling me princess? What have I done to deserve such a nickname?' she asked.

'You command this estate like a princess. Every time I ask for something, the thralls tell me to ask you, rather than Ragnfast or your half-sister.'

'This farm does not run itself. There are many things that need to be accomplished, regardless of who graces our shores. Ragnfast remains very much in charge. I simply do the women's work.'

He raised an eyebrow. 'There is nothing simple about running an estate. My sister, Astrid, reminds me of this every time I return home.'

'I dare say in Viken you like your women to be silently spinning and weaving.' Thyre gave an arched laugh, remembering some of her mother's comments about the violence of the Viken court. 'Silence is not one of my virtues.'

'In Viken, the queen sits next to the king in the Storting and advises him. I doubt Asa has ever handled a spindle. But my late wife was one such as you describe. My comfort was ever uppermost in her thoughts.'

'And what does King Thorkell think about it?' Thyre kept her tone measured. Despite everything, she wanted to ask about the Viken king, the father she had never met and the woman he had finally chosen. Here, at long last, was someone who knew him and knew the sort of man he was. Her mother had said very little when Thyre was young and Thyre treasured every scrap of knowledge. 'Does he approve? Or does he long for a woman like your late wife?'

'I doubt he has much choice. Asa is very strong willed, but he respects her counsel. They are well matched.'

Respects her counsel. Thyre risked a breath. She could not imagine her uncle, the current Ranrike king, respecting any woman's counsel. She could remember her mother complaining bitterly about how her brother, King Mysing, refused to listen to a mere woman's words. 'And do the Viken jaarls respect her as well?'

'You under-estimate Asa at your peril.' A faint smile touched his lips. 'I suspect you also should not be under-estimated.'

'A compliment?'

'If you wish to call it that.' Ivar leant forwards, his hand closed over hers, holding her in his strong grip. 'And, my lady, why does Thorkell the Viken king and his queen fascinate you if you have no wish to know what lies beyond the horizon? What else are you hiding from me?'

Chapter Four

Ivar took a long, considering drink of his mead while his other hand kept Thyre by his side. It had been a long time since he had tasted any mead this fine. There was something about this place that made him long to draw back the layers and discover the truth.

'Curiosity.' Thyre moved with lightning speed, deftly twisting her wrist and escaping from his grasp. 'It is always best to know your enemy.'

'But you do wish to travel, to see what lies beyond the confines of this bay. Why did you lie to me earlier, princess?'

'My home is here. They need me. And I have no need of that name. There are no princesses in Ranrike.'

'Once I get to know you better, maybe I will call you something different. Maybe I will even call you friend. I believe it is possible for the Ranrike and the Viken to be friends. Your stepfather's hospitality has proven it. Perhaps one day you too will visit the Viken court and see its many splendours.'

'I am not your friend.'

'But I do not consider you or any other person here to

be my enemy. Are you asking for something more than friendship?'

A dimple played in the shadows of his cheek. In the dim light, his scar faded to nothing and Thyre could see only the planes of his face.

'Deeds prove friendship. Much has passed between our two countries. There is good reason for the mistrust. It was the Viken who…' Her throat closed around the words and she stopped aghast at what she had been about to reveal.

A few poorly chosen words and he would have taken offence. Or she would have blurted out the truth. How many times had Ragnfast warned her? And what would Ivar do if he knew the truth about her parentage? Would he consider her an abomination for having mixed blood, as her uncle the Ranriken king did? Would he understand why her mother had felt compelled to marry Ragnfast and accept banishment from the court? Or why her mother hid her birth from her true father, King Thorkell?

'The jaarl Sigmund says that the Viken continually challenge Ranriken ships.'

His eyes turned to cold blue ice. 'It is Sigmund who has preyed on the Viken shipping, not the other way around. The Viken have no quarrel with the ordinary Ranrike people. We never have.'

'It is good to hear!' Ragnfast patted Ivar on the back as he returned to the table. He nodded towards Thyre, motioning for her to continue on with the serving. She looked at him, willing him to mime where he had been. Ragnfast simply smiled, one of his overly pleased smiles. He was up to something, Thyre thought. What sort of mess would she have to clean up…this time?

'Here we sit, feasting—eating and breaking bread

together. This is no place for politics. Tonight is for enjoying tales and relaxing, safe from Ran's storms.'

'I could not agree more. I intend to enjoy tonight to the full. It has already provided unexpected opportunities.' Ivar gave a half-shrug, but his hand burnt against her wrist. And she was intensely aware of the latent power in his shoulders and in his forearms. 'It is good that your step-daughter has been attentive. I hardly missed your absence.'

'Where is Dagmar, Thyre?' Ragnfast's eyes narrowed as he toyed with the hilt of his eating knife. 'Her duties involve serving at the high table. No one appears to have seen her since early afternoon.'

'Dagmar's feet pained her. Her new boots pinched her toes.' Thyre made a little gesture, but Ragnfast's frown increased and he tapped his fingers against the drinking horn. Her stomach tightened. Ragnfast was determined on something. His greed often overcame his caution. She had seen it happen before when he bargained for a load of timber.

'Her new boots!' Ragnfast's face became a mottled purple.

'I told her before she had them made that they were too small, but she refused to listen. She wanted everyone to admire them, but now she is forced to sit,' Thyre said. 'We decided the Viken would prefer a steady hand and a smiling countenance to one grimacing with pain.'

Thyre kept her back straight and waited. Ragnfast had to believe the pretty tale. She had kept to the truth as much as possible.

Ragnfast gave a non-communicative grunt and waved his hand, dismissing her, and she knew he had accepted her version of the events. 'Dagmar knows her duty. See that she does it.'

'Surely there is no harm in having your stepdaughter

serving at the high table. Allow your daughter to change her shoes.' Ivar's voice was steady, but there was no disguising its commanding tone. 'Thyre appears to have a ready wit and a steady hand when she pours the drink.'

'A very steady hand,' called a Viken from further down the table. 'Not like this one here.' He grabbed Hilde about the waist and spun her on to his lap as the ale arched out from the jug. Hilde collapsed against him giggling, obviously enjoying the attention. 'I had best keep my eyes on her.'

'And your hands,' one of the Viken warriors called out. Coarse laughter filled the hall.

Thyre raised an eyebrow and pointed towards the kitchen. Hilde immediately sobered and disentangled herself. Ragnfast took another long draught of mead. Thyre willed her brain to work. What exactly was he up to with that calculating expression?

'Otto the Red, the farmer in the next steading, has made an offer for Thyre. An excellent match, given her circumstances. He is a very particular man and I have no wish to antagonise my neighbour.' Ragnfast tapped the side of his nose. 'I am sure you understand.'

Thyre listened with mounting horror as Ragnfast continued to expand on his subject. Otto the Red? Otto the Toothless who had buried three wives? Surely Ragnfast could not mean this! Why hadn't he mentioned it before? She thought it understood that she should have some say in who she married. And she wanted to marry a man whom she could respect, rather than one who spent his time bragging about the number of women he had had in his bed. When had her stepfather been planning to mention this scheme? He had to know her feelings about Otto. The last time he had visited, she had mentioned the way his eyes followed her and Ragnfast had promised that it was nothing to worry about.

She swallowed hard and her hands trembled, nearly spilling the mead. Ivar's hand closed around hers and held the jug steady. 'Did you know?' he asked.

Slowly she shook her head. Ivar nodded.

Ragnfast continued on, seeming oblivious to her distress, explaining why this match was advantageous to a woman with few prospects and why he was certain the Viken would not wish to disrupt it. 'Otto hates the Viken with a passion. Blames them for his son's death. I told him that his son should not have sailed with Sigmund's ship. But it was a bad business, that. Sigmund also lost his brother.'

'That is hardly the fault of the Viken,' Ivar remarked.

'A man must grieve.'

'I have never denied a man that! But grief must not become revenge.'

'You will understand that my stepdaughter does not have many opportunities and Otto can give her much.' Ragnfast put a hand over his heart. 'I am an old man, and I fear the Norns will cut my life's thread soon. Thyre's future must be settled. Her mother would want her daughter safe with a secure future. It is a good offer.'

Thyre's insides twisted. Give her much. She knew what Ragnfast was saying, but she had no desire to become Otto's wife. She stared dumbly at the jug. She wanted to protest, but Ragnfast had timed his news perfectly. She could not risk an argument with the Viken present.

'Serving me at the table does nothing to change her status.' The Viken's eyes flashed blue fire. The entire table stilled.

Thyre looked from Ragnfast to Ivar and back again. Had she inadvertently given the Viken jaarl the excuse he was seeking? Would he now take it as an insult and lay the entire community waste? Her heart thumped in her ears. Silently she prayed to any god that might be listening that she was wrong and the Viken meant no harm.

'What does it matter who serves you, Ivar?' One of his companions reached over and twitched the jug from her fingers. 'All cats are alike in the dark, and mead tastes the same out of the horn whoever serves it.'

Ivar gave a laugh, drained his horn and wiped his mouth with the back of his hand. 'You are right, Erik the Black, it makes no difference. But I still prefer to see a delicate hand pouring my drink to your hairy one.'

The entire table laughed and the tension ebbed away.

'I will send Dagmar out, Ragnfast. She is taking far too long.' Thyre gave a quick curtsy. If she stayed any longer, she would find an excuse to argue with Ragnfast and that would not do anyone any good. After the Viken had left, then she would change his mind about the proposed betrothal. 'The meat needs to be checked. You do remember what happened when the jaarl Sigmund dined…'

'How could I forget it?' Ragnfast lifted his horn. 'Tell Dagmar to bring out the special mead.'

Ivar watched her depart, her skirts swinging about her ankles, revealing their slender curve. It was obvious that the details of her intended betrothal had come as a shock to Thyre. It was inexcusable of her stepfather. But why had Ragnfast thought to warn him? What sort of game was he playing and why was the woman important?

There was something more to this. Ivar swirled his mead and the honey scent wafted up towards him. He hated secrets, but he would not be here long enough to involve himself in Thyre's affairs. He had to be practical. There was little he could do for her. And he had to respect her stepfather's wishes for the moment. As Erik rightly said, if he was in the mood to bed a woman, it did not really matter who it was.

Ivar took a gulp of mead. Erik might believe that, but Ivar knew differently. He no longer needed to prove his manhood by bedding every woman who crossed his path. He wanted something more from a bed partner. Something that Thyre seemed to promise.

'About my daughter…' Ragnfast began. He leant forwards and his mead-soaked breath washed over Ivar in an unwelcomed wave. 'I think you will find her to your liking… She remains free from any betrothal. She would make any jaarl an admirable wife.'

Ivar frowned. The implication was clear. He knew what was expected. He refused to risk insulting his host, but he had no intention of bedding the man's daughter, let alone wedding the woman. She did not appeal. Tonight belonged to Thyre or no one. 'I look forward to being served.'

Thyre sat with her knees curled up to her chest, her eyes lost in the dancing flames of the cooking fire. The noise from the feast had died down a little to a dull murmur. Deep within her a great emptiness welled up. Ragnfast had betrothed her to Otto, after all she had done for this estate. In her dreams, she had wanted a love match like her mother had had with Ragnfast, one where the warrior was prepared to sail into the heart of enemy territory to retrieve her. Or failing that, she had thought perhaps she might never marry and would simply run the estate as she had done since she was a child of eight. Her own little kingdom.

There had to be a way around the betrothal, a way to escape the destiny Ragnfast had laid out for her. How much had Otto offered? Or was it that, having given his oath to King Mysing that his wife's offspring would never trouble him, Ragnfast had at last found a man whom he knew would never lift a sword in her name? Her stepfather should know that she was her uncle's loyal subject. She had no designs on a throne.

Thyre knew she should be doing other things, such as cleaning up and putting away the utensils, but she seemed to lack the energy for anything except staring at the fire and watching the flames dance.

She should have known something was brewing from the way Ragnfast had acted the last time he had encountered Otto. Ragnfast had always hinted that she could not expect to stay here for ever, but he had only ever said it when he was in drink and then he'd sober up and beg her to stay for ever. And she had assumed that when the time came, he would at least have given her a choice, that he'd let her find her own life's partner, not simply sell her off as if she were one of his sheep or a length of cloth. The whispers about how his wives had died swirled around him. How he had showed them no respect when they were alive and even less when they were dead. Thyre drew a shaky breath. She refused to give up on her dreams and accept a life of servitude.

She would find a way to outrun her fate. Her life would be something more. She simply had to discover it.

Dagmar stumbled in, wild eyed with her hair about her shoulders. She appeared to be gripped in some sort of trance, muttering and wringing her hands.

'Is there something wrong, Dagmar?' Thyre pushed all of her own problems to one side. 'Has one of the Viken attacked you? Broken the rules of hospitality? Are we going to be burnt in our beds? Should we be hiding the arm rings? Running to the woods and hiding?'

Dagmar muttered something, before Thyre saw her hand close around a knife. She held it out in front of her, the point turned towards her breast.

Thyre blinked twice. Her mouth went dry. She swiped her hand over her eyes and willed the apparition to be gone. But Dagmar still stood there gazing at the knife, muttering, seemingly oblivious to her. 'Dagmar! Answer me! We can do something!'

Dagmar raised her chin slightly, but ignored Thyre's outstretched hand. Thyre allowed it to drop to her side.

'There comes a time in woman's life when she knows that she has found the one man who will make her happy.' Dagmar looped her hair behind an ear. 'I always thought Father would let me make my own choice, but he is determined to make the Viken pay and in gold. He wants me to share the Viken's bed!'

'There are other ways…'

'Father will not listen. He refuses to even consider you.' Dagmar's eyes flashed and her mouth became pinched.

'You offered me!' Thyre stared at her half-sister. She swallowed hard and tried to make sense of it. 'You might have asked me. Do you think so little of me to treat me like some thrall to be ordered about?'

'Not offered, not exactly… I simply mentioned that the jaarl had asked after you. You were the one that he took the horn from…' Dagmar's voice trailed away and she lightly touched the hilt of the blade. Tears shimmered in her eyes. 'It was wrong of me, Thyre, I see that now. But it doesn't matter because Far would not hear of it. He is determined to marry you off to Otto and wants to keep you for that marriage bed. Why does he care more about you than me?'

'Dagmar…' Thyre said quietly. 'Dagmar, you're scaring me. Sit down and we will talk sensibly.'

'There is only one thing for me to do. I am an honourable woman.'

The knife glinted in the firelight. Thyre's blood ran cold. Who did Dagmar intend to hurt—Ragnfast, the Viken jaarl or herself? 'Dagmar, you are not a character in a saga. If you hurt the Viken, or you die, Sven loses you for good. Sven won't want that. He loves you.' Thyre hated the desperation in her voice. 'Nobody wants that.'

'I swore an oath to Sven. How else can I prove my worth?' Dagmar raised the knife a little higher. The blade glinted ominously in the dying embers of the fire. 'Please tell him that I kept true to my sacred vow, the one we made in front of Var's statue on the night before he departed.'

Thyre kept her eyes trained on the knife, measuring the distance between it and her hand. There was a chance that she might be able to get it before Dagmar plunged it into her breast. Slowly she rose and took a half-step towards Dagmar.

'There will be a solution to your problem. There is always a solution.' Thyre made her voice sound light and soothing. Dagmar could be distracted by her singsong tone. She could save Dagmar's life. She had to try. 'I will find it for you. You can't undo the past, but you do want a future with Sven.'

'Sven will not have me if he knows I have slept in the same bed as another man, especially not a Viken, even if he is a jaarl. I will be cursed for ever, like Mother was.' Tears trickled down Dagmar's face. 'I never asked to be cursed. Our mother lost everything because she slept with a Viken, even if he was the king.'

'Our mother found happiness with your father and you were born. How can you call that cursed?' Thyre risked another step forwards, and prayed to any god that might be listening that her tongue would prove silver and her inspiration would hold true. 'Hear me out! I have thought of another way!'

'What way?' Dagmar tilted her head to one side, the mist seeming to clear from her eyes.

Thyre risked a breath. The crisis had passed. Dagmar would listen and, when the time was right, she'd grab the knife.

'How does your father intend for you to go to bed with this Viken? Are you to entice him there with soft words and tender looks? Or to be a surprise? A gift in his bed for when he retires.'

'Far hasn't said. He simply indicated what he expects from me. Where I am to sleep tonight. You must understand how important this is to him. I swear he has changed ever since his quarrel with Sigmund. Or maybe I am just seeing him clearly for the first time.' Dagmar raised the knife again, screwing up her eyes. 'I must be strong.'

'All cats are black at night. All women appear the same when there is no light.'

Thyre caught Dagmar's wrist and shook it, forcing her to drop the knife. It fell on the table with a loud thunk.

Thyre breathed a little easier. Dagmar would not die tonight. She would ensure that she did not come in contact with any more knives. Tomorrow, after the Viken had departed, Thyre would figure out a way to let Ragnfast know about Dagmar's oath and they would discuss the best way to prevent such scenes in the future. If Dagmar was able to present a substantial morning gift to her father, Ragnfast might become more amenable to the idea of the forester as a son-in-law.

'I don't understand. What is all this talk of cats? We are women. Men can tell women apart.'

'I mean if the lights are out, this Viken will not know

who is in his bed.' Thyre kept her voice calm and clear even as her mind raced. The more she considered the idea, the more she was convinced it would work. 'He does not know you from the meanest serving girl. You are simply a warm body in the night. Whoever warms his bed means nothing to him. He will not know the difference.'

'You are going to send a serving girl to his bed?' Dagmar frowned. 'You scare me, Thyre. What happens when she talks and Far hears of it?'

'No, me. I will go. I would not trust any of the serving girls. They will all want the gift.'

Dagmar's eyes widened as comprehension dawned. 'You would do that for me? You would take my place in that Viken's bed?'

Thyre swallowed hard. She had been annoyed that Dagmar had offered her without consultation, but if this was the only way to save Dagmar's life, then she would do it. She had no other choice.

'We are sisters. I cannot let you kill yourself.' She forced her voice to be light. 'We swore a blood oath, Dagmar.'

'I…I suppose you are right…'

'I'm right. I would stake my life on it,' Thyre said with growing confidence. She would do this. The Viken would remain in blissful ignorance and she would cheat the fate that Ragnfast had planned for her. She would obtain one night of pleasure, before she was condemned to a life of cold servitude. She remembered the way the Viken's hand had felt against hers, the way his breath had stirred her hair.

'But…but…'

'If we are clever, no one will ever know who went into the Viken's bed. He will only care that there is a warm body in it. He is a man, after all.'

Dagmar gave an excited nod, accepting the scheme. 'But what should I do?'

'Go now and tell your father that you are tired and will go to the Viken's bed. Wait for me there. We can change places. You can go and sleep on my pallet, taking care to keep your hair covered.'

'It is such a simple plan. But what happens when he wakes? Or lifts the light? Sometimes men want to have the rush light on…to see your face. Sven likes to look at mine.'

'I will make sure there is no light.'

'But there will be light in the morning…'

Thyre captured Dagmar's cold hands and held them between hers. 'In the early morning, I will slip out of the bed, and you can go back and receive any morning gift that he cares to leave. You can even sit on the end of the bed, and play with your unbound hair. That way you will keep true to your oath to Sven and your duty towards your father. Ragnfast wants the gold and the prestige. The Viken dangles the possibility of new markets for his timber.'

Dagmar bowed her head, acknowledging the truth of the statement. 'But what if we get caught?'

'We won't be. What means more to you—your oath to Sven or your fear of your father? And in any case, it can hardly be worse than dying. You want to see Sven again.'

'I…I…'

'Allow me to handle this, Dagmar. Some day you will be able to repay me.' Thyre closed her eyes and tried to concentrate. Dagmar had to let her do this. It was a way of solving both their problems. She had to seize the chance.

'And you would this for me?' Dagmar's bottom lip trembled.

'I refuse to let you throw yourself away. Pointless dramatic gestures only work in sagas, Dagmar. Trust me on this point.' Thyre put her hand on Dagmar's shoulder, squeezing it when Dagmar returned a weak smile. 'In the name of the mother we share, I love you too much to lose you.'

'And what is this if not a dramatic gesture by you?'

'It is a practical one, forced on us by your father and his greed.' Thyre straightened the pleats of her apron dress and straightened her shoulders. She could seduce the Viken jaarl. It was the only way. All it would take was a steady nerve and a cool head. 'It is my life to make of it what I will.'

Chapter Five

Ivar watched the guttering torches with growing distaste. Soon the hall would be cast into darkness and he would have no choice but to retire to bed. The vast majority of his men had already left the table to find a space to sleep either with or without female company. His orders of no fighting had kept the quarrels to a minimum and nothing had happened that could start a lasting feud. All in all the evening had gone better than he had dared hope. It was not luck, but planning and paying attention to the smallest detail. It represented a potential ally gained and a harbour of safety for the Viken. The route to the markets of Permia would be open to Viken ships again, one way or another, plus it was also a good timber source for ship building.

'Do you intend to remain awake all night? You have been staring at your tafl pieces for a long time,' Ragnfast said, slurring his words. 'I have had a bed prepared for you. The best bed in the hall with all the comforts. After a journey like yours, you could do with a warm bed and a soft pillow for your head. Honour me by accepting my best bed and all its comforts.'

'You do me much honour.'

'It is you who do me the honour.' The old man dug his elbow into Ivar's ribs. 'It will be something to say—one of the great jaarls of Lindisfarne slept in my bed. Enjoy my hospitality.'

Ivar made a non-committal noise. Refuse now and he risked making an enemy for life. This bay would make the perfect place to wait out storms, or re-supply boats with fresh water.

If he returned again, he could continue his pursuit of Thyre. She would fall eventually. 'Lead the way.'

'There you go.' Ragnfast pointed to a raised area curtained off from the main hall. A single tallow lamp guttered in the corner of the makeshift room. As beds went, this one could rival many in Kaupang—piled high with furs, down pillows and linen sheets. Despite everything, the lure of linen reached out and called to him.

Ivar lifted an eyebrow. 'Most unexpected. You live well.'

'My late wife had a taste for luxury,' Ragnfast replied, hooking his thumb in his belt. 'I did manage to acquire a few things along the way.' He gave Ivar a pat on the back. 'Enjoy your…rest. We will speak more in the morning.'

Ivar groaned as he approached the bed. A telltale bump was in the middle of the bed. The blondeness and overt charms of Ragnfast's daughter held little appeal after his encounters with Thyre.

He ran his hand through his hair, contemplating turning on his heel and sleeping in the boat. Immediately he rejected the idea. Excuses should have been made earlier.

Ivar pressed his lips together. He was no longer in the first flush of youth and intent on proving his manhood. Sleep would come easy, no matter who his bed companion. And it would be sleep. He would give the woman a suitable morning gift and all honour would be satisfied.

Ivar eased his body between the crisp linen sheets, placing the tallow light on the bedside stool. The soft pillows and the furs enveloped him. He disliked thinking about the last time he had encountered such luxury. Why had Ragnfast indulged his wife in this manner? Had she really been as penniless as Ragnfast pretended? Ragnfast appeared to have mastered the technique of never really explaining anything. Thyre ran things, but who was her mother? It was a mystery and he hated mysteries.

When he returned to Viken, Ivar resolved to visit Bose the Dark to discover if somewhere in his vast memory Bose knew of a Ragnfast the Steadfast and how he had come by the nickname. He put his hands behind his head. Mysteries were there to be solved.

The woman stirred slightly, stretching. In the dim light, he could see a slender hand, but nothing more. He lifted the tallow light higher, throwing elongated shadows on to the bed. Her body froze, but she remained hidden underneath the covers.

'No light.' The two words slid over his skin, low, musical and full of promise.

'Hush,' Ivar said, placing his finger against her mouth after he had put the light on the bedside stool. Her fresh flowery scent filled his nostrils and held him in its embrace. 'Sleep now.'

Her lips quivered at his touch and her tongue flicked out to taste his finger. An unexpected surge of warmth went through him, causing the need for sleep to fall away and to be replaced by something far more urgent. He frowned. The last blonde who had truly attracted him in this fashion had been Edda, his late wife. Ever since her death, blondes had only served to magnify his loss and to rebuke him for his failure to protect her.

Was Erik right and were all cats black in the dark?

He had forgotten the last time he had felt the need for a woman's body without knowing anything about her. Perhaps as long ago as his first voyage. There was a difference between taking and savouring your partner. The delights of Freya's grove were far sweeter when the mind played a part.

He forced his shoulders back against the pillows. Desire would pass. He would remain in control of his body. 'I want to sleep.'

'Then we shall sleep…and only dream of delight.' Her words were a soft caress.

Ivar stilled. The voice sounded different from the brash, nasal-like quality of Ragnfast's daughter. Completely different. There was an underlying tone of intelligence and quality.

He reached towards the light, intending to lift it higher and satisfy his curiosity. But a gust of wind extinguished it, plunging the room into complete darkness. Ivar regarded the darkened figure. Getting up and relighting the reed would make the woman realise he was on to her and give her a chance to escape. And he had no wish to lose her. With every breath he took her scent further infiltrated his being, making the tiny flicker grow within him, drowning out his earlier intentions. But he would know whom he bedded. 'Or perhaps we should find a little relaxation first.'

'I live for your desire.'

He turned her body towards him, trailed his fingers down her chin, skimming the indention of the dimple. A dimple, not smooth skin. He paused and grasped the chin more firmly, checked to make sure that his fingers had felt true. The dimple was unmistakeable.

He lay back against the pillows and struggled to breathe, reviewing his memory of both women. It was Thyre who sported the dimple in her chin, not the daughter. He was certain of it. His body sprang to life at the knowledge.

'I wish to see you,' he whispered. 'Let me find another light.'

'It is better this way. Darkness has its own embrace.'

Ivar lifted a brow. He was torn between wanting Thyre and wanting to solve the mystery of why she concealed her identity. She would be in his arms come morning. Ivar smiled grimly. He would play the game. First seduction and then revelation with the first light of dawn. 'Darkness it is, then. For now.'

'For ever.'

His fingers traced the outline of her cheekbones. Her flesh quivered at the slight touch, calling to him, tempting him to taste it. His body sprang to life, insisting. Ivar breathed deeply and regained control. He was not some untried youth. He wanted to prolong the encounter, not spill his seed before he had begun. 'You are an unexpected surprise. A welcome one.'

He cupped her face between his palms and lowered his lips. One brush of his lips. One indulgence before the true seduction began.

Thyre relaxed slightly as his lips whispered over hers. It had begun. She had spent so long lying there that she had been convinced he had found somewhere else to sleep. Or that she should abandon her position and let him assume that it was only a bed on offer and risk the insult. Half a dozen times she had started to get out, but each time she remembered her promise to Dagmar and the look in Dagmar's eyes. How hard would it be to fool Ivar?

Then he was here, lying next to her, his musky masculine scent enveloping her as surely as his arms turned her body towards him. And she knew it was more than that. Something about him called to her. She should consider this man an enemy, but she knew tonight he was to be her lover. A singing of the blood, her mother had once said, and now she began to understand. Quick flames of heat licked her insides, radiating outwards from his lips.

The pressure of his mouth increased, calling to her with warm insistence. His tongue traced the outline of her lips, demanded entrance, and she forgot to breathe. Her lips parted and his tongue slowly penetrated her mouth, teasing her. Every part of her suddenly seemed to be alive and tingling with anticipation.

'You like this?' he whispered against her lips as his hand trailed along her shoulder, sending ripples of pleasure coursing through her body, each stronger than the last.

'Yes.' The word was drawn from her throat in a soft sigh.

His lips returned, recaptured hers, plundered and took. They were slow and smooth, but firm, and demanded a response from deep within her. A tide of warmth engulfed her, making her forget everything but the sensation of his lips moving against hers. Each breath caused her to sink deeper into the tide of warmth. Her hand lifted, curled around his neck and held him there, his silky hair wrapping itself around her fingers, his body covering hers, hard muscles pressing into her soft curves.

She knew she should confess about the deception and tore her mouth from his. 'I…'

'Hush now,' he breathed against her temple, smoothing

her hair back. 'The time for talking is done. You are here and I am here, and that is all we need to know. You are free to leave if you wish, but I would far rather you stayed.'

Scorching molten heat infused her. She was not powerless. She had a choice.

Here in the darkness, no one would ever know, would ever guess, and she could indulge in the fantasy of seduction.

'One night,' she murmured. One night of pleasure was all she would have. In the morning he would sail away and she would be married to Otto, becoming little more than a thrall. Her mother would have wept at how far her eldest daughter had fallen. She had trusted Ragnfast and he had betrayed her. She deserved this one night of passion with her chosen warrior.

Tonight she refused to think about the future; she would simply experience the present. Her stomach became heavy with desire. The steady practical self had vanished and in its place she had become someone different, someone who was determined to take pleasure, pleasure she knew instinctively his touch promised.

'One night, one perfect night,' she whispered against his lips.

'One perfect night? If that is what you demand.' He settled her more firmly in his arms, his hot skin burning hers. Intoxicating her. She arched forwards, brushing up against him.

His mouth shifted, slowly moving down the column of her throat. At its base, he suckled hard. Gently nipped. Then he returned to the spot again and again as the ache grew within her. She squirmed slightly at the sudden pressure, but his mouth travelled upwards again, reclaiming hers. His tongue traced the outline of her lips and demanded renewed entrance.

This time his kiss became more insistent, as if it were feasting, calling to something deep within her and she could only feel this growing need inside her, pushing everything else away. It made it impossible for her to think beyond the next pulse of heat. She lifted her hand and silently traced the smoothness of his scars; his skin quivered under her fingers.

His hand stroked down her body, skimming her shoulders, turning her more towards him, making her fall against him, covering her with his body.

He pushed the hem of her shift. Thyre suddenly wished she had taken Dagmar's advice and had gone into the bed naked. But that had seemed odd so she had gone to bed as she normally did. Her back arched, seeking his warmth, and her nipples tightened, thrust up against the confining cloth.

His hand lifted her plait from her shoulder, undid it, and drew her hair over them both, creating an intimate curtain. Thyre's breasts ached and became heavy with the need to feel his touch. Tongues of flame licked her core.

'Soft, so soft.'

He trailed open-mouthed kisses down her throat and when he reached her shift he brushed it aside with impatient fingers. He cupped her breast, exposing it to his mouth, and bent his head. As he breathed, he sent a stream of air over the nipple, causing it to harden to a delicate nub. She arched her back, driving her breast upwards towards his mouth.

His tongue licked, sweeping around and over the tightly furled nipple, exploring its surface. Slow and languid, he took his time as if he understood exactly what he was doing to her and was determined to make her suffer. Her hands gripped the linen sheet. Everything had come down to this gentle tugging on her breast. The suckling became harder, more insistent, as waves of raw heat thrummed through her.

Her hips lifted towards his hard body. He slipped his hand down her back, edging her towards him, her hip hitting his, his arousal nestling against her, demonstrating his desire for her.

Her fingers explored the firm muscles of his chest, trailing over his flat nipples. They became molten heat under the pads of her fingers. She dipped her head quickly and licked them, much as a cat would lick its milk. She tasted faint salt and something indefinably him. She felt the rough points with the tip of her tongue and returned to taste again.

His muffled groan echoed in her ears and his arms locked around her, holding her there, face pressed against the rise and fall of his chest. She lay there, listening to the steady thump of his heart, and knew her heart beat the same rhythm.

His hand tugged at her shoulders, raised her face. Their breaths intermingled for an instant before he reclaimed her lips. Ivar's friend Erik had been wrong. All cats were not black at night. He was not just any man, but this man. He was doing this to her, and her to him.

He lowered his head, returning to the sensitive point of her nipple. A mewling cry emerged from her throat. He stopped and freed the other breast from her shift, captured its swollen peak, taking it into his mouth, and suckled with renewed intensity.

The primitive fire within her raged, consuming her senses, demanding that she become one with him. She pressed her body closer and felt his skin, warm and subtle under her fingertips. He pushed them aside and rolled her over, so she was under him.

Her world began to blur at the edges as his hand drifted inexorably lower and found the nest of curls at the apex of her thighs. A single finger traced her crease, delving inwards and parting her innermost folds. Stroking firmly, he discovered the hidden peak. He lingered, playing, circling it as his mouth covered hers again. His fingers mimicked the playing of his tongue, sliding over her crease and within her. Thyre longed for more. Her hands grasped his shoulders, trying to make him understand.

Ivar's heavy weight came down on top of her. His knee pressed against her legs, wedging them open. The tip of him nudged her, resting there. It seared her. Pulses coursed through her body as she squirmed upwards, seeking more. And then he impaled himself, driving deep within her. She gasped at the unexpected burning pain. His lips touched her brow, soothing her.

'I am sorry,' he murmured. 'I had not considered…'

He lay there inside her, not moving. Thyre moaned in frustration. Her entire being was consumed with him and she needed something more, something to take away the burning itch inside her. She tried to lift her hips.

Gently he kissed her mouth, his tongue coaxing a response from hers. Tangling, twisting, thrusting with his tongue. Suddenly the fire that the pain had held at bay flamed with a new intensity and consumed her, turning her resistance to ashes and forging her from new again. Her hips arched upwards, driving him deeper.

He began to move against her, faster and faster. The pain subsided as the need overtook her. She grasped his shoulders and held him there. It was as if the world had been made anew. A great shuddering engulfed her and a heartbeat later it engulfed him.

Afterwards, they lay together, his hand lightly cupping her back. He started to speak, but Thyre touched her hand to his mouth. 'No regrets.'

As she said the words, she knew them to be true. Despite the pain, despite the knowledge that she would never see him again and he would never know who had shared his bed, she would treasure this night.

His fingers curled around hers, pulling her close. His strong, warm arms went around her. His heart thumped in her ears.

'Sleep now.' His breath kissed her temple, but she lay there listening, savouring, prolonging this special world that she had somehow entered.

Thyre lay awake for a long while, listening to his steady breathing, feeling his strong arm curved around her middle and the way their bodies fit together. She was determined to remember everything. She had to change Ragnfast's plan for her destiny. She had to believe she could. Instead of quenching her desire, tonight had ignited it. What would happen if she stayed? What would happen if she was discovered in his arms? How would he react when he discovered that it was not the daughter of the house, but the stepdaughter? Would he think they intended to dishonour him?

She listened to his steady breathing for as long as she dared. A queer happiness filled her and she longed for the night's great blanket to keep enveloping them. She rested against him for a few heartbeats longer before she eased her body away from his, ignoring the siren call of warmth and protection.

Silently she fumbled about for her shift, discovering it wrapped in a ball on the floor. Quickly she slipped it over her head.

Outside in the empty hall, she wrapped her arms about her middle and headed towards the faint light of the kitchen. Her life began again now today, this morning. Nothing that had happened here had any bearing on the future, but she could not resist taking one last backwards glance at the naked shoulder and the tousled hair against the whiteness of the linen. With a sigh, she let the curtain fall.

The faintest rustle woke Ivar. Instantly his body jerked awake. Seeing the heavily embroidered bed hangings and the piles of furs, he leant back against the pillows, replete, at peace. He found it difficult to remember the last time that such contentment had filled him. He reached out for the woman, ready to reveal her identity and satisfy his curiosity. This time he would watch her face as he kissed her mouth and brought her once again to the brink. He would see the passion in her eyes.

He encountered cold air and an even colder indentation in the bed. Something within him shrivelled.

Ivar slammed his fist into the pillow and cursed his sound sleep. She had gone. He would have wagered any money that she would stay for the morning gift. He pressed his hands against his eyes. Had he merely dreamed the episode? Instantly he rejected the notion. Her floral scent clung to the pillows.

But she had been real, not a figment of his fevered dreams. No phantom, but flesh and blood. And she had been a virgin.

He had felt her maidenhead give way when he had entered her. If he had known, he would have taken her more gently, but he had also heard her cry of pleasure and had felt her move and open under him.

Why had Thyre come to him? It had to have been her. And why had she given him that most precious of gifts and not stayed to receive her own gift? Because of her intended betrothal? But why come and not stay?

He did not want to think how long it had been since he last held a woman in his arms, neither did he wish to think how his arms felt empty without her in them. Silently, he willed her to return. Even now, he wanted to kiss her again. His body quickened at the thought.

'Oh, you are awake.'

Ivar regarded the blonde who pushed aside the curtain. Her chin had no dimple and there was no mark at the base of her neck where her apron dress gaped open. Ivar knew he had suckled long enough between the two bones in her throat to make a mark. It would appear that his caution had not been misplaced. Last night's woman had not been Ragnfast's daughter. He let out a breath, and willed his body to relax. Perhaps there was an innocent explanation for this woman being in his chamber.

'Is there something you require?'

She walked over to the bed and perched on its edge. She twisted her hands and her eyes flicked over the bed hangings, avoiding his face. 'Forgive me. Nature called. I did not want to disturb you after our…'

Her face puckered and she appeared to be having trouble thinking of the correct word as her throat worked up and down. Finally she gave a hopeful smile that did not reach her pale blue eyes.

'Our night of passion,' Ivar finished smoothly.

'Yes, that is exactly what I wanted to say—our night of passion.'

'And what a night it was.'

'Truly?' Her eyes grew wide.

'Oh, yes. One of the most passion-filled I have ever spent.'

He controlled his features as the anger grew within him. This woman had not been in his bed, and now she was attempting to make him think she had been. He knew Ragnfast had expected his daughter to be in his bed. He had made that honour clear, but the half-sister had been there instead.

What had Thyre hoped to gain? Had she been compelled to do it or had she begged for the honour? He frowned. Her response had appeared real enough. No one could feign that amount of fire. There was a deeper story here.

He would find out the reason and punish whoever had done this. No one made a fool of him. And his lady of the night would not slip through his fingers, melting away in the dark of the night.

He could well imagine the laughter in the kitchen early this morning. How they had fooled the hideous Viken. How he had been so grateful for a woman's touch. How they had deceived him and how easy it had been.

Inside he seethed. His lady of the night would pay for this. No one mocked him.

The blonde twisted a strand of hair around her forefinger, dipped her head and gave a flirtatious smile. 'That's right—our night of passion. I only hope you enjoyed it as much as I did.'

'I certainly enjoyed the night.' He waited, raising his eyebrow as his mind raced. He would exact his revenge on Thyre. She would regret her deception.

'One thing remains between us…the gift that lovers share.' She leant back, sticking her bosom out, but averted her eyes as if the scarring on his face bothered her. She held out her hand expectantly. The morning gift. The one she had no right to.

Ivar cursed under his breath. He refused to be manipulated in this way. He had no objection to giving a gift, but only to the woman who had shared his bed. To the woman who had responded so passionately to his touch, but who had not stayed 'til morning. No doubt she had thought she had won, but he would prove her wrong. 'I think we should do this formally.'

'Formally?' Her eyes widened and her mouth turned down at the corners, making her look like a startled owl. 'Why? I like things to be…to be intimate. Kept between the man and woman.'

'Your father has done me much honour while my men and I have rested here,' Ivar said smoothly, clinging on to the remnants of his temper. Revenge would be all the sweeter for prolonging it. He would exact every drop of it from Thyre and she would learn. 'I wish to thank him. How better than to give you a small trinket of my appreciation.'

'In front of the whole house?' she squeaked. 'You want to give me my gift in front of everyone?'

'In front of the household and my men.'

He watched her through narrowed slits as her hands smoothed and re-smoothed the pleats in her gown.

'It will be much more pleasant this way,' he said. 'I can show my true *appreciation.*'

'And there is no way that you wish to keep this between us two. An intimate exchange between two who shared the passions of the night.' Her eyes flickered everywhere but on his face.

'No. I wish to make my declaration before everyone. I must insist.' Ivar waited. Even now, if this woman confessed, he would forgive her.

'Very well, I will do as you request.' She rose from the bed, and her lips curved into a trembling smile. He almost felt sorry for her, and the humiliation that would come, but the conspirators had brought it on their own heads. Seeing her actions, he doubted if she had the brains to think the scheme up. No, it must have been Thyre, and it would be Thyre who would pay. Last night was not the end, but the beginning. Concubine to a jaarl would suit her far better than wife to some hard-handed farmer. He wondered that he had not thought of it before. He would make the offer in his own time.

'Allow me to inform your father,' Ivar replied carefully, watching the woman's face drain of colour. He had to be careful. Thyre must not suspect and have time to plan. He focused on her white throat and renewed anger filled him. 'You may go and make yourself ready. Your face appears flushed. I would have my bed partner looking her best.'

'Of course, it was a unique experience for me as well, but such things…that is to say, it is not our custom.'

'But it is my wish. Your father will indulge me. Trust me. The gift will make it all worthwhile.'

He kept a tight lead on his emotions. The woman who had shared his bed would be sharing it again. And this time, it would be for far more than a night.

Chapter Six

'He knows, Thyre. Your Viken lover knows all about the trick and he is taunting us.' Dagmar burst into the kitchen, her eyes wild and her face pinched.

'Sit down, Dagmar, and take a deep breath.' Thyre made her voice to sound natural and easy as she gave the porridge another stir. 'All this pacing up and down is making my head ache. He has no idea, not unless you told him. And he is not my Viken lover any longer. I hope never to see him again.'

Everything was a drama with Dagmar. She continually fretted about every word and nuance. This morning was no different. It had to be. The plan was without a flaw. All Dagmar had to do was to perch on the bed, give her sweetest smile and Ivar would never guess.

He had failed to stir when she had left the bed. He had taken his pleasure, fallen asleep and that was the end of it. She was only a warm body.

Thyre blinked rapidly. Her heart screamed she was wrong. But if she was, why hadn't he said something or whispered her name during the time they had spent together?

Thyre gave the porridge one final vicious stir, regained control of her emotions and turned to face Dagmar.

'Did you do something, Dagmar? Something that we had not discussed?'

Dagmar caught her tongue between her teeth and slowly shook her head, counting the points off on her fingers. 'I did everything you said…almost everything, I was not able to slip into his bed… I came up with a good excuse though.'

'Why do you think he is taunting you?' Thyre hated the way her stomach twisted and all the air rushed out of her lungs. 'You must have a reason. Simply saying that you have one of your feelings is no good to me. We will have to make plans. Did he kiss you?'

Dagmar recoiled. 'Nothing like that. He never even attempted to touch me. He regarded me with his glacier-blue eyes as if he could see through to my heart.'

The heavy weight on Thyre's chest vanished and she could breathe again. No kisses. No caresses. Nothing to tell him that they were different women. Just Dagmar's overactive imagination and her love of drama. Thyre pressed her fingers to her temples and wished she had had more sleep.

Everything should be over now. Only Thyre knew it would not end for her. Last night was seared on her memory. Every part of her ached with an intense burning. She had not been prepared for this maelstrom of emotions that swamped her senses. She had thought it would not change anything, but instead it had changed everything. Thyre leant forwards and touched Dagmar's cold hand. 'Dagmar, keep calm. All will be well.'

'He thanked me for the pleasant night, one of the best he had ever spent…' Dagmar paused, and her brow wrinkled.

'Is there something wrong with that?' A small spark of satisfaction grew with Thyre. Last night had been special to Ivar. She hated that she wished it could have continued, and that she could have had the words from his lips herself. Face flaming, she turned back to the hearth and concentrated on the bubbling porridge. 'What did he give you for your morning gift?'

'He intends to present my morning gift in front of everyone.' Dagmar twisted the ends of her apron dress, crumpling the ties with her hand. 'I am afraid, Thyre. It is far from normal. These things are discreet—bed talk between a man and a woman, not out in the open where all might gawk. What if he makes an offer for me?'

Thyre struggled to keep her temper. Dagmar was doing it again—seeing shadows where there were none. There was a logical explanation for the Viken's behaviour if only she could find it. 'Ivar Gunnarson is too great a jaarl. When he marries, it will be because his king has chosen him a bride. Ragnfast married our mother only when the king commanded it.'

'But Mother was a princess.'

'Precisely, and you are the only child of a jaarl and will inherit all of his lands. Your father would never allow you to become a concubine to a Viken, even if he is one of the most powerful jaarls in the kingdom. There is a difference between a concubine and a wife.'

'But then why does the Viken want everyone there? These exchanges are supposed to remain private.' Dagmar shook her head. 'I just do not understand Viken warriors.'

'The ways of men are mysterious.' Thyre picked up Beygul and held her close. She inhaled the familiar catty smell and stroked the soft fur. She had to hang on to what was real. Viken customs were different.

'What is the matter with your throat?' Dagmar asked, her gaze becoming piercing. 'Put that cat down and come over here into the light.'

'My throat…nothing is the matter.' Thyre let Beygul go and put her hand over her neck, trying to feel if anything was different. She had not bothered with Dagmar's mirror this morning, not daring to see if somehow her face reflected the night she had spent and the change she felt in herself. She had simply tidied herself up, put on a fresh apron dress and her soft leather boots and tied her hair back with a kerchief. She had taken extra care with washing, had made sure none of his scent lingered anywhere except in her memory. Little things that kept her mind from going back to the night and what had happened. 'Stop giving me that look, Dagmar.'

'What look?'

'As though I am a mouse and you are Beygul. What can you see?'

Dagmar reached out a slender finger and touched the base of Thyre's throat. 'You are bruised. That warrior bruised you. Do you have passion marks anywhere else? Anywhere at all?'

Thyre explored the area with her fingers.

Marked. He had marked her. Deliberately. She remembered how in the beginning, his fingers had skimmed her face and had traced the indent of her dimple. 'Is it that obvious?'

Dagmar tapped her finger against her mouth. 'It may have been unintentional. Some men are just like that. They lose control and do not realise their own strength.'

'But you noticed it straight away. You said he was taunting you. Do you think he was looking for this? Was it light enough for him to see you or was the curtain that separates the room from the hall still drawn?'

Thyre fought against the rising panic in her voice. She was becoming worse than Dagmar. Her mind was playing tricks, making her remember things that had not happened. Had he indeed kissed her there and then caressed her dimple? Or was she just imagining it? She forced air into her lungs, let it go and then forced them to fill again. It was only her overactive imagination.

'He could have been. How would I know? I did not even know you had it!' Dagmar paced the room, then stopped. 'No, that's impossible. I had pulled the curtain back, but it remained dark. His scar was barely visible.'

'But you said that he seemed to know instantly.'

'And you said that it was my nerves. He noticed that I was coming back into the room.' Dagmar glared back at her. 'You know what I am like and I accept your opinion.'

Thyre swallowed hard, trying to think as a small satisfied something twisted in her stomach. He had guessed from almost the first moment. But what was his purpose? How did he intend to use his knowledge? And had he toyed with her? Why had he not asked before they had joined?

'We shall have to hide the mark,' Thyre said, pressing her hands against her head. 'It would look strange if I did not appear with you. We do not want any comment. It would leave Ragnfast open to insult if we did not appear. And if the Viken appear insulted…'

Dagmar gave a small frightened nod as if she understood. 'But how shall we hide it?'

Thyre snapped her fingers. 'Shawls. We must wear shawls. He cannot ask you to undress. There are limits to hospitality.'

Dagmar hurried over to the trunk, and flung it open. 'This one will do.'

Thyre caught the shawl and pulled it tight about her throat. Thankfully Dagmar had noticed the bruising before it was too late.

She did not need any awkward questions this morning. Later after the Viken had left, she would shrug and allow Ragnfast to reach his own conclusions. Whatever happened, last night had prevented the betrothal to Otto. Ragnfast might bluster for a few days, but he would see the sense in her remaining here in the end. 'Does this hide it now?'

'Much better.' Dagmar looped the russet shawl about her shoulders. 'You can always say that you are sickening if Far asks why you are wearing a shawl in the summer time.'

'Dagmar! Dagmar!' Ragnfast's bellow echoed through the kitchen. 'The Viken jaarl wishes to make a goodbye present. He commands that all of the household be present. Everyone. I have no wish for trouble after this visit has gone so well. You and Thyre must be there. He insists.'

'Sister…' Dagmar reached out and Thyre caught her hand, covering the ice cold fingers with her own.

'Shall we go?'

'Hold on tight to me,' Dagmar pleaded. 'You must not leave me.'

'Once we are on the beach, you go and stand by your father. I will stay back amongst the other women. Receive the morning gift with dignity, Dagmar.'

'If you say I must…'

'We have to hope, Dagmar. Without hope, we are lost…' Thyre drew the shawl tighter about her neck, clinging to the thought that men sometimes marked women without realising it. He could not suspect. After all, he was just a warrior and thought with his brawn, instead of with his brain.

She took one last look at the kitchen and the way the

cats lay sleeping by the fire, and the pot spluttering on the fire. Everything was normal and peaceful and it would be the same when she returned.

'It will work out. It has to. Keep your head up and your gaze direct.'

Ivar stood, the hot sun beating against his back, struggling to maintain control of his anger. This had already taken far longer than he had dreamt possible. Ragnfast had offered several more excuses on why his daughter failed to appear until he had demanded that the Ranrike jaarl fetch his daughter.

The tide lapped against the *Sea Witch*. All his men were ranged behind him, waiting for his signal. He would discover the truth, and he would make the woman pay for her deception. Did she really think she could trick him like that?

'Forgive me, my lord. It took longer to discover my daughter than I thought possible. But she is here now along with the rest of the women.' Sweat stood out on the farmer's brow and greed shone from his eyes. 'You do my household and me great honour.'

Ivar released a breath as he saw the women. Most were in their light summer apron dresses with head kerchiefs, but two—the daughter and Thyre—were swathed in shawls.

Ivar forced his hand to remain at his side. The time to play the final round had begun and this time they played by his rules.

'Your hospitality has been a revelation, truly a milestone in the relations between Ranrike and Viken.' Ivar watched him intently.

How much was Ragnfast party to? And what exactly did he hope to gain by the deception? Did Ragnfast think that he was so blind in lust that he would not notice the insult?

'I wish to reward those who give such unsurpassed hospitality.'

'You are too kind, Ivar Gunnarson.'

Ivar signalled towards Erik the Black, who brought forwards a few of the spices from Permia. Ragnfast made a low bow and murmured his thanks.

'And for your daughter, a length of silk.'

Ivar paused, enjoying himself as the blonde simpered forwards and clutched the silk to her breast. But she never let the shawl slip from around her neck. This little scene was playing out better than he had envisioned. Revenge would be sweet. He would keep his temper, but he would make his offer.

'And for the woman who shared my bed...' He held up a golden arm ring studded with jewels, worth more than most warriors would ever possess. He allowed it to glint for a moment in the sunlight.

The blonde hesitated; her eyes grew round. Her fingers twitched. She glanced back over her shoulder at Thyre, who gave an encouraging nod. Ivar raised the arm ring a little higher and waited, keeping all his attention on the woman in the background. When would her greed overcome her sensibilities?

'Thyre?' A single damning word wafted on the wind. 'Help me! My oath!'

Thyre wet her lips and silently urged Dagmar to take the arm ring and to end this farce. Explanations to Sven could happen later. Right now, the Viken had to be appeased. No Ranriken boats appeared on the horizon, coming to save her. In the distance she heard the water slapping against the hull of the Viken.

Why was Dagmar taking so long to take the gift?

It could not be difficult. One tiny action, that was all and the Viken would go. She willed Dagmar to reach out and end this little drama. *Pick it up*, she mouthed. But Dagmar appeared to be turned to stone.

'I believe my daughter shared your bed. I gave her specific orders. My daughter never disobeys me. She accepts my guidance in these matters.' Ragnfast's eyes glittered with greed at the magnificence of the arm ring.

'It was your stepdaughter who shared my bed,' Ivar replied, his deep blue gaze directly on her. His features became harder, his scar more pronounced.

Thyre kept her head and did not flinch or blush under his intense stare, even though her fingers itched to guide Dagmar's hand to the ring to end the ordeal.

Ragnfast went white and then red. 'I gave specific orders to Dagmar. Why would you believe she would disobey me?'

'I marked my bed companion with my mouth,' Ivar said with an arrogant smile. 'Your daughter's throat remains free from any blemish.'

'You are guessing, Viken.' Ragnfast gave a scornful laugh. 'My daughter is swathed in a shawl, presumably because you *did* mark her. Reveal your neck, Dagmar, and show this Viken to be a liar.'

Dagmar threw her a panicked glance as Thyre's stomach lurched. The full horror slammed into her. He knew. He had known all along. He had played her and Dagmar for fools this morning, toying with them like a cat with its prey. And now they were trapped. Dagmar had to obey her father. She had to reveal her unblemished neck. But what happened then?

They should have hidden in the bath house until Ivar

and the other Viken departed. She should have done a dozen other things except stand here on the sand, listening to the steady pounding of the waves and feeling the dampness creep into her boots. This entire situation was her fault.

All she could do was watch, powerless to stop the drama and the destruction that must surely follow.

Why had she ever thought that she could deceive this man? The idea was hers and hers alone. No one else should be punished, but he would use it as an excuse to destroy them all. She could sense it in her bones. She wanted to grab a sword and call the men to her banner. She wanted to turn back time. But most of all she wanted the horror of waiting to end.

'Dagmar, obey your father. Show this arrogant Viken the truth.' Ragnfast reached for Dagmar's shawl. 'You have abused my hospitality, Viken. You are no longer welcome here.'

'It is not I who abused it, but the daughters of this house.'

'I will obey you, Far.' Fingers trembling and white faced, Dagmar allowed the shawl to fall to the ground, but she kept her head erect and shoulders back. A surge of pride rushed through Thyre. Dagmar could have given way to hysterics and run, but she stood proud and elegant. Her slender neck was revealed to all. Thyre had never been prouder of her half-sister. She only hoped that she could display the same sort of courage when her time came.

'Free from blemish.' Ivar made a sweeping bow. 'She is not the woman with whom I shared my bed. The arm ring remains unclaimed.'

'What sort of mischief is this? What sort of spell have you cast to have my daughter's neck clear?'

'No mischief. Nothing supernatural. Another woman waited for me in the bed. A woman who filled the night with passion.'

'And who might that woman be?'

'Your stepdaughter, Thyre.'

'Thyre? Have you been touched by moon madness? Thyre did not share your bed. She has not shared any man's bed. I would stake my life on it. She is far too proud, far too like her mother. I explained about the betrothal and why she must keep herself pure. It is her best chance for marriage.' Ragnfast made a disgusted noise. 'We will find the woman who shared your bed, Viken, and when I do, I will reach the truth of this puzzle. Show him your neck, Thyre. Show him that he lies.'

'If that is your wish, Ragnfast.'

'It is.'

Thyre took several steps forwards so that she was level with her stepfather. Her earlier nerves vanished and a queer calm descended.

The shawl floated to the earth with a soft whisper. She forced her shoulders to stay erect, and prayed fervently that some god would hear her prayer—that somehow the mark would have vanished.

Ragnfast's hissed intake of breath showed that her prayer went unanswered. He clawed at his chest for an instant before recovering and glaring at her and Ivar. 'You disobeyed me, Thyre!'

'I marked the right woman, but you may examine all your other women, if you wish.'

'What sort of dark magic is this? What sort of spell has this Viken jaarl cast?'

Thyre opened her mouth, but her voice refused to work.

'No magic or spells,' the Viken commented in a dry voice.

'She seduced me, rather than the other way around. Then she slipped out of my bed and your daughter thought to get in it, pretending to be the one who had passed the night with me.'

'Do you deny this, Thyre?' Ragnfast asked. 'Is it what happened?'

'The Viken jaarl speaks the truth.' Thyre kept her head up. Her body seemed to have gone numb.

'Dagmar would never have disobeyed me like this. This is your doing, Thyre. This is the last time your will is followed on this steading.' Ragnfast's brows drew together and he raised his fist as if to strike her. 'The sooner you are gone, the better for all of us.'

'No one touches her. She bears my mark. I claim her as my woman.' Ivar's voice rang out as he caught Ragnfast's wrist and held it for an instant, then let go. Ragnfast's hand remained frozen in mid-air. Then, very slowly, Ragnfast lowered it and appeared to shrink.

'Dagmar had a knife, Ragnfast. She is in love with Sven the forester.' Thyre kept her voice steady and calm. Ragnfast could understand love. He had braved the Viken to rescue her mother, when her mother's brother had been content to see her rot.

'Dagmar and Sven? Sven the forester?' Ragnfast did not bother to hide the incredulity in his voice. 'My daughter would never—'

'Yes, Far, Thyre speaks true.' Dagmar stepped between Thyre and Ragnfast. Her chin was held high and proud. Faced with the evidence, Dagmar had not given way to the easy lie; she had told the truth even though Ragnfast was likely to forbid Dagmar ever to seek out Sven again. After today, the future Dagmar and Sven had carefully planned would be shattered.

'You love that…that forester?'

'Sven and I swore an oath in front of Var.' Dagmar kept her eyes on the ground and her voice was barely audible. 'Last night I despaired and would have taken my life but for Thyre and her plan.'

At Dagmar's faltering glance, Thyre put her arm about Dagmar. She had protected Dagmar ever since she had been born. She would protect Dagmar now. Somehow she would make Ragnfast see sense. He wanted a living and breathing daughter, not another corpse in the graveyard.

'You brought this on yourself, Ragnfast,' Thyre said, looking sternly at her stepfather. 'You should never have insisted. I acted in the only way I could save Dagmar's life.'

Ragnfast bowed his head. 'You did mark your bed companion, Viken. Give her the arm ring. Let us be done with this sham. No dishonour to you was intended, as you can see. I will deal with this mess later. Thyre, you will be for ever soiled by this affair.'

Thyre squeezed Dagmar's shoulders and risked a breath. They had weathered the storm. All would be well now. Ragnfast knew. Dagmar and Sven would find a measure of happiness. Some good would come of the Viken's visit after all. Thyre gave the arrogant man a haughty nod. Did he know the trouble he had caused?

'I have changed my mind.' Ivar placed the ring back on his arm.

'Changed your mind?' Thyre exclaimed as her mind raced. What new treachery did this man have planned? He was worse than Loki for twisting words and situations to suit his purpose? Where was the trap? 'You offered the arm ring to your bed companion. We have agreed I was the woman in your bed. You may give it to me and be on your way.'

'Explain yourself, Viken,' Ragnfast growled, his hand going to his sword.

'Ragnfast offered me his life if I was proven right, but it is not much use to me. However, I do want something, something you will give me willingly or else I shall take it.'

Thyre's glance flicked between the two men and knew it would be an unequal contest.

'For Thor's sake, he is an old man. He last fought…' The words were torn from Thyre's throat as she started forwards, then checked herself. The Viken wanted the excuse. He wanted to enslave or kill every man. It had been a trap and she had walked into it. She had handed him the farm on a silver platter. Her stomach clenched. No man should die for her. She had to believe that Ivar had no idea of her parentage, of who her mother was, and therefore who her father had to be. No, this was Viken arrogance in the extreme. His pride was irked. She refused to let others die for her mistake. Ragnfast would not fight. '…before I was born. Have pity on us.'

The Viken merely lifted his brow and his lips thinned. 'You have a better idea?'

'He had nothing to do with last night.' Thyre's fists balled at her sides. This was between her and the Viken. She would protect Ragnfast and this estate. It was her duty. 'You will not use this as an excuse to take this land and to plunder this farm. Your quarrel is with me and me alone.'

Ivar's insolent gaze raked her form, burning through her clothes. Against her will, the memory of what it was like to lie wrapped in his arms welled up inside her. Angrily she damped it down, but not before a knowing gleam appeared in his eyes. 'I did not hear you complaining last night. What passed between us was your suggestion.'

'That was different. And it ended this morning.'

'We are far from finished, you and I.'

The back of her neck prickled a warning. She took a half-step backwards, but his hand shot out, clamping around her waist and pulling her forwards. His thigh hit her hip. Ruthlessly he lowered his mouth. Thyre intended on being a statue, but his tongue delicately traced the outline of her mouth, calling to a deep well inside her. It was far from punishing, but persuasive and seductive. Without her realising it, her hands came up and buried themselves in his hair. She opened her mouth, wanting the warmth to continue.

Abruptly he let her go. Her mouth ached. He ran a finger down the side of her face and neck, stopped at the mark. 'Mine.'

'A kiss proves nothing,' she said.

'Your words war with your body. Which one should I trust?'

'Will you answer the challenge?' Ragnfast thundered.

'I will take this woman with me instead of your life, Ragnfast. You were going to marry her against her will in any case. It will be one less mouth for you to feed.' Ivar looked her up and down. 'It will be my payment, unless you wish to spill blood over it?'

'Take her with you?' Dagmar gasped as the crowd murmured behind her.

Thyre's throat refused to work. This was a disaster. This was not supposed to happen.

'You said that she is without value and the man you wished to betroth her to would not accept someone soiled by a Viken.' His lips curled around the word 'soiled' and spat it out. 'How can I condemn her to death for lying? I am doing you a favour.'

'You understand nothing, Viken—' Thyre began, but he ignored her.

'Which will it be, Ragnfast the Steadfast? Your life or your stepdaughter, the penniless orphan you took in?'

Images of blood-soaked sand rose before Thyre's eyes. How could she ask anyone, least of all Ragnfast, to die for her? Ragnfast kept this bay safe. People depended on him. Once he was dead, there would be nothing to stop the Viken just taking whatever they pleased. She had a chance to stop the blood before it began. This was her responsibility. She had a duty to all who lived here. Besides that her freedom meant nothing.

Thyre knew that the choice meant a death to her dreams. They were dust beneath her feet. She would never meet that gentle warrior who would cherish her and protect her. She would never experience love as an equal to her mate and she would never see her home again. But to keep safe everyone and everything she held dear, she had to do it.

'I will go with the Viken, Ragnfast,' Thyre said, her voice echoing over the harbour. 'It is the only way. I refuse to have blood on my hands. But please, Ivar Gunnarson, give me a moment to speak to my stepfather. Things need to be said.'

It was a little enough request. Ivar Gunnarson had to agree with it.

At first he did not move, but stood there with his hands flexing as if he struggled to maintain control. Then, just when she had given up hope, she saw a glint in his eye. 'Very well, if you must.'

Thyre led Ragnfast a little way away from Ivar. They did not have much time, and he would have to understand that this was the best way, far better than marrying her off to an elderly man.

'The Viken are far from trustworthy.' Ragnfast gripped her arms and his face became intent. 'What will you do when he discards you? You should have a choice. Remember who you are, who your mother was—the Ranriken Swan Princess. She did not intend for you to become a Viken's concubine. If I were a younger man, I would have fought him for his impudence, but my sword arm is weak.'

'My mother died a long time ago. There are few who remember her story. They will not think me the Swan Princess's daughter. King Thorkell will not question. You acknowledged me. No one will use me to try for the Ranriken throne. I will not permit it. The safety of this estate must come before all things. I have a duty.'

'You are so very like your mother.'

Thyre put her hand on Ragnfast's shoulder, and he loosened his grip on her arms. Behind him the farm hands and foresters stood. She knew their wives, their children. If they fought they would die and the outcome would remain the same. But it did not mean she would not miss them. She scanned the crowd, trying to memorise faces. She would hold them in her heart until her dying breath. She turned towards the hills for one last look at her home and saw the faintest curl of smoke. The bonfire still burnt! Her heart leapt.

'I lit the bonfire and Sigmund should arrive soon,' Thyre said. 'You send him after me. It is what the system of beacons was for.'

'You did what?' Ragnfast stared at her. Sweat gathered on his brow.

'I worried that we would need help to get the Viken to leave.' She leant forwards and kissed his cheek. Ragnfast should be pleased. 'Sigmund explained it, in case you were ever ill and I needed assistance.'

'Woman, you have destroyed us all. Sigmund will use this opportunity to finally crush me and to take this bay. He will say that I sent you to the Viken king to make a new alliance.'

'No, he won't,' Thyre said with a faint sense of unease. She had done the right thing by lighting the bonfire. Her mother would have done the same thing. 'He is an honourable warrior. He will want to right the wrong.'

'You do not know him the way I know him, Thyre. He will use this to crush me.'

'The tide is starting to turn,' Ivar interrupted, coming to stand between them, preventing any further discussion. 'This woman comes with me now.'

Thyre forced her lungs to fill with air, concentrating on the simple act of breathing. Ragnfast's paranoia about Sigmund Sigmundson would not take away her last ray of hope.

'I have made my choice. I will survive. I promise you that.'

'I did try to protect you, Thyre. The marriage to Otto would have kept you safe,' Ragnfast said, clasping her arm. 'But the gods have seen fit to put you on another path.'

'You never consulted me!' Thyre crossed her arms about her waist and tried to control the ice-cold shivering. She longed to pull the discarded shawl about her shoulders, but that would show the Viken her weakness. She refused to be weak, even though she was heartsick. Even now, Ragnfast didn't understand her duty towards Dagmar and this steading.

'I have held true to my promise to your mother. You confuse words with deeds. When have I ever done anything wrong to you? When were you mistreated?' Ragnfast hung his head. 'You should have honoured your mother's memory.'

'I honour her memory now. My mother would have approved of my decision. Above all things she loved you, and this land. She taught me my duty,' Thyre said slowly. She turned towards the glowering Viken. 'If you will give me leave, Ivar, I will get my trunk.'

'Someone else may get it for you.' His hand clamped around her wrist. 'You remain at my side where I can see you.'

'I have said that I will go with you.' Thyre twisted her wrist and he allowed her to go free. 'Allow me to take my leave. My half-sister needs to know things. She will need to know how to give the women orders.'

'Why should I wait?'

'I will get your trunk,' one of the thralls called. 'It will be here. You saved my daughter last winter with your gruel.'

The sting of tears pricked Thyre's eyelids. She missed them all already. Angrily she brushed them away. The Viken would not see her cry.

'If there is ever anything I can do…' Dagmar whispered, darting forwards. 'Send word and I will try to help. You just see if I don't find a way. I will make him go to Ranhiem and tell the Storting. I can be brave like you, Thyre.'

'I will always remember that.' Thyre gave a watery smile at the thought of Dagmar making Ragnfast do anything.

'The tide turns, Ivar!' The cry came from the boat.

'I love you, Dagmar,' Thyre said. 'Remember that.'

'And I love you as well. We are sisters!'

'Come, concubine. I have tarried long enough.'

'I will go now, Viken. And my name is Thyre, Sainsfrida's daughter.'

'Your name is whatever I choose to call you. You belong to me now.'

Chapter Seven

Thyre sat perched on the small iron-bound trunk, watching the shoreline disappear. Dagmar and the rest had become small specks and then dots on the horizon.

The outline of the buildings lingered a little while longer. And Thyre felt certain that she had had a glimpse of the serpent gable long after it was possible. She had half-hoped that Sigmund's ships would round the bend as Ivar's pulled away from the bay, but the sea remained stubbornly empty.

Would Sigmund be bothered about her once he did arrive? Would he risk an open breach with the Viken? Or were his words about the beacon system merely an empty promise?

As the boat left the inlet, it began to toss and pitch. Salt spray washed up over the side, getting into her hair and nostrils. Thyre put out her hands, trying to stay on the trunk.

Some day, she would see Dagmar again, and they would tell stories and exchange confidences. And she would discover little things, like how many kittens Beygul had had and if Tregul had been in the cream. Little things that had once seemed so inconsequential, but things she knew she would miss. And whatever lay in her future, she knew she would carry the image of her home in her heart for ever. It would remind her that she had done her duty, and that the estate had been saved. They would go on as before—free and happy.

What had her mother felt when she'd been taken hostage by the Viken? Then her mother had gone as a princess, the jewel of Ranrike. Now her daughter went as little better than a slave.

She glanced up to where Ivar stood, barking orders as the long ship glided over the waves and the oars began to move as one. Remote and commanding. The master of all he surveyed. But she knew little about him and how he treated his men. What sort of leader was he? He certainly appeared to be everywhere at once, sorting out the problems of cargo shifting and making sure the rowers were in their correct places.

She hated how, despite everything, her body had re-membered the passion and had responded to him on the shore. And she doubted that she could ever be friends with him, not in the same way that her mother had been friends with Ragnfast. She could remember the shared laughter from before her mother's death, and how Ragnfast had changed afterwards, becoming withdrawn and bitter.

And what had her mother been to the Viken king? a treacherous voice whispered at the back of her mind. What storm of passion had conceived her? And what would King Thorkell do when he discovered how his former lover had cheated and kept their baby alive?

Would he forgive or would he demand her death?

Ivar had said she was under his protection, but did that protection extend to this? She hugged her knees and wished she had planned more carefully before she had gone into Ivar's bed. What if she conceived? She doubted that Ivar would ever respect her. He probably thought that women occupied a specific niche and that was all.

Idly she traced the runes on her trunk, naming each one out loud as her mother had taught her. Her head pounded slightly. She did not even want to think about having children with Ivar. Her arms might long to hold a baby, but she had no wish to have that child torn from her. Children belonged to the father. It was the custom, even though her mother had defied it. Her mother had sworn at first to Thyre that she was Ragnfast's, and simply born early. But one day, shortly before her mother died, she had heard them quarrelling, and her mother begging Ragnfast to look after her daughter. Much later, Ragnfast had told her the story about how he had rescued her mother from Viken, and how the new king of Ranrike, her brother, had threatened to kill her for being pregnant with the Viken king's child. It was only because she accepted banishment for herself and her children, along with Ragnfast, that King Mysing had spared her life.

'Do you know runes?' a young boy asked, leaning on his oars and looking over at where she sat. 'Come and speak with me.'

Thyre started and then moved towards the lad, hand over hand, clinging to the side until she sank down on the bench beside him. His light brown hair tumbled about his forehead and he had the look of Ivar in the shape of his chin and shoulders.

'Yes, I do,' she said carefully, keeping her voice neutral. 'I learnt when I was a little girl. My mother also made me learn lots of poetry.'

'I want to carve my mother's name on a comb.'

Thyre gave a small smile. Wanting to carve his mother's

name was something she could understand, a little action. Maybe the Ranriken and Viken were not so different after all. 'It is an easy thing to carve a name, if you concentrate hard.'

'Is it? I keep making mistakes with my runes.' He gave a rueful smile and half-shrug. 'I need to learn them, or else I will never be a great warrior like my uncle.'

'Is your uncle…?' Thyre let her voice trail away as she nodded towards where Ivar sat, hands on the oar, muscles bulging as he brought the oar back another time. A faint sheen of sweat glistened on his forearms, making them appear sculpted and powerful, almost as if they belonged to Thor himself.

'Ivar is my uncle. He and the jaarl Vikar Hrutson saved us last summer when we were attacked. He promised that I could come on his next voyage, no matter what my mother said about it being far too dangerous.' The boy raised his chin. 'And my uncle keeps his promises. When I grow up, I want to be like him and sail over the seas as the leader of a mighty *felag*.'

'It is good to keep your promises,' Thyre replied slowly. She watched where Ivar took his turn at the oars, exchanging jokes with his men. She doubted if any of the Ranrike jaarls would do such a menial task. Even Ragnfast boasted that he had never pulled at the oars. But she could see the respect in the men's faces that Ivar was willing to take his turn. 'Why did you get your mother a comb?'

'I promised her something for her hair. I want it to say that it belongs to Astrid. The last one she had, someone stole from the bath house when she visited Kaupang to see me off. You should have heard her complaining!'

'Where did you get the comb?'

'In Birka. Uncle Ivar advanced me part of my share from the *felag* and he helped me bargain for it.' He scratched his nose. 'My uncle says that I am spelling comb wrong, but I don't believe him.'

'Does your uncle know his runes?' Thyre leant forwards, eager to learn more about the man.

'Enough to get by.' The boy gave a careless shrug. 'He has spent most of his life fighting and trading. Building ships. But he says that a true Viken must be able to read runes and figure, so you won't be cheated.'

'And the women of Viken…'

'Some do, but my mother can only work out her name.' His face wrinkled with concentration. 'I think Vikar's new wife can read runes, and maybe my aunt could before she died. The Queen can. She even composes poetry.'

'Your Uncle Ivar's wife,' Thyre said slowly, a cold creeping over her. She had to know. 'When did she die?'

'Aunt Edda died a few years ago, before he left for Lindisfarne. I know very little about her except my mother thought her weak as cow's milk in winter.' He tilted his head to one side and his blue eyes assessed her. 'He has never had a concubine before. I thought he preferred blondes to dark-haired women. It is the fashion to be blonde. My mother says that Queen Asa dyes her hair.'

'You will have to ask your uncle why he compelled me to be here.'

The lad ran his hand through his hair, making it stand on end. 'Nobody asks my uncle anything. He tells them.'

'I have discovered.' Thyre gave a rueful shrug. 'But then I did what I had to.'

The boy's merry laugh rang out. 'You remind me of my mother.'

'I can help you with the runes…if you wish.' Thyre leant forwards. 'It will help me pass the time. I have never been on board ship before and the rocking unnerves me.'

'I would like that.' The boy gave a shy smile.

Thyre breathed a little easier. She felt like she had made a friend. Or at least someone she could help, instead of missing home and wondering what Dagmar and Ragnfast were doing.

'Asger! The horn sounded! You pull the oar at the second blast. Pay attention to when it is your turn, if you wish to become a Viken warrior!'

The boy flushed and glanced at the oar. 'I was too busy talking.'

'We have spoken about this before. You are to be ready. The *felag* is only as strong as those who are in it.'

'I forgot…'

'Remember next time or it will go worse for you.'

'Ivar, your nephew did not mean any harm.' Thyre stood and faced Ivar. 'He wanted to carve his mother's name on the comb. If anyone is at fault, it is me. I distracted him.'

'You will not do my nephew any favours. His mother already keeps him wrapped in sheep's wool.' Ivar's hand pulled her away from where Asger now laboured with his oar. 'He will have to play a warrior's part soon and he must not fall into bad habits. You should stay where I told you. This is not a pleasure outing.'

'It is one of my more infuriating habits—having a mind of my own.' Thyre forced her voice to be sweetness and light and took a perverse pleasure in Ivar's furious glance. 'Is that a problem?'

'No,' he said, through gritted teeth. Primitive anger surged through Ivar as he looked down at her unrepentant face. Even after what had happened to her this morning, this woman still underestimated his intelligence. This time he would keep control of his temper. On the beach, when her stepfather had used the word 'soiled', Ivar's control had snapped. It had been years since he had last lost his temper. And this time, it was all down to the maddening woman who stood before him, chin tilted upwards and eyes blazing, daring him to go on. 'Asger is a full member of this *felag* and must pull his weight.'

'Am I a member of your *felag* now? Will you force me to take my turn at the oars?' Her eyes flashed fire.

'Women can never be members of a *felag*. You will have other duties.'

She wrapped her arms about her waist, but not before her tongue had flicked over her lips. 'You will no doubt inform me what they are. Very well, I will do them as long as I deem them appropriate. I came on this voyage to save lives, not to give you any pleasure. It was my duty to save my people.'

Ivar clung on to his temper. She lied. She had experienced pleasure with him. Her response was far from feigned. But if she wanted to play games, she would learn. Today, he hoped her people had learnt a lesson that they would not soon forget. No one played him for a fool. 'You will not cause a disruption on my ship. Mischief-makers are dealt with…severely.'

'I was helping your nephew with his present for his mother.' Thyre put her hand to her throat and her eyes grew wide. Ivar's insides twisted. He was no monster. He had never forced a woman. This morning, he had thought to save her. It made her rejection all the worse. Ivar pushed his confused thoughts away and contented himself with glaring at her as her voice faltered. 'He wanted to know the correct runes. He bought his mother a comb in Birka. We were having a pleasant conversation. I did not think.'

'That boy is a member of my crew. He has other duties than amusing my concubine.'

'And whose job is that?' she asked.

'Mine, when I deem it fit.'

She opened and closed her mouth several times, but no sound came out. A sense of satisfaction filled Ivar. She would learn. He leant forwards so that his lips were inches from hers. A ghost of a caress. 'Remember that.'

She turned her face away, but not before he saw her mouth tremble. Her pretended indifference would cease in time. 'It is not in my nature to be idle. I wanted to assist him when he asked. He wants to be a great warrior and so must learn his runes.'

'And you know runes? Very few women know how to read runes.'

'My mother taught me.'

'Your mother?'

'Women are capable of reading when they try. I have tried to teach Dagmar, but she refuses. Reading runes is important. Brains can often outwit brawn.'

'You are a puzzle, Thyre. Why would Ragnfast wish to give you to someone you hated when you are obviously such an asset to the farm?'

'You would have to ask Ragnfast,' she replied, her voice high and tight. 'But I had no plans to marry Otto. In the end, Ragnfast would have come around to my way of thinking. I did not intend to tell him of our time together.'

'Why did you speak to Asger and offer to show him the runes? He is a loyal nephew. He will not help you escape.'

'He is a boy. He misses his mother and wants her to think well of him. He certainly thinks well of you.' Her jaw became set and her fingers twisted the folds of her apron dress. 'Was there any harm in that?'

'I have no wish for Asger or any of my men to become counters in a game of *tafl*. Do not play games with me and expect to win, Thyre. You will be my concubine for as long as I need you.'

'Was I playing a game?' The wind whipped several strands of her hair, pushing it across her face. 'If so, then I lost. I lost everything today, Ivar Gunnarson. What more can you take from me?'

'It is an intriguing suggestion. I prefer my women to give.' Ivar concentrated on the creaking mast rather than on her white throat and its mark. Seduction had no place on a boat. 'I do not have time to watch out for you. I have a ship to command. Men's lives depend on me. Your life depends on me.'

'I have no intention of dying. That would be far too easy. I intend to plague the life out of you.' She smiled sweetly.

'I wonder who will tire of the game first.' His hand caught a lock of her hair and twisted it between his fingers. 'You made me lose my temper once, Thyre. You will not make me do so again.'

'But why did you bring me? Surely you have no need of me—a woman on board ship,' Thyre protested, looking up at him. The way the wind pushed his dark blonde hair across his forehead made her fingers long to push it back. After all he had done to her, how could she even begin to think about the way his lips moved against hers or how soft his skin was? She shook her head to clear it. Was she under some sort of spell? She wished Dagmar was there to ask. Dagmar seemed blessed with the innate knowledge of how men reacted.

He stopped. A half-smile appeared on his face as he stared intently at the mark on her neck. 'After the night we spent together I would say there was plenty of need.'

'It was never supposed to be repeated.' Thyre started to

draw the edges of her shawl together. His eyes gleamed and she forced her hands to go back to her sides. 'One night's madness. That is all it was.'

'And why were you there? The truth, this time.' His fingers reached out and grabbed her chin, held her in a pincer-like grip. 'Some day you will tell me all your secrets.'

She moved her head and he released her. She struggled to take a steady breath. 'That will be the day after they cease to have meaning.'

He gave a crooked smile and a shrug, but his eyes flared and their breath mingled. 'You will share my bed for as long as I wish it.'

He rubbed his thumb across her lips, causing a deep ache to fill her.

'And my wishes count for nothing,' she breathed, trying to ignore the growing heat in her body. She despised her body for welcoming his touch. She should loathe this man and all she could think about was the shape of his mouth and the way his muscles had felt under her fingertips.

'I have yet to force a woman, Thyre. What we enjoyed last night was pleasant and it should remain thus.'

'Do you simply use women and discard them? I have never been a concubine before.'

'I am well aware of the fact.' His fingers gripped her chin and she was forced to gaze into his piercing blue eyes. 'Drink had not dulled my senses. My bed companion was enthusiastic but untried, an intriguing combination. And now you seek to challenge my mind. What more could a man ask for?'

'You have not answered my question.' Thyre kept her voice steady, but her stomach knotted. Was this all about hurt pride or something more? Did he intend on humiliating her, making an example of her? She wished she could remember more of her mother's tale. But then her mother was never anyone's concubine. She had taken a lover when she was hostage to the Viken king. She had even thought she might marry, but then they had quarrelled and Ragnfast had rescued her. 'What will happen to me when we reach Kaupang? How will I fare at court?'

The steady rhythmic sound of the oars hitting the water surrounded them.

'I will protect you, but you will not be part of the court.'

'I had understood…' Thyre breathed easier. She had to stop borrowing trouble. She might never meet her father. 'That is…the customs of the Ranriken court allow for concubines.'

'The queen does not permit it.' He looked somewhere off into the distance. 'Court etiquette is complex and re-volves around the queen. Trust me.'

'I will take your word for it.'

His eyes crinkled. 'You are showing a flicker of intel-ligence.'

'I am being practical. You know the Viken court and it has a reputation of being a dangerous place.'

'See the prow of a dragon ship!' The cry resounded around the ship and Ivar's demeanour instantly changed.

Thyre's heart leapt into her throat as she saw three dragon ships sail into view. Warships, bristling with shields and spears. It was far too soon for Ragnfast to have orga-nised anything. Was Ragnfast wrong? Had Sigmund actually intended on protecting them?

'What happens now? You are outnumbered,' she said.

Ivar stared at the horizon and silently cursed. Three ships in perfect position, lying in wait for him. He should have thought of the possibility. Ragnfast had been far too effusive in his welcome.

When would he learn? He had only his own stubborn pride to blame. He had been so certain that he had outrun the storm, and the ships had perished. The beach had been littered with the flotsam and jetsam of at least one ship. A decoy?

His fingers went to the hilt of his sword. Three warships and so soon after they had left the safety of Ragnfast's harbour. And he had been prepared to swear that none survived the storm. Perhaps he had been unlucky. But he preferred to think otherwise. Men made their own luck. Someone had signalled to them.

'Did you know about these warships?' he asked Thyre, capturing her elbow with his fingers. He would get the truth from her…this time.

'How can I know anything? I am merely a woman.' Thyre tilted her head to one side. 'Many ships travel up and down this strait and not all are bent on trouble. Perhaps you should turn around and go back to Ragnfast's. Perhaps he can save you from your countrymen.'

'They are not Viken. These are Ranrike warships. See the diamond pattern on the sails. You know whose they are.'

He waited, watching her. A myriad of emotions crossed her face. Had she been hoping for them? If he had been in her place, he would have.

'They are Sigmund's. I can recognise the shield pattern now. But they are coming from the wrong direction.' Her brow knit together. 'They are coming from the east. They should have been in the west. There are no beacons to the east.'

'And what will Sigmund Sigmundson say when he discovers you are on a Viken ship?'

'He will rescue me.' Thyre thrust her chin upwards and her eyes flashed. 'Once he realises. It is the duty of any

Ranrike warrior to rescue one of their women. You are best to return to Ragnfast.'

'You came on to this ship freely.' Ivar's neck muscles ached. 'He might think Ragnfast sent you to Viken.'

'Sigmund would never do that.' Thyre swayed slightly and then righted herself. Her eyes went to her trunk with its intricate runes. 'Would he?'

'You only hope that.' He looked down on her. In his anger, had he missed something obvious about the situation? Had Ragnfast manipulated him into taking this woman? In many ways, it had been too easy. He had been thinking with his nether regions, rather than with his head. After the danger passed, he would examine that trunk and search its contents. He should have done it earlier. 'Why doesn't Sigmund use Ragnfast's bay? It is an ideal place to strike at passing ships.'

'Because…Ragnfast refused and King Mysing respected his decision. My mother never wanted anything to do with such things. But Sigmund knows that Ragnfast would never send me…unless…' She shook her head decisively. 'Ragnfast is loyal to Ranrike. You know who alone is responsible for me being on board. The jaarl Sigmund is an honourable man. He would rescue me, rather than use it as an excuse to punish Ragnfast for standing against him.'

'You had best pray to the gods that we outrun the ships and you never have to put your theory to the test.' Ivar started to turn away, but she grabbed his arm.

'But were you able to do all your repairs?' Thyre tilted her head to one side. 'Your mast is creaking. Even I know that you do not raise a sail on a creaking mast.'

'Watch and learn.'

'You are proud, Viken. Gods punish pride. It is in the hands of gods now.'

'No, it is in mine.'

He glanced at the creaking mast. She was right. It would not wear the sail, that much was clear. And the other ships held the advantage of speed. Even now, they were manoeuvring into position. He knew in his gut that someone on the farm had a system of signalling to Sigmund and his fleet. They had been waiting for this opportunity. Very well, he would make them pay.

'We fight. We win. It is how the Viken behave.' Ivar reached for his helmet. 'Raise shields. Prepare to ram the lead ship.'

Chapter Eight

With a bone-jarring crunch, the Viken ship collided with the lead Ranriken ship, ramming a hole in its centre. Confused shouts rang in Thyre's ears as Ivar ordered the oarsmen again and again to put their backs into it.

Thyre went down on her hands and knees and crawled her way back to her iron trunk. Her hands closed around its familiar proportions. With shaking fingers, she undid the lock and retrieved her mother's dagger. The feel of the hilt with its engraved swans and twin rings in her hand gave her courage. She had a weapon of sorts and was far from defenceless. Not daring to look, not daring to hope, she crouched beside the trunk, hugging the knife to her breast.

The final jolting crunch rocked the boat, making her fall flat. She turned her head, expecting to see water rushing in, but the Viken ship remained whole. At Ivar's command, his men pulled as one and the ship lurched away, revealing a gaping black hole in the side of the Ranriken ship.

The air teemed with the prayers and pleas from the stricken ship. Soon Ran would be out with her net, capturing the souls of the drowned, if no help came for those men.

Above her, the seagulls circled, cawing loudly. Or were they something more sinister—Valkyries searching for warriors to take back to Odin's halls?

Thyre tightened her grip on her mother's dagger and whispered prayer after prayer. For the stricken ship. For her. For this battle to end. Surely Sigmund would go to the aid of the men. It would enable the Viken to escape, but it had to be done. Ivar's logic now became clear.

Sigmund would not risk losing able warriors. His ships would go to the aid of the stricken Ranriken ship. Like any good commander, he could not leave his men to drown.

She squinted and saw Ivar silhouetted against the sun, helmeted and shouting orders as his men rowed as one. The Viken boat swung around, moving sluggishly in the water, but moving away.

Her heart stopped as one of the Ranriken boats picked up speed, bypassed the sinking ship and headed straight for the Viken ship. But rather than ramming it, the Ranriken ship pulled alongside, bumping up against them.

'Lift shields! Prepare to defend!' Ivar's voice thundered above the noise.

She glanced towards Ivar's nephew and saw his face was pale and resolute. He appeared barely old enough to lift the broad sword he carried. 'I might wet my sword in battle today!' he cried.

Thyre's stomach twisted. He was far too young. She waited, her knuckles shining white against the handle of the dagger.

The shouts increased and she heard metal meeting metal. But the Viken appeared to prevent the Ranrike from fitting their boarding plank.

When the third Ranrike ship put its boarding plank on the side, she knew how it would end. The sagas were suddenly horribly real. How many times had she listened to tales of battles with her heart in her throat? The reality was a thousand times worse.

Despite the noise, the cries, and the confusion of the current battle, there was a certain measured calm in the way Ivar led his men, exhorting them to defend here and to attack there. He appeared to be everywhere at once.

'Watch out, Thyre! Duck now!' Ivar thundered and Thyre went flat. An axe hit the side of the boat, directly above her. She stared at him in wonder as he lifted his sword and engaged another warrior in battle. Despite all the noise and confusion, he had known where she was and had saved her life. She pressed her hands against her eyes, not quite able to believe it.

Quickly she crouched down once again between the trunks and the sacks, forming a sort of tunnel, a barricade, hoping against expectation that she could survive and somehow repay the life-debt she now owed Ivar.

Asger backed towards her, his sword held aloft. Somewhere he had lost his helmet, but his eyes were alight with excitement.

She watched the axe rise again and pulled Asger to safety. 'You should be more careful.'

His eyes gleamed. 'Do you think I will get to Valhalla today?'

'I hope not.' Thyre gripped his shoulders and held the boy firmly, preventing him from wriggling away and re-joining the confusion. 'Your mother will want to see you again. Stay here with me. Keep safe.'

'No, I want to die like a warrior, not skulking like a

woman. Only warriors go to Valhalla.' Asger wriggled free and went back out into the fighting.

Suddenly the sound of battle fell away, to be replaced with an eerie silence. Thyre peeked out from behind her makeshift barricade and stifled a gasp.

Bodies littered the ship, men who had enjoyed Ragnfast's hospitality and who had survived the storm only to die in battle. They had not done anything to warrant the attack. They had treated Ragnfast with respect. They had not come to plunder. They had come in peace and had been attacked without warning. Nothing could justify that. And she knew that her bonfire had alerted Sigmund. It must have done. Her stomach heaved.

A sickening sweet scent hung in the air, and decks were wet with sea water and red blood. She knew the dead would go to Valhalla, but it was not the same as being alive. And she hated to think what had happened to Ivar. She owed him her life and it was a humbling thought.

Heavy footsteps resounded on the wooden plank connecting the boats.

'Ivar Gunnarson, how pleasant it is to meet this way,' Sigmund's voice rang out. Instead of his usual fawning lisp, Sigmund's tone dripped irony and contempt. 'I do believe your ship has experienced a mishap.'

'Ah, Sigmund Sigmundson, I thought it was your stench that hung on the breeze, but as you chose to hide your face I could not be certain.' Ivar's voice rumbled from some place to her left.

Thyre lifted a bit of sacking and risked a glance towards it. Thin trails of blood trickled down his face, and his hand held a red-stained sword, but Ivar lived and without any obvious wounds. Thyre hated the way her heart rejoiced to see him alive. She knew she should be cheering Sigmund's victory, but something about his sneer and the manner in which he had left the men in the sinking ship to Ran's fabled net made her recoil. A leader should look after his men.

'You can be certain now. I am the victor of this battle.'

'For now. Victory can be a fleeting thing.'

'For always.' Sigmund wiped his hand across his mouth. 'My brother died when we last met.'

'Your brother died because he attempted to stab Vikar Hrutson in the back—always a dangerous thing to do after you surrender.'

'He was my brother and now his shade will cease to cry vengeance.' Sigmund waved his hand. 'I knew you were too cunning to go down in that storm. In which bay did you hide?'

'The sea is like a mother and father to my *Sea Witch*.'

'My best ship went down in that storm, chasing you and your goods. Nothing could have survived it on the open sea.'

Thyre risked a breath. Her mind reeled. Ivar had told the truth. Sigmund had chased him, and had been hunting him still. He was supposed to be protecting the shores of Ranrike, rather than going after trading vessels, waiting in his bay until someone lit a beacon, signalling their need. She remembered how he explained the system of beacons to her, in case there should be a need. How many more lies had she believed?

'But we survived, as you can see.' Ivar gestured about him. 'Viken ships are hardier. It is why we travel to far-off lands to trade and you are forced to prey on passing vessels.'

'Ah, you have fresh rope, Ranriken rope,' Sigmund said with a curl of his lip. 'You need not worry. I will discover who dared give you such a thing.'

'Is hospitality now a crime?' Ivar asked. 'How curious Ranriken customs are.'

'I will enforce my will and the king of Ranrike agrees.' Sigmund raised his blade so the tip of it touched Ivar's cheek. 'No help given to the Viken vermin.'

'Your sword appears to be bright and shiny without a drop of blood on it,' Ivar said.

Thyre narrowed her gaze. Ivar was right. Sigmund's sword was without a stain. He had not taken part in the battle.

He had risked his men's lives, but not his own. Sigmund had hidden in his boat until victory was assured. It was his way—to move in the shadows and strike like a snake, then to claim everything for himself. Ragnfast had complained bitterly of his habit once when he had drunk too much mead. Now she saw, he had not even understood the half of it. Sigmund Sigmundson was a coward with little or no honour.

Silently she slipped the dagger into her boot, grateful she had realised Sigmund's treachery before it was too late.

'Are you volunteering to spill yours?' Sigmund asked, pressing the shining blade into Ivar's cheek.

A thin line of red appeared, but Ivar remained still. 'I never volunteer *anything*.'

'Brave words, but you will surrender to save your skin.'

'Surrender? A Viken never surrenders. You must remind me of that unique Ranrike custom.'

'Your head is addled, Viken. You are in no position to dictate terms.' Sigmund coughed and brushed a speck from his black cloak. 'You have lost. The day belongs to Ranrike. You will kiss my rings and beg me for mercy.'

'Victory can prove fleeting if the leader proves to be somewhat less than a warrior,' Ivar replied, looking Sigmund straight in the eyes.

Every muscle ached, but he had fought until they were

overwhelmed. Both the Viken and Ranriken warriors knew the difference between a battle-stained sword and a bright one. If he could get Sigmund to react and challenge him to single combat, there was still a chance that he could win the day.

All of his muscles contracted, waiting for the briefest of openings. Behind him, he heard the shuffling of his men's feet, and their groans. But Ivar did not permit his gaze to waver. Sigmund had to take the challenge.

'I am proud of my men, proud to have fought alongside them. We are a *felag* bound by blood-oaths.'

'Some customs are overrated. Counters are always expendable when guarding the king in *tafl*.'

'Men are far from being glass counters.'

'That is your opinion. What did your men give their life for?'

'The men who died will even now be dining at Valhalla, but it is not a place for men with bright swords,' Ivar said softly, taunting Sigmund.

'Why is there any need to risk my sword arm, Ivar?' Sigmund's mouth curled and he spat on the ground. 'I have already proven its worth…even against vermin like the Viken.'

'You should not insult my people,' Ivar replied steadily, willing Sigmund to respond with a sword thrust. Such a move would signal the start of the combat. 'Viken warriors have more honour in their little fingers than the Ranrike do in their whole bodies. The concept of honour has no meaning to you.'

'Only those who have clothes on their backs, and food in their bellies, can afford such words. I know what traitors Viken can be. How they boast of their prowess with the sword, but yield at the slightest hint of gold.'

'Are you describing yourself, Sigmund?'

Ivar drew in his breath and willed the warrior to respond. His guards had slackened their hold on his arms. Most Viken warriors would be raging with anger at the insult, but not Sigmund. An amused smile played on his lips.

'How would you describe me, Viken?'

'A man who moves in the shadows and sends out untrained boys to do his dirty work.'

'I know what drives people, even people like you, Ivar Gunnarson.'

'Honour and duty are worth the price.'

'Brave words, but foolish for someone who has lost.' Sigmund's smile turned cruel. 'You will have to be taught a lesson.'

'By you?' Every muscle in Ivar's body tensed. Despite the tiredness from the battle, his muscles itched for the chance to cross swords. 'I welcome the opportunity to fight you—man to man. We will settle this quarrel as Norsemen.'

'I had another form of punishment in mind. This is for my brother, Gorm.'

Sigmund landed a punch in the middle of Ivar's stomach. Ivar forced his body to stay calm and to ignore the sudden audible female gasp from behind a pile of trunks and canvas sacking. Thyre had to remain where she was. Once he had achieved victory, then he would seek her out and discover the full truth of why Ragnfast had allowed her to come with him.

'It would have been better if we had met in battle,' Ivar said, raising his voice to drown out the gasp. 'Then we would know who is truly the better man.'

'We did and I won. There is little to stop me slitting

your throat now, Ivar Gunnarson. You with your tales of fabulous wealth and invincibility. What will the skalds say then? Will they sing of how you fought the wolf, or will they only remember that you died unlamented on the deck of a ship?'

'I have never claimed such a thing. Skalds are notorious for embroidering stories…I scarcely recognise the Lindisfarne saga now. But at no time have they claimed I hid during battle. What claims will the skalds make for you?'

'You should get ready to welcome the embrace of Hel, rather than boasting about your past exploits.'

'My men and I are worth more to you alive than dead.' Ivar forced his shoulders to relax. His first plan had failed. He had to adapt. He would prevail in the end or die a warrior. 'The Viken will pay the ransom. Else you risk war. Is that what you truly want, Sigmund, war? If it is, you can have it.'

'With what will you pay?' A cruel smile crossed Sigmund's face. 'Your ship and everything in it belongs to me. I should sell you as slaves, but I don't know who would want such an untrustworthy lot.'

'Send my nephew as proof to Kaupang if you like. Ask your ransom and the price will be paid out of Lindisfarne gold.'

He waited as the gleam grew in Sigmund's eyes.

'What you say has merit, Viken. The blood price of a jaarl is high, and the king prefers the gold from Viken ships to outright war. This could prove worth my while.' He snapped his fingers. 'Very well, you had best hope he returns with enough gold to cover my head.'

'He will.' Ivar removed his glove and gave his nephew a gold ring. 'Give this to your mother, Asger. She will know what to do. Tell her to give the men what they ask for.'

The boy nodded solemnly as his hands clasped the ring.

'And be sure to tell Astrid how proud I was of you today,' Ivar said.

'No, let me go! I will take the boy's place.' Erik the Black stepped forwards. Blood ran down his face but he stood. 'The Viken Storting will listen to me. The boy might be disbelieved. Send me in his stead, Ivar. I ask you this on our bond of friendship.'

Ivar closed his eyes. Erik's words had merit. The jaarls in the Storting would believe Erik more. The Storting needed to decide their response. Was his hide worth ransoming? Or should they prepare for war? He knew Erik the Black would say the right words. The Viken would avenge this insult. 'It is not my choice to make. Sigmund Sigmundson is the one offering the hospitality of his boat.'

Sigmund stroked his chin. 'It matters not to me who goes. Let the Viken warrior run away. Keep the boy here. He might prove a useful hostage.'

He gave a signal and his men bound Erik the Black's arms and legs.

'I will remember the insult, Sigmund.' Erik the Black bowed low as he was led off the ship.

'Good. And you may have this to remember as well.' Sigmund aimed another blow at Ivar and then the two men dropped him hard on to the blood-soaked wood. Ivar lay on the hull of the ship and willed the pain to go.

Thyre watched for a long heartbeat. The remainder of the Viken stood in a dispirited huddle, wounded and fearful. Asger rubbed his eyes, trying to fight off tears.

The ship rocked violently as the Ranrike ship with Erik the Black in chains pulled away, but Ivar remained lying, unmoving on the deck.

Would no one help him? Were the Viken too fearful? Someone had to make sure that he breathed. Silently she willed the Viken to rise up as one. He had saved their lives. He was willing to give his gold for them. And they let him be treated like a dog.

Sigmund aimed a kick at him, connecting his boot with the centre of Ivar's back. Then he turned away and barked a few orders, laughing.

Unable to bear it any longer, Thyre darted over to Ivar and lifted his head up, and heard his ragged breath. He gave a crooked smile and shook his head, motioning for her to go away. She shook her head back. She used a corner of her apron dress to wipe the blood from his face.

'You have a woman, Ivar.' Sigmund's voice rang out, sending ice-cold chills down her back. Thyre froze. In her haste and concern, she had revealed her existence on the boat.

'I wasn't aware that I needed to inform you of my domestic arrangements…' Ivar sat up and rested his head against his knees.

Sigmund's hand snaked out and grabbed Thyre's hair, twisting it painfully. Thyre clenched her teeth and refused to scream. Then he kneed her in the back and the cry was torn from her throat, echoing out over the water. She knew now what some of the maids had whispered earlier in the year was correct. Sigmund was a man who enjoyed hurting women.

'Who is she? Why do you have a woman on board?'

Thyre looked up at the clouds skittering across the sky and willed the pain to go. This morning she had been convinced that her life would go back to its usual routine, and now before the sun had even begun to dip, she knew she never could.

Declaring her identity would put Ragnfast and Dagmar in danger. She could see that now. Sigmund would punish them for offering hospitality to the Viken.

An ice-cold chill went through her as the knowledge hit her—Sigmund had wanted to destroy Ragnfast for a long time. That was what the beacons were about. He wanted that anchorage and she had provided him with the means to obtain it.

'Does it really matter to you, Sigmund? She is a woman I picked up somewhere. Her life is worth but a little.'

Thyre heard the faint hiss of a sword being drawn, felt the cold steel against her neck. 'Then you will not mind if I cut her throat.'

'Your quarrel is with me, not my concubine.'

'Sigmund Sigmundson,' Thyre croaked out, wiping her hand across her mouth. 'How good it is to see you again. I have not seen you since you last stopped at Ragnfast's steading. How does your wife fare?'

'Ran's net, it is Thyre, Ragnfast the Steadfast's step-daughter!' one of the Ranrike called out.

Instantly the sword relaxed and Sigmund stepped away from her. His black eyes glittered. 'I should have guessed. Ragnfast gave you shelter, and now he gives you his step-daughter as a concubine. Interesting. Today the gods have shown me their great favour.'

'There is nothing interesting about it,' Thyre snapped, resisting the temptation to put her hand to her neck. 'Ragnfast counselled me against welcoming this ship and you can see what has happened to me. Captured by the Viken and forced to be a concubine.'

Thyre waited. He had to believe her. She had to protect them from Sigmund.

'Ragnfast has been a thorn in my side for far too long.

And it is little use attacking without all of our men. When I make war, I want to be assured of victory.' Sigmund stroked his beard, ignoring her comment. 'It is intriguing, is it not, that Ragnfast's stepdaughter is travelling with a Viken *felag*? Who knows what messages Ragnfast might have for King Thorkell? Finally King Mysing will have to order the Ranrike Storting to destroy Ragnfast and he will give me that bay.'

Thyre's stomach heaved. Sigmund was going to twist this. He was going to say that she was being sent as a peace offering to the Viken. He would drip poison into her uncle King Mysing's ears and the Ranriken king would agree to destroy Ragnfast. And it was all because of her. The entire steading would be burnt. All the thralls, all the people she had known all her life would be destroyed. The lucky ones would die and the rest would be sent into slavery. All because of her and her blind trust in Sigmund.

There had to be a way that she could prevent the unthinkable happening to Ragnfast and Dagmar.

'It was not by choice, I assure you.' She made her voice sound stronger. 'Ragnfast had nothing to do with it. He loathes the Viken. He was responsible for…for bringing the Swan Princess home and securing the throne for King Mysing. He has never been a friend to the Viken. What proof do you have of his disloyalty?'

'Yes, show us the proof, Sigmund,' one of the Ranrike shouted. 'Show us that Ragnfast is a traitor.'

The swell of Ranriken murmurings grew. A flicker of hope rose with Thyre. Someone might believe her. Perhaps not everything was lost. Perhaps she could save everyone on the steading.

'Her story rings false,' Sigmund said, and the murmurs

fell silent. 'Ragnfast would never have allowed his step-daughter to become a concubine.'

'I took her,' Ivar said.

'What did she bring on board?' Sigmund's eyes narrowed as his fingers drummed against his thigh. 'What did Ragnfast send? Search the ship.'

'I brought my iron trunk. My mother's sole bequest,' Thyre called out before Ivar could say anything. There was no point in hiding or denying it. 'It contains nothing.'

Sigmund raised his hand. 'Find it. Search it.'

Thyre tried to swallow and concentrated on the knot of wood in the decking. She tried to think what was in her trunk. Was there anything that he might use against Ragnfast? Even now, she knew Sigmund was proceeding with caution, because of Ragnfast's past loyalty and because of her mother's connection to the king. But if he could find one thing, the Ranriken warriors would be baying for Ragnfast's blood.

'Would you mind enlightening me as to what you are searching for?' Ivar said, struggling to stand. 'Ragnfast has assured me that his stepdaughter is penniless. He was pleased to have her off his hands. A man with hopes does not give up any woman as concubine.'

'I will know, Viken, I will know.' Sigmund's right eye twitched and he rubbed his hands together. 'I have longed for this day—the day that I finally prove to the king that he was wrong to trust Ragnfast. One cannot simply attack a man under his protection without cause.'

The iron trunk was brought forwards, and its pitiful contents spilled out on the deck. Several brooches from Dagmar, her spare apron dress. A stone from the beach. A piece of wood that she had collected from the embers of her mother's funeral pyre. A scrap of cloth, red shot with gold, from her mother's court gown. Thyre's shoulders relaxed slightly. Nothing. Sigmund would not dare act. Ragnfast and Dagmar would be safe…for now.

Sigmund ran the cloth through his fingers and then motioned to the men to toss the contents overboard. A small squeak escaped from her mouth. Her entire life would be destroyed.

'Is there something you want to tell me? Some reason why I should not toss these things?' His hot breath touched her.

Thyre fought against the bile rising in her stomach, but she kept her face forward. 'No reason that I can think of.'

'You may keep this.' He dropped the scrap of red cloth.

Thyre allowed it to flutter to the ground and then crushed it beneath her boot. She hated the way the sole left a muddy imprint. But what did it matter now? 'It was a childish thing.'

'As you wish…' Sigmund shrugged.

'What happens to my concubine?' Ivar demanded. 'As you can see, all she possessed was a few worthless trinkets. The Viken are not so poor that we seek bits of wood and stone. Ragnfast has not offered Thorkell anything. There was no coded message here.' Ivar's voice was hoarse and rough as he stood up and faced Sigmund, towering over him. 'Are you going to slit her throat and be done with it? Or do you have something else in mind?'

Thyre felt her throat close. She was dead. She knew that. It was everyone else on the steading she worried about. Sigmund would destroy them, and all because of her.

'Not yet, she may have her uses.' Sigmund's smile was cruel and without a hint of warmth. Ice filled Thyre's limbs, leaving her numb and devoid of any feeling. She was aware of the little things—the way her boot pinched her ankle because of the dagger, and the way her mother's amulet hung between her breasts. At least the pain from Sigmund's blow had vanished. He could no longer hurt her. 'What better way to convince the king of Ragnfast's treason than to present him with this creature and her Viken lover? He forgave his sister's treachery, but will he forgive this? He will have to listen to me. It is the final proof I need. A way to crush Ragnfast once and for all time.'

'You would not dare!' The words were torn from Thyre's throat and hung in the air.

'I would dare,' Sigmund said, slapping his gloved fists together. 'He cheated me once. He will not cheat me again. I will have what is rightfully mine.'

Thyre reached down, and withdrew her dagger from the boot. Without pausing to think she rushed towards Sigmund. Her hand trembled as the knife connected with his leather tunic. A burning pain went through her shoulder, which somewhere in her mind she registered as a sword thrusting through her flesh, but blindly she tried again. This time her knife connected with his chin and the soft part of his neck.

'This should have been done years ago!' she yelled. 'This is for my family!'

With a sureness from many years supervising in the kitchen, she dragged it down, but before she could deliver the final blow, she was roughly shoved away.

'Will no one save me from such a pitiful creature?'

'It is time, Sigmund—' Ivar's voice rang out '—that you met a real Viken!'

Above her a sword flashed and she heard Ivar's roar, calling the Viken to him. The world appeared to slow. Every movement was a single and distinct image. Sigmund's sword hung in the air, poised. Ivar lunged and missed.

Thyre ignored the throbbing pain in her shoulder. She launched her body forwards and connected with Sigmund's sword arm. Another burning pain went through her as his sword hit her forearm. A huge heavy weight fell on her body, pinning her to the deck. All around her rose the chant of 'Viken, Viken, Viken'.

Chapter Nine

Thyre was never sure how long she lay there, looking up at the sky. Ever after, in her dreams, it seemed like several lifetimes.

She only noticed eventually that the roars of the Viken had stopped. The boat rocked violently once and then became much calmer. Her hand clutched the dagger to her chest and she wondered idly whether she would have the strength to use it to end her life since Sigmund's sword thrust had only wounded her in the shoulder? Surely a dead woman would not prove anything. A wave of exhaustion hit her and her eyes fluttered closed.

Strong arms lifted her up, freeing her from the heavy weight on her legs. 'You are lying in a pool of blood, but your chest is moving, Thyre. Open your eyes! Speak to me!'

Her heart leapt at the sound of Ivar's voice. It seemed so strange that before the attack she would have been happy to consign him to Ran's net, but now she wanted to see his face and hear his voice one last time. He leant down and she could see that, other than the thin trickle of blood on his cheek where Sigmund had marked him, Ivar bore no true injuries.

'Yes, yes, I am alive.' She winced at the sudden pain shooting through her shoulder as she tried to sit up. 'But this is far worse than when I fell off the ladder two summers ago. Sigmund's sword went into my shoulder.'

'But it is far from fatal.' His fingers closed around hers and then gently prised them open. The dagger fell into his palm and he calmly tucked it into his belt without really looking at it.

'Has Sigmund…?'

'Sigmund is dead. And after he fell, his men fled in the one remaining boat. They lost all stomach for a fight when confronted with a dagger-wielding woman.'

Her heart rose in her throat. Sigmund dead? How could it be possible? Sigmund had loomed over her life for as long as she could remember. She had learnt today how truly black his heart was. She knew she should not feel pity, but she could not help whispering the traditional Ranriken lament for him and the brave warrior she had once thought he was.

'By whose hand?'

'Yours. Your final blow caught him in the throat. A man does not recover from a wound given in that manner. And no warrior will follow a man who cannot withstand an attack from a woman.'

Thyre put a hand to her head and tried to think clearly despite the pain in her shoulder. 'Ragnfast? Dagmar? We will return there now, won't we? Sigmund's ship…they must be heading there. They will burn the steading and kill everyone.'

Ivar shook his head. 'No, we go to Viken. Sigmund's other ship is heading to Kaupang even as we speak. I will not have tribute sent. The captain will not dare attack Ragnfast, not without your king's consent.'

Thyre stared at him in dismay. She had to have heard wrong. Go to Kaupang? How could they?

'But…but there are not enough alive to man the oars.'

'Nevertheless, we sail to Kaupang. We will make it, Thyre. You will see Kaupang before you ever see Ragnfast.'

'Women can't go to Valhalla, can they?' she said with a weak smile. 'So I shall have to live.'

'Some women become Valkyries, but this is not your fate, Thyre.'

Thyre looked at the assorted men who were left. Battered and bruised to a man, they did not look fit to do anything, let alone row for the distance that must surely be required. She doubted that they could even row as far as Ragnfast's. 'How will we get to Kaupang?'

'We raise the sail.'

'But the mast is cracked.'

'Do you have another suggestion?' He put an arm around her. 'I do not intend to die on water, Thyre. And we will get there before the Ranriken ship.'

'How? They have a full complement of oarsmen.'

'We have one thing they don't.' Ivar put his hand in his pouch and withdrew a blue crystal stone. He lifted it up to the sun and it sent out beams of light stretching over the ship. 'It is a sunstone. It means I can navigate without a coastline to guide me.'

'That stone can do all that?'

'How do you think the Viken crossed the open ocean to Lindisfarne? To sail in summertime, when the sun never sets, you need to navigate by the sun. This crystal allowed me to. Here, you look at the sun.'

Ivar held out the wondrous stone. Thyre gazed through and the world suddenly took on a blue tinge. She handed the stone back with a shaking hand. 'I could almost think it was magic.'

'Not magic, skill. It is where the beam falls on this board. One without the other is useless.'

Thyre looked out at the vast expanse of water. She had to hope for everyone's sake that Ivar knew what he was doing.

'But Ragnfast…needs to know what happened here.'

'Your stepfather is wily. One boat will not harm him. Those men are leaderless, Thyre. Do you think they have the stomach to go against a jaarl, one of the more important jaarls in the kingdom? They will return to Sigmund's lair and lick their wounds. They might petition the king, but it will be sorted in the Storting, rather than by a raid. It is what would happen in Viken.'

'I suppose you are right.' Thyre shifted slightly and a fresh wave of pain washed through her shoulder. She was totally dependent on his leading this boat to safety. But after that, she would do everything in her power to make sure that Ragnfast learnt of the danger. 'I feel responsible.'

'You did not cause those ships to attack us.'

She regarded the bruised and battered men and then glanced up at his chiselled face and knew she had to confess. 'I lit the bonfire. The second one so that neither you nor Ragnfast would guess. Sigmund was supposed to sail once he saw the bonfire. I calculated it would take him two days. If you broke your word, then we would need help.'

'Sigmund came from the west, Thyre. Your fire did nothing.' He gave a crooked smile. 'But it confirms that you are a lady to be reckoned with. You think rather than reacting like most women.'

'You are not angry?'

'You saved every man's life on this boat, Thyre. Think on that. Whether you want it or not, you are a Viken now.'

She turned her head and saw the affirmation in the remaining Vikens' faces. Asger gave a little wave from where he sat with his hands on the oar. She was one of them. Her blood had won through. No, she screwed up her forehead. It had been a matter of honour. Her heart remained firmly wedded to Ranrike and her whole being had to be devoted to saving her family. She had to right the wrong she had inadvertently caused. She felt only gratitude towards Ivar. Somewhere deep inside her, a little voice called her a liar.

'I see you failed to make Valhalla, Asger,' she said, pushing away the conflicting thoughts.

'Some day I will,' Asger said, puffing out his chest. 'Uncle Ivar says that I am a true Viken warrior now that I have been blooded in battle. My mother will be proud.'

'Your mother is more likely to skin me alive,' Ivar answered. 'I worried for my future well being, but luckily Thyre pulled you to safety when you failed to stop the berserker with the axe.'

'Asger will have to take better care next time.' She put her hands on to her head. She needed to move and to get away from the images that were clogging her brain. She began to go back towards where she had sat before the battle.

'Stay still, your wound is open and you have lost blood.'

Thyre regarded the dark stain on her shift. A wave of nausea washed over her. Her arm seemed to belong to someone else and refused to respond to her attempt to make a fist.

'You promised I would live.' She tried to make her voice sound unconcerned. 'I do not see you tending your men.'

'They are not my concubines. They can tend to their own wounds.' Ivar reached into a bag that hung from his belt. 'I think this calls for touchwood.'

'Touchwood?' Thyre gave a strangled laugh and tried to ignore the ever-growing stain on her shift. 'Are you going to light a funeral pyre? Surely you can see that I am still breathing.'

'It works to stem bleeding. Annis, Haakon's wife, taught me the trick. It has saved other lives, including Haakon's prize elk hound when he was savaged by wolves.'

'Annis? What a strange name.'

'She is from Northumbria. Like you, she has a tendency to want to fight.' Ivar's eyes danced as he withdrew the piece of touchwood from his pouch. 'She once killed a berserker.'

'I have heard the Lindisfarne saga.' Thyre closed her eyes as Ivar's fingers moved the cloth from her shoulder and exposed the wound. 'But I was certain that was an exaggeration.'

'No, it was one of the truths.'

'And what is the truth about my wound?'

'Sigmund's sword was sharp and clean. The wound should remain clear of infection.' He crumbled some of the touchwood on the wound. Then he stripped off his jerkin and fine linen tunic. With a great rip, he tore a sleeve from the tunic and, using his dagger, cut it into strips. He wrapped the strips around her shoulder, fashioning a bandage, and then put on his jerkin again.

'You will need a tunic.'

'I have found a better use for it.' His cool fingers touched her cheek. 'The entire boat owes you a life-debt, Thyre. Remember that.'

'I was trying to save my own life, not theirs.'

'Unintended consequence.' His hand stroked her hair, capturing it between his fingers. 'These men would be willing to give their lives for you. When are you going to be honest with them?'

'Honest? I have no idea what you mean.' Thyre kept her head upright, even though the temptation to lean against him nearly overwhelmed her.

'When were you planning on telling me that you were the Swan Princess's daughter?'

Thyre had to force the breath back into her lungs. After all they had been through, it seemed such a little thing to reveal. She allowed her head to collapse against her chest. 'How long have you known?'

'Since I saw the scrap of material from the chest—it was her court dress. And the light opened on my mind. It was why Sigmund became so angry. He was practically foaming at the mouth. He thought you were being sent as an emissary from Ragnfast the Steadfast.'

'You know the truth.' Thyre shifted uneasily. How much of the story could she reasonably trust him with? Would he guess that King Thorkell was her unacknowledged father?

'You should have trusted me.'

Thyre stared at him, her pain and discomfort forgotten. 'But how did you know the dress?'

'When I was younger than Asger, the Swan Princess resided at the court. Everyone was in love with her, including me. She was the most beautiful creature I had ever seen. She once stopped and wiped my face after I had had a fight in the hall.'

'Ragnfast liberated her. He brought her back to her brother King Mysing,' Thyre said carefully. She had not even considered that Ivar might have personal memories of her mother. Would he be able to remember the dates?

Would he guess that King Thorkell was her father and that her mother had cheated by not fulfilling his wish and murdering any sickly child? How much would his life-debt to her count then? 'She died when I was eight. My mother and Ragnfast were happy. I think they were friends before she was sent as a hostage…before everything happened.'

'That was what confused me. I thought she had died much earlier.'

'Then you were wrong. Her brother Mysing, then the new Ranriken king, banished her. She became dead to him.' Thyre pulled her shift down so it covered her ankles. She refused to explain that the quarrel had to do with the child her mother carried, and how King Mysing wanted the baby strangled at birth. There was no guarantee that King Thorkell would accept her if he knew the truth. Ragnfast had explained the full significance of the dagger when Thyre had found it amongst her mother's things after her death. How King Thorkell had given it to her mother. If she had had a son, she was supposed to send him to be raised a Viken. And her mother had known that the dagger was a sign that she was to kill the child, should it be a girl. Thyre glanced up at Ivar's face. Would he protect her against King Thorkell's wrath? No, it was better to allow her father to be a mystery. She could not be sure whom to trust. 'Had we best get the sail up? Night will come soon. My shoulder pains me.'

'We will speak of this later, Thyre.' Ivar's face was set in planes of chiselled stone. 'After you are rested, you will tell me the full truth, the true reason you wanted to go to Kaupang. Why you seduced me in that particular fashion. I dislike game playing and will not be used as some counter in an imaginary game of *tafl*. Nor will I allow my men to be used.'

'I have told the truth. This is no game of *tafl*. My being here had everything to do with my duty towards my family and nothing to do with the Swan Princess. That story is history,' Thyre whispered to his retreating back. She settled her body against the bulwark, away from the splash of the waves. Everything ached and all she wanted to do was to sleep. Later she would plan. There had to be a way to warn Ragnfast and to prevent anyone else from being harmed. It was the only thing she had left worth living for.

Thyre woke with an abrupt start as the pain in her shoulder throbbed. The horrors of the day came rushing back at her and she knew that it had been no dream. The sun had set and the dark velvet of the night sky twinkled with silver stars. The mast creaked slightly, but the sail was full of wind and the ship glided over the waves. All around her was a comforting darkness. The snores of the Viken filled her ears. She started to settle down again when she saw a figure sitting with his hand on the oar, moving it slightly every so often so that the sail filled, but not too much.

She inched her way forwards. Hand over hand, hanging on to the side of the boat. 'Ivar?'

He kept a hand on the steering oar, but his other hand closed around her wrist and gently eased her forwards so that she could sit next to him. 'I thought you would sleep longer. The rest of the company are sleeping.'

'The pain in my shoulder woke me.' She stared at him. The starlight had turned his skin to silver.

'Someone has to steer. When we get to Kaupang, then I shall sleep. Safety and home and then rest.'

'Isn't there anyone else? You were not steering earlier when we left my home.'

'I would only trust Erik the Black with this boat and he has gone to Kaupang as a hostage.'

Thyre gave a nod. She could understand the need to make sure a job was properly done. She had often done that. But it made Ivar more dangerous. It would be so easy to start to care for him. A day ago, she thought she would never see him again, and now she did not want to think about what would happen when he went out of her life. She took a deep breath. 'Ragnfast never sent me. What happened today is not part of some elaborate game. Ragnfast is above all things loyal to King Mysing.'

'I want to believe you, Thyre.'

'It is the truth. Ragnfast may depend on my counsel, but what sort of man would send a woman like me as an emissary?'

He glanced up at the sky, and then moved the steering oar. Thyre began to hope that he might believe her. 'You should have said about your mother being the Swan Princess.'

'And would that have stopped what happened? Ragnfast was overcome by greed and Dagmar had to be protected. Would you have taken me as a concubine? Or would you have found some other way to punish my step-father?'

'I do not know. It is an honest answer, Thyre. Many in Viken were upset when the Swan Princess left, but Bose said…' He paused, and his fingers caught her chin, turning her first one way and then the other, before abruptly releasing her.

'Is something the matter?'

'It is ancient history, Thyre. I do not delve into what might have been, but if Bose the Dark is at Kaupang when we arrive, I think we will be having a chat. Things are missing.'

'Missing?'

'Ragnfast managed to escape with your mother. By your own account, he is not a good sailor. There should have been a chase. I had never thought of it before.'

Should have been a chase. Casual words, but ones that caused a stab of fear to run through Thyre.

'It is all history. But Ragnfast never had any time for Viken after that.'

'When did your mother marry Ragnfast?'

'She chose marriage to the man who rescued her after her brother the king turned against her. She thought there should be peace between Ranrike and Viken and the *frithe* should be kept. He disagreed. Is it important?'

'I had wondered what happened to her and why we were never told the truth. King Thorkell never wished for her death.'

'What is court like? My mother used to tell stories when she wanted Dagmar and me to behave.'

'It was a very different court when she was there. Queen Asa, when she married King Thorkell, made changes.'

'Good or bad? My mother told me tales of the hunts they had and the feasting. How the men would fight bloody battles in the hall and the women would be made to watch.' Thyre gave a hiccupping laugh. 'I was so relieved when you said that concubines were not allowed there. The fights in Ragnfast's hall are bad enough and the foresters only use their fists.'

'It is now more refined. Asa has had a civilising influence. She likes a woman to be womanly. She brought a number of women from Denmark, including Edda, my late wife, and banished concubines from taking an active role in court life.'

'I like to think that I always behave in the appropriate manner.' Thyre shifted so there was air between them. 'You were the one who made me into a concubine.'

Ivar reached out and gathered her towards him. His arm went about her waist and she could feel the bulk of his muscles against her thin shift. He lowered his mouth to hers.

'Court is far from everything. Neither Queen Asa nor any of her ladies could have fought Sigmund,' he said against her lips, 'let alone killed him. You must have some Valkyrie blood in you.'

Thyre drank from his mouth. She needed this man. She did not want to think about the future. Or how unsophisticated she was. She had never experienced the intrigues of court.

Then he put her from him as the sail filled out and the mast gave a loud creak. 'Now I need to concentrate.'

'What was that kiss for? For luck?'

'Because, daughter of Skathi, I wanted to. I make my own luck.'

'I am no warrior.' Thyre paused, remembering the tale of how the goddess Skathi had donned her father's armour and demanded satisfaction from the gods as they supped at Asgard. Eventually, they accepted her as a goddess and she married the god of the sea.

He ran a hand down her arm. 'You are all night-time promise and daytime fierceness.'

'Something to be admired?'

'To me it makes you interesting, a puzzle. I am finding that I quite enjoy puzzles.'

They sat there, with his hands on the steering oar in companionable silence. She relaxed against him and did not think beyond the moment. Somehow, she drew strength from the steady beat of his heart under her ear. They would get to Kaupang, and she would ensure Ragnfast's safety without revealing her parentage.

The wind caught the sail and, suddenly, the mast began

to twist with an ear-splitting crack. The entire ship woke. Ivar swore loudly.

'The mast is going.'

Thyre looked out at it. If the mast collapsed, they would all perish out here in the ocean.

'Something will be needed to bind the mast together to prevent it from crackling more. To keep it from completely splitting,' she said.

'But what? There is no time.'

'My apron dress,' Thyre said, warming to the idea as her mind raced. 'It will make for a strong padding. It is good honest wool. Wool absorbs water.'

Ivar was silent for a long moment. 'Why are you willing to do this? I could use the silk in the hold. It will serve the same purpose.'

'The silk is not as strong and there is no time. That mast needs to be bound now.' Thyre struggled out of the dress and stood in her shift. 'Wool will be better. Later if you need more, use the silk.'

Ivar held the dress in his hand as if he were weighing up the offering. 'If you like, I will use it. Anything to save the ship.'

'Do it quickly.'

Rapidly he bound the mast, and the creaking stopped. The sail filled again with wind and the boat began to move.

Thyre concentrated on securing the rope. Her shoulder tugged, but somehow she seemed far more alive out here next to Ivar than she had ever been back at the steading.

Ivar watched the horizon in the dull grey sky. Instead of the sea meeting the sky, a brown line appeared. It was impossible to tell where Erik the Black and the Ranrike ship were. He suspected that the captain would spend the night in a bay and that they were ahead of the ship. But he could not be sure. He knew the tricks the sea could play.

He waited a few breaths more until he could make out the vague outlines of the rock islands that guarded the entrance to the harbour. Then his life would start again. It was very different from when he had sailed out of the harbour earlier in the year. Then he had thought that he would marry whomever Thorkell recommended. But now, he knew that he could not. He had seen how two households had torn his father apart. A jaarl could not marry his concubine. It was not done in Viken, even though Haakon had married Annis. Then the circumstances had been very different. Annis was a great lady, whereas Thyre was simply the bastard daughter of a disgraced princess.

'Time to get the sail down,' he called.

'The gods have favoured us,' Asger cried.

'The gods? What about my skill? Or Thyre's quick thinking and reflexes?' Ivar asked.

'If I compliment you on your skill, Uncle, I would have to compliment Thyre's apron dress and that would not be right as she is in her shift.' Asger's ears became bright pink.

'You have acquired an admirer, Thyre.' He glanced at her dark black hair. 'But we need to get this boat into harbour.'

Instantly the remaining crew cheered. The whole boat came to life as the warriors bustled about and grabbed the oars. A number of places sat empty. Ivar thought of each man. Every family would share in the bounty from the venture, but he wished the cost had not been so high. Some day, he would avenge their deaths, but today, today was a day for rejoicing.

Against the odds, they had made it home. He had proved that the passage was far from being cursed, but it was patrolled by Ranrike and Sigmundson and that menace would have to be considered.

'What is going on?' Thyre asked from where she sat. She turned her head slightly, revealing her long white neck. Ivar never tired of watching her. He wondered who her father was, but that was the least of his concerns. Certainly the father had never gone looking for her. Nor had her mother ever sent her. Perhaps he did not acknowledge her, or did not know. She was his now and he would fight any man who said differently. Once things were more settled, he would make discreet enquires, starting with Bose the Dark.

'Kaupang is on the horizon. We will row in. The shoals are tricky for a sail.'

'I thought there were not enough to row this boat.'

'Not over a long distance, but it is safer to row than to sail in the harbour.'

'Then I shall row as well.' Thyre sat down opposite and grabbed an oar.

'Women do not row,' Ivar said.

'Women do not kill jaarls either, but I seem to recall doing it.'

Ivar made a non-committal grunt, but allowed her to take an oar. Carefully, he slowed the tempo down. Thyre deserved her moment of triumph and if she wanted to celebrate by rowing, then they would match her speed.

'They will have to write a saga about this voyage,' Asger declared as he began to row.

'Your first voyage and already thinking of sagas.' Ivar gave a laugh. 'My sister will barely recognise this battle-hardened warrior as her son.'

'I never finished her comb.'

'Your mother will be pleased to see you,' Thyre said,

her hands only lightly resting on the oar. 'You are more important than any comb.'

'I suppose.' Asger shrugged.

Ivar turned his attention back to the shoreline and cursed under his breath. Amongst the multitude of ships in the harbour, the Ranriken ship was pulled on shore. Erik the Black must have navigated the ship with a great deal of accuracy and rushed home to secure their freedom. But whatever happened, they could not be more than half a day behind. He wished now that he had risked the full sail. But he looked forward to the astonishment on the Ranriken faces when they realised that their ship now belonged to him.

'There is a crowd on shore!' Asger called out from where he was stationed on the prow.

'I see them!'

'I wonder what the Ranrike will think of our story. I bet they never expected to be bested by a woman!' Asger shouted, warming to his theme.

'I want you to keep silent about Thyre's role until I tell you. You are no skald, Asger. People do not need to know the story.'

Thyre tried to concentrate on the buildings and forget Ivar's words. She doubted if she had ever seen so many people in one place at one time. Ragnfast had always steadfastly refused to take her to Ranhiem, but she knew from her mother's stories that Kaupang surpassed the meagre Ranrike capital. It had a prosperous air. She had given up trying to decipher where the ships were from. Some she could see must come from the kingdom of the Franks and others from Charlemagne, but the vast majority were the Viken's fabled fleet.

'The jaarl Ivar Gunnarson lies imprisoned in Ranhiem.'

Erik the Black's voice floated over the harbour. 'Who will be with me? Who will bring the ransom?'

'Who will attack the Ranrike?' someone called.

'I gave my bond. They will kill him if we go into Ranhiem with shields raised. Ivar Gunnarson has brought much prosperity to Viken. He needs our help.'

'But did Ivar make it to Birka and Permia? Have the Ranrike taken possession of all the spices and silks?'

'He should have taken more ships!'

'There is a curse on that strait! Ivar Gunnarson should never have taunted the gods.'

'Erik the Black, you have little faith in me.' Ivar's voice resounded across the water. 'You should know that I never surrender and I remain undefeated. You should have stayed aboard the *Sea Witch* and joined in the fun.'

The entire crowd drew its breath. People started racing down towards the shoreline. Two large Viken jumped in the water, heedless of their fine clothes, and waded out to the boat.

'Ivar, what has happened?'

'Sigmund was defeated,' Ivar said with little emotion. 'I had help in the shape of this woman.'

Both men stopped. Their eyes immediately turned towards where she sat at the oar. Thyre put her hands on her lap. Out in the ocean, it had seemed easy to give up her apron dress and even to row. She felt part of the *felag*, but now they were here, in Kaupang, everything was different. She was alone and dressed only in her shift. Her other apron dresses were at the bottom of the ocean. Would Ivar supply her with new ones? Or would she have to beg? She refused to beg. She would find a way to get around him. It was merely a matter of dropping hints and making sure that he understood the consequences. It was how her mother had taught her to manage Ragnfast and it worked.

She crossed her arms and hoped no one would say anything about the indecency of her costume.

'You have a woman on board.'

'She is my concubine,' Ivar growled. 'And you should talk, Haakon. You have never had any qualms about having a woman on board ship.'

'Annis has never pulled the oars,' the dark-haired one replied with a scowl. 'I never forced her to do that.'

'It was Thyre's choice. Her quick thinking also kept the mast from splitting. Otherwise, we might have never arrived.'

'A concubine? From Birka?' the dark blonde one asked.

'I am from Ranrike,' Thyre said, using her firmest voice. 'I was involved in the fighting.'

Both jaarls burst out laughing. 'And, Ivar, you always said that you wanted a gentle woman, just like Edda. Biddable and not inclined towards a cross word. It appears you have seen sense after all.'

Edda. She saw a muscle jump in Ivar's jaw. The name held significance. His late wife? She swallowed hard and tried not to feel jealous.

'Thyre is my concubine, not my wife. She was wounded in the battle. Now if you will let me get ashore, there is much I must discuss with Thorkell.'

'You will have to wait,' Vikar said. 'Thorkell is off hunting moose. He has a new elkhound from Haakon's latest litter and is determined to trial him.'

'When is he expected back?'

Thyre held her breath. She was not ready to meet King Thorkell yet. What could she say to him? How could she explain? She noticed that neither Vikar nor Haakon had asked her if she was related to the Ranriken Swan Princess.

She had prepared a little speech, but it appeared unnecessary. Would Ivar tell them?

'A few days. The Storting will start on Freya's day. He will be back to preside then.'

'Ivar Gunnarson,' a male voice resounded over the water, 'your queen wishes to greet you.'

'Did you bring the spices she so desired?' Haakon asked.

'I kept my promise,' Ivar said.

Thyre looked out over the water and saw the silver blondeness of the queen, standing splendidly dressed. Her stomach churned. Her father's wife stood with malice shining from her pale blue eyes.

'My shoulder pains me a great deal. You go on ahead and greet the queen,' Thyre said, putting her hand to where Sigmund's sword had sliced her flesh. The shoulder only niggled, but she needed a moment to compose her mind after the queen's look of pure hatred. She would think of the right words. A woman could be dignified no matter what she was wearing or the state of her hair. It came from her inner self. Her mother had repeated the words many times over. Now more than ever, Thyre wished her mother was standing next to her, telling her what to do and how to behave.

'Haakon, is your wife at Kaupang?'

'Yes, Annis is here for the start of the Storting. She demanded that we bring both children as well. A priest from Charlemagne's court is supposed to be here, and she is determined to have them baptised.'

'Thyre was injured in the battle. I have dressed the wound as best I could, but I would like Annis to have a look. Ever since I saw what she did to Thrand, I have held her work in the highest esteem.'

'Yes, of course. I will go and inform Annis. She will be pleased to help.'

'And, Vikar, I want you to take Thyre quietly off the ship. There is no need to expose her to all this.' Ivar waved a hand towards the ever-growing crowd. 'Her dress is—'

Thyre stared at him. 'Ivar!'

'For once in your life, Thyre, obey me! You are my concubine, not my wife!'

Both Vikar and Haakon burst out into laughter. Thyre crossed her arms. This time she would obey him, but somehow she was going to have to find a way to speak to King Thorkell on her own to stop this madness. Ragnfast and Dagmar, they were important. War with Ranrike would benefit no one. She had to remember them and the danger they were in and not that she suddenly wondered what it would be like to be Ivar's wife.

With Vikar's help, she stumbled from the boat. Her legs could barely remember what firm land felt like and, with each step, the land appeared to pitch and roll.

Off to her right, she heard Ivar addressing the crowd, explaining his story.

She glanced up and saw again the silver blonde radiance of Queen Asa. Their eyes met and the queen's expression turned ice cold. A chill went through Thyre and she knew she had made an enemy.

Chapter Ten

'This bandage will have to come off. I will be as gentle as I can, but it may hurt.' The woman's lilting voice filled Thyre's ears as she stood in the middle of Ivar's bedchamber. The chamber was not as well appointed as Ragnfast's, but it had a certain amount of comfort. Thyre ran a hand over the silver wolf skin that lay proudly on top of the bed. Ivar's boast had been far from idle. The fur proved it.

Vikar had delivered her to Ivar's house; then, within a few breaths, Haakon's wife had arrived. Thyre watched her with curiosity. She was the captive from Northumbria, the one who had slain a berserker, if the saga was to be believed.

'Can you keep still, please? I am trying to be as gentle as possible but I do need to see the wound.'

'I understand.' Thyre kept her body rigid as Annis started to undo Ivar's makeshift bandage. As she promised, she was gentle, but moved with sure expertise.

'It is better than I hoped. Ivar obviously took heed of my instructions.' Annis probed the wound with her fingers. 'It is healing well with no sign of infection.'

'Is it true what Ivar said, that you have the power to heal?'

The woman gave a musical laugh. 'I have no idea about power. I have a small skill with herbs and God does the rest.'

'God?' Thyre started at the singular use of the term. 'You mean like Thor or Ran.'

'I am a Christian and believe in one God.'

Thyre shook her head. Only one god? It made no sense. But she had no wish to offend as the woman was clearly skilled in healing. 'I am sorry, but I have lived quietly. Ragnfast, my stepfather, might be interested in a god that can heal.'

'It is a bit more complicated than that. Do not worry. After two years here, I am used to pagan ways.' Annis gave a merry laugh and Thyre shifted, uncomfortably aware that she had made an error.

'I hope I have not offended.'

'Not at all. I dare say everything here is strange. I know it was when I first arrived. How did you come to be Ivar's concubine? Did Ivar capture you? All of Kaupang will want to know. I suspect several skalds will be competing for the honour of composing the saga.'

'All?' Thyre took a step backwards. Her stomach knotted. Would any guess about her parentage? She wanted to keep it hidden until she had petitioned King Thorkell. He needed to hear the story from her lips. 'It is a very boring tale, hardly worth bothering with. I am sure the skalds will concentrate on Ivar's part—the journey out to Birka and the way he navigated the ship back to Viken.'

'He was not expected to return—that is true. Everyone thought he was foolish to taunt the gods, but once again he is the hero of the hour. Ivar and his miraculous boat and seamanship. Thorkell will undoubtedly throw a feast in his honour. I understand from Haakon the boat has returned full of spices, silks and furs. Thankfully, Haakon thought to finance part of it. I look forward to a new silk gown.'

Thyre's heart skipped a beat. A feast for the returning heroes. Here was a golden opportunity to speak to the Viken king and to plead for Ragnfast and Dagmar's rescue. If an expedition was organised, they might even arrive back there before Sigmund's followers reached her uncle, King Mysing. 'And will I be expected to attend?'

Annis developed a sudden interest in putting away her herbs and ointments. 'I have no idea about a welcome-home feast. It depends on the queen. If she goes, concubines will not be welcome. Otherwise, it would be up to Ivar. Personally, I am not overfond of the singing and the wild dancing. The Viken tend to sing rather loudly and very badly. And that is only their skalds.'

Thyre gave a weak smile and tried not to concentrate on the word—concubine. She wanted to think of herself as free and independent, not as a concubine who was subject to the whims of her master. 'I understand. I doubt I would have liked the court. Soon Ivar will take me off to his estate. It was just the feast I had wondered about.'

Annis placed a warm hand on her shoulder. 'I know Sela, Vikar's wife, finds the customs of the court difficult. Perhaps you had best speak to her. She is here for the start of the Storting and has already been complaining about the strictures Asa requires of her ladies, but Vikar insisted she attend.'

'I want to avoid making obvious mistakes…'

'And do you have clothes? Your shift is only fit for rags.'

'They went overboard.' Thyre gave a little shrug. 'Other things seemed to be more important.'

To her relief, Annis did not pursue the subject.

'I will send something over. Ivar, if he is like Haakon, will have no sense about clothes. Or that you might need them.' Annis put some honey on Thyre's wound and then put a clean cloth over it. 'And now, I believe you need a draught to make you sleep. Tomorrow, I will inspect it and you can tell me the full tale of what happened.'

'You asked to see me, my lady, the moment I returned.' Ivar made a bow before the queen and then held out a little cedar box. 'I bought the spices that I promised.'

Asa clicked her fingers, dismissing the rest of the court. Ivar lifted his brow. His nerves were instantly alert. The last time they had spoken alone was after Edda's death and she had informed him of whom she blamed for her favourite's demise. They had agreed to differ. The queen rose from her chair.

'I have been pondering your need for a wife. If you will recall, Thorkell and I spoke to you about this before you left. You are far too important a jaarl. You must make a wise and considered match, one that benefits the kingdom as well as your bed.'

'And we decided that it was a subject best left until I returned as the prospects for the voyage's success were not high.' Ivar kept his tone measured. A twinge of guilt ran through him. Had the queen spent time on the matchmaking? He had not expected Asa to do much; now, with the advent of Thyre, the need for a wife vanished.

'And now you have returned.' Asa tapped her forefinger against the arm of her chair. 'I have drawn up a list…'

'I will have a look at the ladies when I have time, but there are other pressing matters at hand.'

'I had wanted to make sure the most suitable served you at the welcome-home feast.' Asa batted her lashes and a smug smile touched her lips. 'A woman must think of such things and allow men to get about their business.'

'There will be time to decide later.' Ivar gritted his teeth. He had no wish to offend, but he would not be marrying. Thorkell would understand his decision, once he had met Thyre.

'I understand you have brought a concubine home from the voyage. A dark-haired woman.'

Ivar kept his face impassive. Now they came to the true reason why Asa had called him here—Thyre. What was the queen's interest in his concubine? 'News travels fast.'

'Thorkell will never allow you to marry her.' Asa's pale eyes glittered with some quickly masked emotion. 'He will insist on you marrying a woman of good breeding and character. And you must marry, Ivar.'

'You know nothing about Thyre.'

'I held your late wife in high esteem, Ivar. We both know I would have saved her if I could, if she had been at court where she belonged.' Asa raised her hand imperiously. 'I am merely offering an old friend some sage advice. Concubines have a way of leaving.'

'Indeed.' Ivar choked down his anger.

Ivar knew that, despite Asa's protests, she had had a hand in sending Annis away before Haakon had realised what was happening. After Annis had saved the king's life, the queen had prevailed on him to free Annis and then she had put her on a ship bound for Northumbria. It was only through Annis's quick thinking and her desire for justice that Haakon had been able to claim the woman he loved. The queen might have tried the trick once, but she would not try it again. Thyre was no high-born captive to be ransomed, but his concubine. And he would keep Thyre as his concubine as long as he desired it. He would not dishonour her or some unknown future wife by having two women at the same time. He refused to yield on this.

'My sole concern is for the well being of your future.' Asa batted her lashes.

'Other than returning home from my voyage with a woman, what have I done to earn this lecture, my queen?'

Asa gave a little shrug and toyed with the tassel of her kirtle. 'I merely wanted to make sure you understood. Where did you say this woman, this Thyre, was from? Birka?'

'No, Ranrike. She grew up on a remote estate between here and Ranhiem.'

In the torchlight, Asa paled slightly. She sank gracefully back down on her chair. 'From Ranrike. I thought they were all blonde in Ranrike. All except…but she died without children. Bose was quite clear on that.'

'Is something wrong?'

'No, no.' Asa put a hand up to her face, shielding it from his gaze. 'Perhaps it is best that Thorkell does not meet her. After the feast, you may take her off to your estate. Keep her there until you tire of her. Yes, perhaps that is best.'

'She played an instrumental part in securing our freedom from the jaarl Sigmund Sigmundson.'

'I have no doubt she did, and she is to be commended for it. I will personally see to it that she returns to her home…unharmed and as soon as possible. It is the least Viken can do to honour such bravery.' Asa gave a long sigh and her lashes swept down. 'But Thorkell hates the Ranrike, particularly those with dark hair. He has a long hostility towards them. If you value your concubine's life, keep her from this court.'

Ivar clenched his fists. Asa would not do to Thyre what she had tried to do Annis. Thyre would remain his concubine; she would not be sent home. But perhaps Asa was correct about the king. Thorkell might not be willing to meet the Swan Princess's daughter. He needed to discover the truth behind the Swan Princess's stay in Viken before Thyre's parentage put her life in danger.

Ivar held out his hand. 'I will take a look at your list.'

Asa tapped the rune stick against her lips. Her entire being glowed. 'I knew if I explained the situation to you, Ivar, that we could reach an agreement. Any one of these ladies would make you an admirable wife. Take your time, but do not delay too long as I wish you to have your first choice.'

Ivar waited until he was out of the chamber before he threw the stick into the nearest fire.

Thyre's troubled dreams swirled about her. Sigmund's face leered up at her before the sea covered it. She leant out but fell down into the water, tried to scream, but no one heard her. She reached out an arm to grab a spar, but her hand encountered empty air. She was drowning in the sea. Sigmund reached up and started to drag her down towards Ran's net. She kicked out, cried out.

'Thyre! Thyre!' Ivar's voice reached her through the dream and held her.

She sat up with a start and saw that a single rush light burnt. Ivar sat on the bed, looking at her. The light highlighted the planes of his face, obscuring the scar. Her heart turned over.

'You were shouting for me,' he said, smoothing a strand of hair from her face. Thyre fought the temptation to turn it in towards his palm.

She took deep steadying breaths and drank in his reassuring male scent. His hair curled slightly at the ends as if it were damp.

'I fell asleep,' she said.

'A restless dream, from the sound of your cries.' He made no move towards her.

'Annis visited. She gave me something to drink. It has made my head go fuzzy. I am unused to sleeping in such a large bed.'

'Perhaps, you would like to sleep alone.'

'No!' The word was torn from her throat. Thyre hated how desperate it sounded. More than anything she wanted to have his arms about her. 'I mean…it is fine. Dreams have no power to hurt.'

His hand picked up a tendril of her hair and brought it to his lips and all the while his eyes watched her. 'Are you sure?'

'Hold me?'

Ivar's arms went around her as her body began to convulse in cold shivers.

'Hush, it is all right. You are alive. He is dead.'

'You knew what I was dreaming.' Thyre looked up into his eyes, eyes that had become deep pools. 'How did you guess?'

His hands stroked her back. 'It is not hard to guess. The first time you kill someone…'

'I had to…'

'I know. You were brave, Thyre. And you were brave again today.'

'Today?' Thyre tilted her head. Had he guessed how seeing the hatred in the queen's eyes had unnerved her? It had been as if Asa could see into her soul and realised who her parents were. A strong son would have been different from the sickly creature she had been as a baby. But now she was a woman.

'I understand you walked to my house with your head held high.'

'I have done nothing to be ashamed of.' Thyre stretched slightly, pleased her shoulder only mildly throbbed. While she had waited for sleep, she had rehearsed her speech to Ivar. She would seduce him into agreeing to help Ragnfast. Sometimes, it was the only weapon a woman had. 'It worries me that King Thorkell is away. He needs to know the situation as soon as possible. Ragnfast and Dagmar…'

'It will be taken care of. I promise you that. Asa assures me that the king will return tomorrow. The feast is planned for the following day.'

Asa. He had been to see the queen. Thyre wondered if she should voice her fears and explain why she needed to see Thorkell alone, without Asa being there. Ivar would probably laugh at her and say that she imagined things, but Asa's look had dripped with hatred.

'I should let you sleep. In the morning, we can discuss things.'

He started to move off the bed, away from her. She might never get another opportunity to plead for Ragnfast and Dagmar, unless she could put him in a good mood.

'Please…please stay.' Thyre curled her hand about his neck and brought his face closer. 'It is your bed, not mine.'

He groaned, but his hands went to her body and pulled her so that her breasts were crushed against his chest. 'Your shoulder needs to heal.'

'We can be careful,' she whispered against his lips. 'Annis says that it is healing nicely. It was a clean cut.'

She claimed his mouth. Their tongues touched briefly. The swirling warmth inside ignited and she deepened the kiss. This was what she needed to keep the dreams at bay.

Her hands buried themselves into his hair and held him there. She arched forwards, her breasts straining against the clean white shift Annis had found.

His arms held her close again, but as if he were holding some precious object.

Thyre lifted her mouth from his.

'You are overdressed.'

'Am I, indeed?'

'Yes, we have light tonight and I want to see all of you.'

He froze and seemed to withdraw from her. Had she said the wrong thing? She worried he would find another excuse, a reason to leave, and she knew she needed him tonight. She wanted him to keep the dreams away. Nothing could hurt her if he was near. He had whispered that on the boat and she had believed him. Together, they were safe.

'Please let there be light,' Thyre whispered. 'Allow me to see you. Allow my eyes to feast. This does not have to be something that happens in the dark.'

His eyes deepened to a midnight blue. 'Very well, if you wish it.'

'I do.' She leant towards him and cupped his face with her hands. 'I do.'

'Edda…my wife. She was shy…we never had light.'

Thyre put her fingers against his lips as her insides convulsed. She knew it was wrong to be pleased about doing something different than the other woman. She had never met her and already she resented her. And she knew that was wrong. 'We can speak of her another time. Tonight is for us.'

He nodded and she released her breath. His hands lifted his shirt to reveal his golden skin with its traces of scars over his muscles and sinews. The desire to trace each of the scars with her tongue and taste his skin swamped her senses. She dug her fingers into the fur that covered the bed.

He stopped and looked at her with a raised eyebrow.

'Continue.' Thyre barely recognised the husky rasp that had become her voice.

His fingers went to his trousers and allowed them to drop. He stood there, his rampant arousal thrusting outwards towards her. Thyre's mouth went dry as she thought of him fitting inside her. She was pleased she had not seen him this way before as it would have made her even more nervous. But now she knew, and she knew this was for her and not for some mysterious lady in the night.

'Do I meet with your satisfaction?' he asked with a husky laugh.

'There are advantages to the light.'

She held out her arms, but he shook his head. 'You need to remove the shift. It is only fair.'

'Since when have you been concerned about such things?'

'I want to see you, Thyre.'

With trembling fingers she lifted her shift and tossed it on the floor. As she tugged the shift over her breasts, her nipples tingled. Under his hot gaze, they ached even more.

He knelt down on the bed, gathering her in his arms. His skin brushed hers. She gave in to her impulse and used a finger to trace several of the scars on his back, glorying in how the muscles shifted and changed under her hands.

His mouth slipped lower, nuzzling a line down her neck until he reached her breasts. Answering her unspoken plea, he cupped her breasts. His tongue flicked over one nipple and then the other, toyed with them. He suckled each one in turn, making the nipples become harder and more pointed.

Her back arched up off the bed and molten heat thrummed through her body. She teetered on the edge of a swirling maelstrom of heat and fire. Her hands clutched at his shoulders. She needed him, needed him to assuage this great aching well of desire that engulfed her and threatened to overwhelm her senses. He held her for a few moments while her body convulsed.

'Slowly,' he said. 'I don't want to hurt you. We have all night.'

'And beyond.' She gave a little laugh and tried to control the trembling in her limbs.

'That as well.'

His hands eased her back against the pillows. He loomed over her as the shadows from the guttering light played on his body, shifting and dancing. 'I want to enjoy you and to give you pleasure.'

'I want to touch you,' she said, her fingers curling in frustration. She wanted to do something, not simply to lie there like some doll. She wanted to be an active participant.

'In a little while.' He kissed her temple. 'Allow me to explore your body. Some things are best taken slowly.'

His hands stroked down her body, gently exploring, but with the same precision with which he had steered the boat earlier. He knew precisely how to elicit a response, from the underside of her wrist to the point just beyond her ears. Each tiny particle of her commanded the same diligent attention. There was nothing rough or sudden. It was firm and assured. He seemed to be aware of each movement that she made, each quiver of her body as a new touch evoked a different tingle of pleasure.

His fingers lingered on the underside of her breasts, stroking and cupping them before continuing inexorably to the apex of her thighs.

Slowly, he parted the curls, and his finger stroked her innermost core. Again the banked fires built within her to a raging inferno. She glanced up at him and saw his face had become intent. Slowly he lowered his mouth and where his hand had been, his tongue went. Gliding over her, tasting her, he devoured until her body bucked upwards and she could only whimper.

He lifted his mouth. 'More?'

She tugged at his shoulders. Slowly his mouth moved upwards, covering hers. An intermingled taste of her and him filled her mouth. Both together.

'My turn,' she whispered, pushing him back on to the pillows.

He raised an eyebrow. 'Like this?'

She smiled. 'Lie back.'

'As my lady commands.' He put both hands behind his head. 'I am at your tender mercy.'

Using the way his mouth had played on her body as a guide, she began to explore the contours of his. Her fingers stroked the ridges and delved into the valleys between his muscles. Her tongue lapped his flat nipples and felt them harden to nubs. She suckled and heard his sharp intake of breath. Ivar's hands held her arms, but she ignored the temptation to obey his unspoken request; instead, she allowed her mouth to drift lower, to circle his belly button and finally to encounter the heat that was his erection.

She glanced up, but his lashes covered his eyes and he appeared deep in concentration. Emboldened by the tiny taste, she wrapped her fingers about him and cradled the hard silkiness. Then she deliberately closed her mouth over him and, suckling, she felt him come alive in her mouth.

'Thyre, I need to be in you.' His voice was a hoarse rasp. 'Put me in you.'

She nodded, understanding his desire. Swiftly she positioned her body over his and guided him in. He surged upwards, meeting her. Her body opened and welcomed him. He put his hands on her hips and helped to call the rhythm. Faster and faster. Each time, he drove deeper, longer. Then his hands moved and cupped her breasts, brought them to his mouth and a great shuddering went through her, a shuddering that echoed his.

As the rush light flickered and died, Thyre regarded Ivar's sleeping face. His arms were tightly around her as if he could not bear to let her go. Guilt stabbed her. She had meant to ask earlier about Ragnfast and then had forgotten.

She had to find a way to get to Ranhiem and expose Sigmund's treachery. Somehow, being here and being happy made it worse to think that Dagmar could be suffering. And Dagmar had said that men were happier after they had made love.

'Ivar…'

'Yes,' he murmured without opening his eyes. 'You cannot want more, but I will be happy to try. Had I known having a concubine would be this much work…'

Thyre felt her cheeks grow hot and the curl of desire started again in her belly. In a few breaths, she would have forgotten everything except the feel of his mouth against hers. She shook her head and cleared her mind. She had to concentrate, instead of letting her body rule her brain.

'Will you help to petition King Thorkell? Now we have…'

He stiffened and his arms withdrew. Thyre shivered and knew she had said the wrong thing. 'Why, why do you need to see him?'

'He might be able to help… My mother used to speak of him. They had a friendship of sorts, I believe. He should know about Ragnfast's predicament.'

'Was what happened between us just now in aid of your request?' His voice was chipped from ironstone.

'No! I was simply thinking out loud afterwards.' Thyre shifted uneasily, knowing she had started with the intention, but their joining had turned into something far more. 'The request to aid Ragnfast might be better coming from me. Perhaps I could say something about my mother. Perhaps he would listen and see that Viken has to help.'

'If you want me to do something, you should learn something about timing.' Ivar withdrew his arm. 'My late wife was a master at using her seductive skill to get a new arm ring or a dress. You ask before and not afterwards. Or at least that was her method.'

'And was she successful?' Bile rose in her throat. She had made a mistake. A dreadful mistake.

'Most of the time. I was young and naïve. I have grown up, Thyre. Such tricks do not move me. Never try them again. They do not do you any credit.'

'Perhaps I should have asked before, but my mind was on other things. I only asked because I was feeling safe in your arms.'

He slid out of the bed, pulling on his trousers.

'Where are you going?' Thyre asked, trying to keep the rising panic from her voice. She should never have said anything. He had to understand. 'You need to say that you will help. You must say it. I am asking for—'

'I shall sleep on the floor, where it is more honest.' He left the chamber, his back unyielding and upright.

Thyre hit her hand against the pillow. This was all her fault. She should never have tried to seduce him into agreeing. But she had enjoyed his lovemaking and had felt safe in his arms. And now she had lost his regard and it hurt worse than she imagined.

* * *

Ivar sat looking at the fire. Part of him hoped that Thyre would come after him, but mostly he was glad that she did not. Her actions reminded him of the reasons why he had hated being married to Edda—how she had used to use their lovemaking as an excuse for another present, or another favour, until he had found more and more excuses not to return home. He wanted it to be different with Thyre. He wanted to feel that she was in his bed because she too shared his passion.

How could he begin to explain about Asa and her not-too-subtle hints about Thorkell and his hatred of the Ranrike royal family? Thorkell's hatred must come from when the Swan Princess had departed so abruptly. Thyre would not understand that King Thorkell could easily take against her and then they would have no hope of saving Ragnfast or any of her family. Thorkell would proclaim the straits were forbidden. To defy Thorkell would mean challenging for the kingship, and Viken needed King Thorkell's leadership.

Once his business was complete, he would take Thyre to his estate. There they could live peacefully without interference and court intrigue. He refused to repeat the mistakes of the past, but a concubine was very different from a wife.

'Here is where you hide your concubine.'

Ivar raised his eyes to the ceiling. He should have known that his sister Astrid would call at the earliest opportunity and without warning. The last thing he needed now was a lecture from her.

'What do you have to say, brother of mine? I have been waiting for an invitation, but nothing has come.' Astrid's shawl quivered with indignation. 'You invited Haakon's Northumbrian lady, but not your own flesh and blood.'

'Thyre was injured. Annis is a healer.'

'You think I know nothing? Asger told me again and again about how she saved everyone from that snake of a Ranriken jaarl. Don't you know how much I value my son's life?'

'Astrid, it is too early in the morning.'

'I want to see the woman who saved my son.' His sister tapped her foot on the ground. 'And you will grant me this request, Ivar. Do you wish the gods to curse me?'

Ivar shook his head. 'You and your curses. Always when things go against you, you threaten me with curses.'

Astrid sucked in her breath. 'You are far too arrogant, Ivar. Some day, your pride will destroy you.'

'Ivar.' Thyre came into the room and stopped as she realised another woman was there. She straightened the far-too-short apron dress that Annis had lent her and swept into a low curtsy. 'You must be Asger's mother. His eyes are like yours.'

The change in Astrid was immediate. Gone was the overbearing sister and in her place, the doting mother. Ivar shook his head in wonder. Thyre had managed exactly the right note. It was as if she had an instinct with people. 'You brought my son home.'

'Ivar guided the boat home,' Thyre said swiftly. 'Without his leadership, the boat would have been lost.'

'Asger tells a different tale.'

'He is young and impressionable.' Thyre smoothed the skirt of the apron dress. She liked Astrid instinctively. The way she had chided Ivar showed that she did love her brother.

'I wanted to make sure I properly honoured the lady who saved my son's life, even if no one else did.' Astrid gave Ivar a dark look. 'If there is ever anything in my power that I can do for you, I will.'

Thyre ignored Ivar's low growl. 'That is very kind of you, Astrid. I thank you for the sentiment.'

'Astrid, Thyre is my concubine and that is the end of the matter.'

'She saved my son. She saved you. Think on that and then tell me that she is not due honour.' Astrid's eyes flashed, making her look like a feminine version of Ivar. 'I refuse to argue with you, brother, and I know when you think about it, you will realise that I am correct.'

She nodded to Thyre and departed in a swirl of skirts and shawls.

'Do not even think about it,' Ivar barked.

'Think about what?' Thyre concentrated on the fire. There were so many reasons why it would be wrong to involve Astrid.

'Using my sister. She dislikes court and is not one of the queen's favourites. She has no influence.'

'Your sister offered to help me. To decline her help would be rude. And you are not interested in my family's fate.'

'Do not try to twist me or my sister about your fingers, Thyre. I know what you are on about. Remember I was married to a woman who took pleasure in manipulating me. I am immune to tears.'

'I was wrong earlier.' Thyre bowed her head. 'You have no idea about me. I do not use people.'

'If you try to manipulate me again, you will lose,' he said, reaching for his leather jerkin. 'Not everything has been unloaded from the boat. I will go out and you will remain here, recovering in safety.'

'I…I understand.' A huge weight settled on Thyre's chest.

'Allow me to protect you.' He put a finger against her lips. 'My steward will watch over the house and make sure you do not leave and that you are not bothered by well-wishers.'

'After all I have done, you are making me a prisoner? I am no thrall!'

'For once, Thyre, will you obey me? This is my country, not yours!'

'I never asked to be brought here! I am doing the best I can!' Thyre began to pace the room. 'You promised to help Ragnfast. And nothing is being done. No *felag*. Nothing. They could…could…' A huge lump rose in her throat.

'You are mistaken. Only the king can make a *felag*.'

'How can King Thorkell if he knows nothing?' Thyre placed her hands on her hips. 'You have little knowledge of the situation. Take me to him. Let me plead my cause. My mother—'

'Credit me with some intelligence, Thyre!' Ivar made a cutting motion with his hand. 'When the time is right, I will mention it to the king. That is the end of the discussion.'

He stormed from the room without waiting for an answer.

'I can't risk your life after you saved mine.' She sank to the floor and rested her head against her knees. She would find a way without involving Ivar or his family, but something had to be done.

Chapter Eleven

As Ivar peeled the final piece of Thyre's apron dress away from the mast it collapsed, hitting the hull of the boat with a loud thump. Ivar held the scrap of material in his hand and stared at the now useless mast. They had been a heartbeat away from disaster on the sea. Thyre had saved him and everyone on that ship with her quick thinking and unselfish behaviour. But if Asa was correct, she was in danger in Kaupang from the king. How could he explain that to her?

'Asa is up to her old schemes.' Vikar announced, climbing aboard the ship.

'Should this concern me?' Ivar lifted one brow and turned from the fallen mast. 'Since when have Asa's actions ever affected what I do? Or how my life is led?'

'Sela thinks it should. She is worried about your concubine's prospects.'

'Why should Asa be bothered about my concubine?' Ivar stared at his friend in amazement. He had hoped that after their conversation yesterday, Asa would choose to ignore Thyre's existence, but for some reason the queen disliked her. 'I kept Thyre away from Asa because she was not suitably attired. There was no disrespect intended.'

'Sela thinks it is because she hates it when another woman triumphs. Asa has re-issued her decree about concubines not being welcome at Viken feasts and made several comments about concubines who wish to draw attention to their exploits. Sela is certain that it is pure spite.' Vikar rubbed his hand on the back of his neck. 'Sela sometimes sees more than I do. She insisted that I say something to you to put you on your guard. And I have learnt the hard way to trust Sela's judgement.'

'Sela is hardly one of Asa's greatest supporters.'

'Sela understands Asa better than I do, better than any man.' Vikar ran his hand through his hair. 'The women's court is not nearly as straightforward as the Storting, The queen often prefers to hide her true purpose.'

Ivar took a piece of damaged wood from the ship and pretended to examine it. He had come out to the harbour to leave these troubles behind. Out here he could usually forget about the court strictures and the difficulties. However, every inch of the hull reminded him of Thyre and how she had saved them with her quick thinking. 'Who am I to believe? Asa wants the best for me. She feels guilty about Edda, and the way she died. She feels that Edda should have had a place in court as Edda had begged for, rather than allowing her to remain on the estate.'

'Asa does appear to be going to a lot of trouble over this feast.' Vikar made a show of straightening his cloak, rather than meeting Ivar's eyes. 'I hear she has handpicked the servers for the high table—all highly eligible women with Danish connections. Your quiet life in the arms of your new concubine does not stand a chance.'

Ivar snapped a piece of board with his hand. Matchmaking was at the root of this trouble. 'Asa is merely pleased that the ship returned from Birka and brought her spices. She wishes to honour me.'

Vikar took the board from him. 'The last time she hand-picked servers at a feast, she was trying to marry me off. It is why we left on the *felag* to the north.'

'And you returned married, thereby ending her grand scheme.'

Vikar's eyes took on a faraway look. 'Marriage is a wonderful institution. There is something to be said for coming home to your wife.'

'I was married once.' Ivar regarded the white caps on the harbour. The long-suppressed memories of Edda crowded his brain. She had had her faults, but in the end he could not love her as she deserved. He had wanted her to take more control of her life and to run his estate, instead of being at the queen's beck and call the entire time. And she had done as he had ordered, then she had died—alone and pregnant.

'But yours was a happy marriage.' Vikar raised an eyebrow, encouraging him to continue. 'Or so I always thought.'

Ivar put his hand on the mast and gripped a tiny scrap of Thyre's apron dress. Asa's oblique warning about Thorkell's hatred of the Ranriken royal family rang in his ears and he knew there could be no compromise. 'Why should I settle for anything less?'

'Why indeed?' Vikar put his hand on Ivar's shoulder. 'There are all sorts of happiness. But do not let your former marriage cast a long shadow.'

Ivar frowned. He had to approach the problem from a different angle, much as he had solved the problem of the need to skim over the waves, rather than having the ship be buffeted by them. Ivar tapped a finger against the wood. 'Vikar, is your father-in-law in Kaupang?'

'Bose?' Vikar ran his hand through his hair. 'He decided to stay in the north with Kjartan. Kjartan is busy with the horses. The boy never stops riding. I will say this for Bose the Dark, he adores his grandchildren. Was there any particular reason?'

Ivar swore under his breath. One more avenue closed. If anyone knew the truth, it would have been Bose. Although getting him to tell the truth might be a different matter. The answer to his problem lay in the past. Vikar and Haakon were too young to truly remember the Ranriken Swan Princess and he could hardly ask Astrid without alerting her to the identity of Thyre's mother and possibly putting her in danger should King Thorkell turn against Thyre. He had to consider everyone and not just his own wishes. 'I had hoped to use his memory. I wanted to know more about the time when the Swan Princess was here and why she left. The skalds have distorted the story, or so Thyre's stepfather claimed. I wondered if her story was at the root of the trouble with Ranrike.'

'You are asking the wrong man.' Vikar shrugged his shoulder. 'I was not at court when the Swan Princess came to stay, but I have heard the story that Bose tells. Sela says that there is always another truth, a deeper truth in her father's stories. The Swan Princess did vanish. And I believe Thorkell was devastated and threatened to run Bose through when he returned from hunting.'

'It is the other truth that I am interested in.' Ivar leant forwards and dropped his voice. 'Can you ask Sela if she remembers anything, no matter how insignificant it might seem?'

'And you think it is the reason that the Ranrike have

been attacking our ships?' Vikar shook his head. 'The tale I heard was that one night she flew too fast and too long and failed to find a resting place before she turned back into a woman. With her final word, she cursed the strait between Viken and Ranrike. King Thorkell fears her curse.'

'The mystery intrigues me.' Ivar closed his hand around the hilt of Thyre's dagger. The swan shape bit into his palm. Until he understood the past, he could not protect her from the future. 'For too long we believed in the curse without questioning the source.'

The fire that had blazed so brightly before Ivar had left the house that morning was now a pile of ash and cinder. The thralls had refused to feed the fire, saying that Ivar had not left specific instructions and that it could be easily lit when he returned.

There had to be a way of ensuring Ragnfast and Dagmar were safe without making things worse with Ivar. Thyre paced the floor of Ivar's house. She had considered a dozen plans and rejected them all as being unworkable. She could find no other way around it. She had to speak with King Thorkell and confess the truth. She could not ask Ivar to do it for her. She had to do this on her own. Her mother had sworn that King Thorkell would listen if approached in the correct manner. King Thorkell was no tyrant like her uncle, King Mysing. But Ragnfast had remained unconvinced. The dagger he had given her mother had had a darker purpose—to kill any girl child she might bear. As a baby, Thyre had been sickly and had hovered between life and death for many months. It had only been her mother's determination that saved her. Was it any wonder that her mother had refused to pay homage to the custom?

She wished she knew why her mother had kept the gift, instead of throwing it far out to sea. Had her mother thought the same as Ragnfast? Was there something else?

Thyre stirred the embers with a stick, causing sparks to leap up and dance. In the twisting flames, she thought she could see Dagmar begging her to help them as the hall was overrun with Sigmund's warriors, bent on revenge. Despite the warm room, a cold shiver went through her. Something had to be done to save them from that fate. And she had to do it with or without Ivar's assistance.

The welcome-home feast was her only hope of ensuring a *felag* was sent to rescue Ragnfast and Dagmar, regardless of what Ivar thought. She had to try or die.

She would have to go, hand King Thorkell the dagger, and demand he save the family of the Ranriken Swan Princess. Before she changed her mind, Thyre ransacked the trunks from the ship but the dagger had vanished.

Thyre pressed her palms against her eyes, trying to recall the last place she had seen it. On the hull of the ship, just after she had killed Sigmund. It probably rested there.

She grabbed her shawl and started towards the door. The huge bulk of Ivar's steward blocked her way.

'What does the lady require?'

'I wish to go out, down to the harbour.'

'The master has forbidden it. You are to rest.'

'Can I go and make sure? I believe he is down at the harbour.'

'The master's order was quite specific. You are to rest. Nothing is to disturb you except the Lady Annis.'

Thyre crossed her arms. 'You will regret this. When Ivar returns…'

'When the master returns, you may speak with him. I

am only his servant.' The steward turned on his heel, leaving Thyre fuming in the chamber.

She would have to do it. She would have to brave the feast and her father without proof. It no longer mattered that Ragnfast had predicted her death should the Viken king learn the truth about her parentage.

But how could she get in if Ivar had forbidden it?

Thyre tapped her finger against the table, considering the problem.

'The Ladies Annis and Sela wish to visit,' Ivar's steward announced.

'How is your shoulder faring? Hopefully your dreams were not confused. I gave you a stronger draught than is perhaps wise, but you seem none the worse for it,' Annis said, bustling into the room. She cast a meaningful glance at the steward, who withdrew. 'Sela, Bose's daughter, was determined to meet you despite Ivar's opposition.'

A tall blonde followed Annis. In her arms, she carried several apron dresses. 'Vikar explained the problem of your clothes. I thought I would bring a few more choices. Ivar will have nothing for you. And his late wife…well, she was much shorter than you and I think far more whey-faced and delicate.'

'Sela, it is not good to speak ill of the dead.'

'You never met Edda, Annis.' Sela dropped the clothes on to the table. 'I speak the truth. Edda took the lead in plaguing the life out of me when I was a young bride. She was so dainty and non-assuming that she made me feel like I had two heads, and she never did anything without asking permission first. She used to sigh and say how much better things were in Denmark. It drove me insane.'

'Surely a crime to your way of thinking,' Annis said drily.

'Vikar respects my opinion…' Sela gave a throaty laugh.

Thyre attempted to keep her face bland as a stab of jealousy hit her. She wanted to have a relationship where her opinion was respected and even honoured.

'And here I thought you wanted an excuse to meet the woman all of Kaupang is talking about, rather than to trumpet your good deeds or your past misdemeanours.' Annis gave a merry laugh and it was immediately clear the pair were good friends.

'That as well.' Sela cupped her hands and said in a loud whisper, 'I knew that if she had caused Asa that much discomfort by just arriving in her shift, I would like her.'

'Thank you for the dresses.' Thyre inclined her head and attempted to ignore the pulling of her shoulder. Already she enjoyed both Annis and Sela. 'I do appreciate it.'

'Kindness has nothing to do with it. You saved the ship and its spices as well as bringing Ivar home. Vikar owes you a debt as he invested in the voyage. If there is anything else I can do…'

'I am going to the feast,' Thyre said before she lost her nerve. 'My stepfather and sister are in danger. Their only crime was to offer hospitality to the Viken.'

Annis and Sela exchanged quick glances.

'What does Ivar think about it?' Annis asked.

'He refuses to consider it. He thinks I am some sort of delicate creature, but my injury is healing.' Thyre held out her hands and willed them to understand. 'I have to do something. They are my family.'

At the women's expressions, she rapidly explained why she was responsible for the predicament and what she wanted done about it.

'Asa will not like it.' Annis pressed her lips together and started to arrange various herbs on the table.

'Annis, Thyre will make herself ill with worry. And we

both know how overbearing Viken men can be. King Thorkell is a reasonable man. She deserves her chance,' Sela said.

'In Ranrike, it is the custom for women to be able to petition the king or the jaarl just after the skald has finished the first saga,' Thyre said. 'All I want to do is to exercise my right.'

'In Viken as well, or at least before Queen Asa arrived,' Sela said, nodding. 'It is her family she wants to save, Annis. You or I would want to do the same if it was our family in danger. I will help you get to the banqueting hall, Thyre, but what you do after that is your affair.'

'Thank you.' Thyre clasped Sela's warm hand. 'The chance to plead my case is all I ask.'

The torchlight threw elongated shadows across the high table as the noise of the Lindisfarne saga rose in the background. For the last two years at feasts like this one, the skalds recited the story. One would think people would tire of hearing it, but always a great cheer went up when the skald said the first line.

Ivar took a sip of the mead and awaited his opportunity. A few more stanzas and the skald would finish and he could petition Thorkell for a new *felag* to rescue Ragnfast and his daughter. He would volunteer to lead it.

There was every chance that Asa was wrong about Thorkell's hatred of the Ranriken Swan Princess, but challenging her directly about it could make an implacable enemy for Thyre. Soon he would be back on the sea and Thyre would need help. Kaupang could be a lonely place if Asa had set her face against you.

'You will have to choose a wife, Ivar, now that you have returned with such success,' Asa said as the skald reached the final stanzas. 'You will agree, Thorkell. Our victorious jaarl must be married. There is any number of heiresses who would suit. Unfortunately, Ivar neglected to tell me his preference and I have not seen him smile at any of the women who have graciously served him this evening. He is too great a jaarl to remain unmarried.'

'I have a new concubine.' Ivar kept his voice mild. 'I believe your Majesty is aware of the situation.'

Asa gave a little laugh and an airy wave of her hand. 'Since when did a concubine mean anything? A man can have both. A concubine is for lying with and a wife is for creating a dynasty.'

'And your point is?'

Asa's smile dripped honey, but her eyes were cold. 'You and your exploits deserve a dynasty, Ivar Gunnarson. It is a pity that Edda perished before you could start a family, but as much as I miss her, I do want you to be happy.'

'I am gratified you think so.'

'I do.' Asa began to play with her necklace. 'There is a world of difference between a concubine and a wife. Thorkell, Ivar is the last of our Lindisfarne jaarls to remain unwed. He must be married without delay.'

'Is that your petition for the night, wife?' Thorkell glanced up from his horn of mead with dancing eyes. 'The custom is to wait until the skald has completely finished his recitation.'

Ivar took a long considered sip of mead. 'I have seen what it can do to a man. My father had a complicated life.'

'Your father was a warrior to be reckoned with, a good man to have with you when hunting moose or bear. And you are the same.' Thorkell drained the horn of mead and held it out to be filled. 'Marriage is far more solid. It keeps a man grounded. Now, about the moose hunt—'

'You see, Ivar, even the king agrees with me.' Asa put a hand on Thorkell's arm. 'All I ask for is your choice from my maidens. Your late wife enjoyed her time in my court. You can understand the need to have the proper bride who can take her place at my side.'

Ivar reached into his tunic and withdrew Thyre's dagger, held it up to the light and allowed the torchlight to hit the inlaid jewels. 'I believe a good marriage depends on the people, rather than the size of the estate involved. But if the king is considering petitions, I would ask him to consider mine.'

'Where did you get that dagger?' Thorkell asked as his eyes became intent.

'My concubine used it to dispatch Sigmund Sigmundson. A pretty thing, isn't it?'

At Thorkell's gesture, Ivar passed him the knife. Thorkell balanced it in his hand as his fingers traced the swan markings. 'Did she say how she came by the knife?'

'I believe it belonged to her mother, given as a morning gift. But it is about her stepfather I wish to speak. He needs—'

Asa choked on her mead. Several of the guards rushed forward to pat her on the back, but she waved them away. Ivar raised an eyebrow.

What was the dagger to her? She had never had dealings with the Swan Princess. The episode had happened at least seven years before she had arrived in Kaupang as a young scared princess sent to bolster a fragile trading relationship. The marriage, despite its rocky start, was counted as a success.

'Is your concubine here?' Thorkell's voice rang out over the din. 'Why have you not brought her to meet me? Where is she? I understand that she killed a

Ranriken jaarl. She should be at this feast. We in Viken honour our heroes.'

'In deference to the queen, she has remained at my house.' Ivar looked hard at Asa, who lowered her lashes and pretended a sudden interest in the remains of her food.

Asa put down her knife and folded her hands in her lap. 'I cannot make exceptions, Thorkell. Once one concubine is allowed at the high table, all will be clamouring. The order of the court will be broken for ever.'

'King Thorkell,' Astrid called out from where she stood, serving mead to her husband and his companions. At the king's gesture, she came forwards and stood before the high table. Her hands were raised in supplication. Ivar wondered idly how many times she had practised that particular gesture. But he had to admit the pose was effective. 'Your Majesty, the lady saved my child, my only son. I owe her a life-debt. Ivar follows the rules far too slavishly. I believe that such a woman has earned a right to be here at this table. In your father's day, he made no distinction between wives and concubines at the feasting hall. The current practice is a Danish custom and not a Viken one.'

'This is the first time you have accused me of such a thing, Astrid,' Ivar retorted quickly. 'The custom has become a Viken one. And it is only for the high feasts.'

The entire hall burst out laughing as Astrid flushed slightly. Ivar frowned as he felt the situation begin to slip from his grasp. There were undercurrents in this hall he could only sense. King Thorkell continued to turn the dagger over and over again in his hand.

'I would speak with this concubine. The Viken must honour its heroes,' he proclaimed finally. Astrid smiled broadly and hurried back to join Asger and her husband, but not before she gave Ivar a smug look. 'I wish to hear as well how she acquired this dagger. It is…of Viken origin and one I never thought to see again.'

'Honestly, Thorkell, I cannot see why you would be interested in how this concubine acquired a knife.' Asa toyed with her goblet. 'Perhaps I should have relaxed my restriction, but I did feel it important to maintain order.'

'Will you never learn when to be silent, woman?' Thorkell thundered.

Ivar blinked in surprise, as Thorkell never rebuked his wife in public. Asa closed her mouth with a snap.

'Shall I bring Thyre to you tomorrow?' Ivar took a sip of the mead. Thyre would now have her chance. He looked forward to telling her and to her gratitude. He had found the perfect way to heal the breach between them.

'Thyre is here!' Sela called from where she sat before Thorkell could say anything. 'You can question her now! She waits in the antechamber. She had planned to petition the king.'

'Get the woman. Now.' Thorkell said, gesturing to his bodyguard.

Ivar gritted his teeth. How badly had Thyre played him for a fool? How many other people had she enlisted in her scheme without consulting him?

Thyre walked slowly, head held high and shoulders back as she followed the guard into the feasting hall. The smoke from the torches momentarily blinded her and made her stumble. Everywhere she turned table upon table of warriors sat eating and drinking. Growing up, she had often imagined this moment. Sometimes it was dreadful and the stuff of nightmares with Thorkell demanding her immediate execution, but other times, she was triumphant as Thorkell claimed her for his own. Now, she felt neither fear nor victory but merely a queer calmness. It no longer mattered what he thought. All she wanted to do was to rescue her family.

As she walked towards the high table, a hushed murmur rippled through the assembled throng. She forced her steps to be measured. Ivar glowered at her, but she concentrated on the man next to him, her father and the man who held the power to rescue her family. Her life was unimportant now. Saving Ragnfast and Dagmar was all that mattered.

When she reached the high table, she clasped her hands together and bowed low.

'Your Majesties, I have come to beg for your help in righting a wrong. My stepfather did nothing more than offer hospitality to the stricken Viken ship and now I fear he will be punished for it.' Thyre could hear murmurs behind her and knew her voice needed to echo off the rafters. All of Kaupang had to hear her. She cleared her throat and tried again. 'I come here not for myself but to plead for the innocents—my stepfather and half-sister. You sit here feasting and toasting the success of the *felag*, but they remain in danger. They offered hospitality, that is all.'

'The name of your stepfather is…?' the king asked.

'Ragnfast the Steadfast. Once he enjoyed your hospitality for a day and a night.'

'I know the man and I know of his exploits. We raised our swords together in the battle for the north lands when I was a young man.' The king leant forwards and his eyes were intent. 'And who is your mother?'

Thyre's fingers reached for her mother's amulet and drew strength from that. In her mind, Thyre heard her mother's tones giving her the exact title and her admonition to speak distinctly if she should ever encounter the

Viken king. 'Sainsfrida, who some called the Swan Princess because of her mother. My grandmother was called the Black Swan on account of her hair and her long neck and my uncle Mysing even now occupies the throne of Ranrike. But I was born out of wedlock. It was my step-father who gave me my name—Thyre.'

The feast hall drew in its collective breath. Thorkell leant forward and the dagger dangled from his fingertips.

'Did your mother ever say who gave her the dagger?'

'The dagger was a gift from the Viken who is my father.' Thyre kept her gaze directly on Thorkell. 'She received it as a parting gift before she left Viken.'

'I understood the Ranriken Swan Princess died without a child. Bose the Dark had investigated the rumour years ago,' Asa said in frigid tones. 'This woman, this concubine, is clearly lying.'

'Am I?' Thyre lifted an eyebrow. 'Why would I lie about such a thing? A disgraced princess who chose ban-ishment in her own kingdom rather than give up the child she carried? My mother married Ragnfast. Bring my step-father and sister here. Ask them, if you do not believe me. All I ask is for them to be rescued.'

Thorkell held up his hand, silencing everyone. 'And why did Princess Sainsfrida leave Viken?'

'She had quarrelled bitterly with my father over a game of *tafl*. It was the final fight of many. What they had was over. There was no need to stay when Ragnfast arrived to tell her that her father had died and her brother, Mysing, was now king. My father knew of her intention to depart and gave her the dagger in case there should be a living child. Rather than see her go, he went out hunting with his hound and hawk. Later it was put out that she flew away, but the truth was that she simply walked out of the hall and

Ragnfast carried her trunk to the ship. The king's chamberlain helped push the boat out.'

'And where was the king?'

'He had gone hunting with his favourite elkhound.'

Thyre stood before Thorkell, ignoring all the curious stares and shocked exclamations.

'The king was very young then. He only learnt later that a woman of great virtue is worth more than a day's hunting,' Thorkell said, tapping his fingers. 'But your mother was stubborn and refused to wait. Come, woman, let me properly look at you. The torchlight is a bit dim. Why do you appear before me now? The events you speak of were many years ago.'

'There is no one else I can turn to.' Thyre waited while several of the guard brought more blazing torches.

'You have your mother's hair and her mouth, but I fancy you have your father's eyes and chin,' King Thorkell proclaimed. 'You certainly have his courage. There are not many women who would have killed a jaarl, or would be willing to face a king and demand his assistance. You are definitely your father's daughter, a daughter any man would be proud to claim as his own.'

Thyre forced her body to stay upright as her knees began to buckle. Without even asking, King Thorkell had acknowledged her and in such a way that there could be no doubt. Her heart soared. Ragnfast had been wrong. She stumbled forwards and two guards caught her arms, held her upright. She gave a small shrug and they let her go.

'What is going on?' Ivar thundered. 'Who is my concubine's father?'

'Your concubine is my daughter,' Thorkell said in a clear echoing voice. 'Her mother should have sent her years ago. Sainsfrida cheated me, but then she always played by her own rules. She knew what the intention of the gift was. I have always honoured my obligations.'

'My mother would have sent a son, but she felt a daughter's place was at her mother's side, particularly as I was a sickly child,' Thyre said. 'Then she died and it was far too late. Once the Viken came and she spoke to the king's chamberlain. Then shortly after her death, the man came again—cloaked and with muffled oars. After that last visit, Ragnfast told me the truth about the dagger and why I must never seek you out.'

'We will retire.' King Thorkell stood, and lifted his hands upwards in an imperious gesture. The guards scurried to open a door behind the high table. 'There is much we must say to each other.'

Thyre nodded her head. She hardly knew where to put her feet as the company rose as one, bowing their heads. Her heart thumped loudly in her ears. She was the king's acknowledged daughter.

'Why did you hide your parentage from me, Thyre?' Ivar asked, grabbing her arm as she passed. 'Did you know what would happen when you gave the dagger to the king?'

Thyre looked at the white knuckled fingers gripping her sleeve. 'You had already made me your concubine. Who my parents were was not going to change that.'

'Ivar Gunnarson, that woman you are detaining is the king's daughter,' King Thorkell said, turning back from the doorway. 'She cannot be a concubine to a jaarl. Kindly allow her to leave with dignity.'

Chapter Twelve

The quiet of the king's antechamber filled Thyre's ears after the noise of the banqueting hall. She walked at a steady pace, hoping that Ivar would come storming after her, but he hadn't and now she had to face her father and his wife alone.

'Come closer, Thyre,' Asa said with a frown between her eyes. 'I am sure you understand why we must keep court gossip to a minimum.'

'Hush, wife,' Thorkell said, raising an imperious hand, and Asa shrank back. 'Thyre, things must be said, things long overdue. Your mother should have sent you as soon as you were weaned, but that is a stain on your mother, Princess Sainsfrida, rather than on you.'

'My mother acted how she thought best, based on her knowledge of your character.' Thyre gave a decided nod. 'I would have sought an audience with you earlier, but was told that kings do not meet with concubines.'

'You are my daughter. You should have come immediately to me.'

'Ivar had little idea about my parentage.' Thyre kept

her voice calm. 'I come here not to petition for me, but for my stepfather and half-sister. You must launch a *felag* immediately.'

'*Felags* take time,' Asa broke in. 'Why should we risk Viken lives?'

'Because Ragnfast risked his life for the Viken. He knew the danger, even if I didn't. He knew of Sigmund Sigmundson's treachery. Ask Ivar.'

'Are you seeking to excuse Ivar's behaviour?' the king thundered. 'He made you his concubine. He had to have guessed about your parentage. You and I look alike.'

Thyre glared back at her father. 'Until my father recognised me, I had no father but Ragnfast. I kept the truth from Ivar.'

'I have recognised you as my daughter,' King Thorkell said. 'And from now until the end of time, I expect you to be treated like a princess of Viken.'

'The king also wishes you to conduct yourself like a princess,' the queen said in a dry tone. 'I devotedly hope this is possible.'

'My mother was a Ranriken princess and this is where my heart lies.'

'Your heart should always lie with your father's country,' Queen Asa retorted. 'We shall have to ensure you do not disgrace him again with ill-considered words, dress or behaviour.'

'Hush, wife, now is not the time. Thyre, let me look again.' Thorkell captured her chin with his fingers and turned her face from side to side. 'You have your mother's hair, and her nose. Even the shape of her face is the same. I fancy you are about the age she was when she resided here.'

'I am surprised you remember,' Thyre whispered. 'It was long ago.'

'Some things are forever engrained on your memory,' Thorkell answered.

'But her nose and the way she carries her body are pure you, Thorkell.' Queen Asa's low voice made a chill run down Thyre's spine. She turned her head and saw no warmth in the glacier-blue eyes. 'Years ago, Bose told me the story. I had him to go and investigate, but he returned saying that Sainsfrida, the Swan Princess, was dead and the child would bother me no more. I knew how the incident played on your mind. I have heard you cry out in your dreams.'

'But you did not seek to inform me, wife. You have been more than remiss. I would have had my daughter at my side.' The bellow from King Thorkell shook the walls. 'She should never have had to endure such humiliation.'

Asa fell down on her knees and raised her hands beseechingly, a motion so smooth and elegant that Thyre wondered if it was practised. Immediately she hated herself for the thought. A tear trickled down the queen's face and she made to grab Thorkell's cloak.

'Can you forgive me, my love? I was young and jealous. I failed to think straight. She was happy. Bose told me that she was happy. Then the other day, I saw this woman and I knew in my heart whose child she had to be. She had the look of you when you return from the sea. After all these years, to have her appear… You must understand.'

Thorkell held her off. 'We have a son. For many years, the guilt of Sainsfrida the Swan Princess's death has haunted me. I took the loss of our ships as a judgement from the gods.'

'You know how I longed for a daughter, and now you have one. It was wrong of me, but I feared opening old wounds. I loved you so much.'

Thorkell made a gruff noise and Asa flung herself into his arms. Delicate sobs racked her body as the king awkwardly patted her back.

Thyre watched the scene with wary eyes, remembering how the Viken had come before. What bargain had her mother made then?

'I do not like secrets, wife.' Thorkell put his hands on Asa's shoulders.

'Bose said—'

'You were young then, but we have been together for a long time. You should have told me today when I returned from the hunt. You made no attempt to. Enough of the tears. I want the truth. Why did you seek to keep Thyre from me?'

Asa paled and stepped backwards. 'The truth was bound to be revealed. Who was I to demand it? And if you had not wanted to accept this woman? What could I have done? I am merely a woman and you…you are king. Could I have the death of this woman, this concubine, on my mind?'

'Have I ever refused a child?'

Asa's eyes darted about the room and she appeared genuinely terrified. 'Your happiness is all I desire.'

'My mother died when I was eight. If you must blame someone, blame her,' Thyre said, filling the silence. She might not trust Asa, but what had happened had happened before Asa had arrived in Viken. 'She had a peaceful life and few regrets, or so she said at the end. I can remember the Viken coming and my mother sending them away. She wanted me with her. Ragnfast believed you would kill me.'

'And was she happy with him?' Thorkell asked, his eyes narrowing.

'They loved each other and she found peace and contentment. That bay was her kingdom.' Thyre smiled. 'She had decided ideas on how to bring daughters up.'

'That is something we never had—peace. We were far too young to be content,' Thorkell said with a laugh. 'Always fighting, always. We were both too young and stubborn. In the end I let her go, knowing she carried my child. I knew what she was like. But there were times that I wondered, could I have tried harder?'

Thyre bit her lip. The time for recriminations had long passed. What could she say? Her mother had chosen her own path. She had known what her brother Mysing could be like and his feelings about the Viken, but had desired to return to Ranrike. It was not her place to judge either person. 'I think she did mean to send me, if I had been a boy. Dagmar, my half-sister, and I once overheard a bitter argument between my mother and Ragnfast, just before she died. He raged for days and days about letting past mistakes stay in the past.'

'And she gave you the dagger after the argument?' Thorkell asked.

'On her deathbed, she showed me the dagger in case I ever needed to go to Viken.' Thyre swallowed hard and kept her voice steady. 'In case Ragnfast ever failed me.'

'Why did you travel to Viken?' Asa asked. 'Surely you owe us an explanation. Your mother has been dead for years. Why do you need King Thorkell now? Do you seek the throne of Ranrike? Would you have the Viken make war on King Mysing?'

'I have never sought the throne of Ranrike. Ivar threatened the entire estate unless I agreed to be his concubine.' Briefly Thyre recounted the tale. She made the vaguest references to what had passed between Ivar and her. 'I must put right the harm I caused. It is my duty. I believe King Thorkell will understand.'

Thorkell began to pace up and down the room. 'Ivar overstretched. He should never have made you his concubine.'

'But there must be something you can do about Ragnfast and Dagmar,' Thyre said. 'They…they are my family.'

'Your family is here now. You are a Viken. As should have been all along. Had your mother sent you, we would not be having this conversation,' Queen Asa said. 'The problem is what to do with your new-found daughter, Thorkell. Everyone knows she is Ivar's concubine. The king's daughter, a concubine. She must marry Ivar. There is no other way to keep order in the court since you chose to recognise her without consulting me.'

'You give wise counsel, wife. Marriage it will be. Marriage or death.'

'But the *felag*. You—' Thyre protested. Thorkell had not said anything about rescuing Ragnfast and Dagmar. And she knew that she did not want Ivar if he was forced to marry her.

'The king has spoken, Thyre.' Queen Asa's voice was sharp and final. 'You should be pleased that he has seen fit to recognise you as a daughter and rejoice. Not many men are as forgiving as Thorkell.'

'You are my daughter now and must be treated as such.' Thorkell put a heavy hand on Thyre's shoulder. 'I will not have you treated as a common concubine to be passed from man to man. I will have you properly dowered and wedded. You will reside here until you are married. I will have to ponder the best way to aid your stepfather, but it will need to go before the entire Storting.'

'And I will expect you to take a full part in my court. My ladies are its beating heart.' Asa's eyes glittered and Thyre knew that, despite the soft words, the queen's enmity had not vanished.

'My daughter will add lustre to the court, Asa. Her forthcoming marriage will solve your problem of which of your ladies will be his wife.'

Thyre stared at the king. His words slowly sunk in. She was no longer to be Ivar's concubine, and she was to live at court. As Ivar's wife! Sela had spent most of the afternoon warning her about it and the spiteful ways in which some of the women behaved. 'I want a choice in my future.'

'Ivar is a very important jaarl, Thyre,' her father said.

'Forcing me to marry anyone is wrong!'

'You will marry, Thyre,' Queen Asa retorted. 'Your father commands it. A princess is never free to choose. You should be grateful that he wishes to see the stain of your present circumstances removed from you.'

'I will see this wrong righted before I lift one finger to help your stepfather.' Thorkell laid a heavy hand on Thyre's shoulder. 'I promise you that.'

'Which wrong is that? Thyre is mine and I will have a say in her future,' Ivar said, bursting into the room, filling it with his presence. His eyes flashed with blue fire and a muscle jumped in his cheek.

'Are you denying any knowledge of her circumstances? You held the dagger in your hand, Ivar Gunnarson.' Thorkell's fingers dug into Thyre, keeping her by his side.

'*Someone* neglected to tell me its importance. Someone played me for a fool.'

Ivar advanced forwards but Thorkell raised a finger and two guards came to stand between him and Thyre. He rolled his eyes upwards. A cold ache descended on Thyre and she hugged her arms about her waist. What they had had before had vanished, shattered.

'Didn't you tell him? How perfectly delicious.' Asa's

voice dripped with honey and she gave a simpering smile. Thyre clenched her fists. She hated the false concern and pretended sweetness. Asa's only interest was in humiliation. She might be able to fool the men, but her hidden knives were painfully obvious. 'Why ever not? Surely you must have exchanged confidences. Not that I would know what goes on in a couple's pillow talk, but he did appear to know who your mother was.'

'Hush, wife. Do not seek to cause trouble.'

'I am merely pointing out the flaws in Ivar's argument. And he needs a wife, we have discussed this before, Thorkell.'

'Unless you wish to challenge me for the kingship, Ivar Gunnarson, you will marry my daughter.'

Thyre sucked in her breath. Kingship in Viken must be different from Ranrike. In Ranrike, only warriors who had kinship to the royal family could challenge for the throne.

'I am your loyal servant, as always.' Ivar bowed low, but his eyes bored into Thyre's. She shivered at the depth of his anger. 'I will be happy to marry your daughter, now that I know who she belongs to.'

'Until my father recognised me, I could hardly claim a father such as King Thorkell.' Thyre glared at Ivar.

'And that is supposed to suffice?' Ivar lifted an eyebrow. 'You enjoy playing games, Thyre. Well, now you have been caught in your own trap. We will marry, despite your wish to the contrary.'

'Thorkell, I think we had best leave the two alone.' The queen laid a restraining hand on King Thorkell's arm. 'It would be wrong to intrude on such a moment. Ivar Gunnarson is an honourable man.'

Thyre turned towards the coals in the fire. The worst thing was that she did want to spend the rest of her life with

Ivar. She would like to be married to him and to have his children, but mostly she wanted to be with him. *This*, however, was wrong. He was only prepared to marry her because Thorkell had forced his hand and he was loyal. And she knew from his reaction that he would never have defied Thorkell and married her if she had remained as she was—a woman with a nameless father.

'When did you begin planning this?' Ivar demanded after Asa had led Thorkell from the room and they were left alone.

'Did I plan what?' Thyre put her hands on her hips. 'I know what you are thinking. I planned all this. I planned for you to threaten my family. I planned for you to bring me here just so that I could meet my father. Then I planned for him to react in this way. How much mead have you been drinking? Next you would have me believing that little men with tails really exist.'

'Speak to Sela and Vikar before making statements about *tottr* men.'

'I had no desire to be forced into a marriage with you!' Thyre tapped her foot on the ground. 'I wanted to save my family! I sacrificed my life for them! I gave up my dreams for them!'

Ivar's scar rippled in his cheek. 'You were the one who waited in my bed.'

'To save Dagmar's life.' Thyre jabbed a finger at him. 'You were never supposed to guess the difference.'

'There is world of difference between you and your half-sister. You also wanted to sabotage the proposed betrothal between you and that Ranriken farmer.'

'I would have found a way to prevent my marriage to Otto without your assistance.' Thyre put her fists on her hips. Ivar had to accept the blame for this situation. 'You were annoyed and lost your temper. Why don't you admit the responsibility?'

'We cannot undo the past, Thyre, however much we might wish.' Ivar ran his hand through his hair, making it stand on end. 'Even now, you might be carrying my child.'

'I have no wish to marry you under such circumstances,' Thyre said around a large tight lump in her throat. Earlier, she had thought marrying him would be the most wonderful thing, but not like this, not because he was forced to.

'That is your problem. Thorkell is my king. I have given my oath of obedience. Why should I condemn my people, my relations, to a life of misery, simply because I refuse to honour my king's wishes? I will marry, but I will take no joy in our union.'

'Then we will marry. The choice has been made for us.' Thyre's heart shattered into a thousand separate shards. Her body appeared to be made of ice. More than anything she wanted him to take her back to the house and make love to her, but that was impossible. 'I doubt either of us will find much pleasure in the match. It is unwelcome to us both.'

Ivar traced his thumb over her lips and despite everything, a white hot heat surged through her. 'Do not lie, Thyre. There is an attraction between us, and I will expect you to warm my bed, whenever I happen to be in it.'

'Who allowed you in? Are you lost?' Thyre said to a half-grown cat who entered the antechamber where Asa and her ladies had gathered for an afternoon of sewing. She put down her embroidery. Her neck and shoulder ached from the intricate stitching. No matter how fine she had sewed the stitches, Asa always seemed to find fault and to imply she was doing it on purpose in order to sabotage the wedding. Earlier Asa had decreed that Thyre would keep sewing until that section of the sleeve was completed.

The cat gave a small meow and purred against her legs. Thyre glanced over to where the other women were sitting. Mostly they were Danish or daughters of women Asa had brought with her when she had first come to Viken. And they always followed Asa's lead.

Defiantly, Thyre put down her sewing and picked up the ginger cat. Holding the small cat reminded her of how much she missed Beygul and the friendly banter of Ragnfast's steading.

'Thyre, cats belong in the kitchen and not in the court where delicate silks are sewn.' Asa's sharp voice jolted Thyre from her musing. 'Imagine what would happen if the gold and silver became tangled. We are behind as it is.'

'The cat wandered in of its own accord.' Thyre struggled to keep her voice calm. Inside she seethed. Asa had not said a word about cats to three of her ladies who earlier had brought in a litter of kittens to play with.

'I must have order in my court. And you keep insisting on sewing to your own pattern.' Asa's eyes glittered and the remaining ladies scurried out of the room, leaving Thyre standing, holding the cat. Over the last few days, she had seen how cruel Asa could be when she was crossed. Several times, women were reduced to tears when the queen had deliberately set one woman against another with a few carefully chosen remarks.

'I merely sought to improve my wedding dress. It should reflect my Ranriken heritage as well as my Viken one. You wanted to use Danish designs.'

'There is nothing wrong with Danish designs.'

'I am not Danish. You are.'

'You go too far, Thyre, with your words. You are not in some back-of-beyond estate any more. Your father will be informed of your insolence.'

'I spoke with him last night. You were there, but I do apologise for my sharp tongue.' Thyre swallowed her anger and made a curtsy. 'I will return the cat to the kitchen. Obviously he has lost his way.'

'Grunhilde can do it,' Asa pronounced with an imperious wave. 'I need you here. The bodice of your gown needs to be fitted properly.'

'But the design will be as we agreed with my father without you trying to change it behind his back.' Thyre glared at the woman. Asa looked away first.

'Very well, I will let you make the modifications.' Asa inclined her head. 'I do want a quiet life, Thyre. But this is my court and I make the rules. When you are on your estate, you may do as you please.'

'I have never tried to undermine you and I have tried to adhere to your rules,' Thyre returned quietly. She would insist on moving out to Ivar's estate and would rarely return to Kaupang again. It would be the only way to survive. Much more time in Asa's company and she would be tempted towards murder. 'I will not have it said that I shirk my duty. After all, once I am married, my father has promised to send a *felag* to Ranrike and I intend to be on it.'

A tiny smile played on Asa's lips as she graciously inclined her head. 'I am pleased you understand my reasoning.

'Is everything ready?' Ivar asked Haakon's half-brother Thrand several days later. As they inched towards the wedding day, he kept himself busy, repairing and refitting the *Sea Witch*.

'The ships are loaded. We can sail whenever you want.'

'The morning after my wedding. Thorkell will not allow us to go before then, even though I know the debt I owe to Ragnfast.'

'The Ranriken king will learn what it is like to tangle with the Viken. Think of the cargo they owe us.' Thrand gave a laugh. 'Still, there is nothing like an outraged father, even if he has come lately to fatherhood.'

'Thyre bears the blame.'

'When was she supposed to explain—before or after you bedded her? And more to the point—would you have believed her?'

At Thrand's smug look, Ivar glared at him. 'She had her chance.'

'You might want to believe that, Ivar, but I have seen the lady in question. You know better than I who her mother was, and therefore who her father had to be. Stop judging her.'

Ivar put his head in his hands. 'The truth is that I was not aware of who her mother was when I bedded her the first time. Afterwards, I only knew that I wanted her on my terms. And now I am determined to keep her safe. She would join the *felag* if she could. I fear Asa wants Thorkell to use her as a counter. Asa argued that Viken needs a friend on the throne of Ranrike and that the Ranriken people might accept her.'

'Is that what Thorkell wants? Or is it merely Asa wanting to get rid of a potential rival?'

'King Thorkell agreed with me that Thyre should remain in Kaupang.'

'Has anyone asked Thyre what she wants? She is a sensible woman. She will understand what you are doing,' Thrand argued.

'She needs protecting from herself and must not know

until it is impossible for her to do anything.' A cold chill went through Ivar as he recalled how Thyre had attacked Sigmund. Would Thyre want to be queen? How would she challenge her uncle? 'I have had Asa keeping her busy. No easy task, I assure you. The queen has even in desperation set Thyre to composing with the skald. Asa thinks—'

'Since when have you paid attention to the queen and her whims?'

'If I had paid attention to her before, Edda would be alive. Thyre must stay here in Kaupang. I cannot be worried about her and fighting the Ranriken at the same time.'

'I hope Thyre understands.'

'It is not a question of understanding. My marriage to Thyre will be on my terms.'

Chapter Thirteen

The final cheers from the crowds rang in Thyre's ears as they reached the hall.

The banqueting hall was covered in fine tapestries. The prows from the Lindisfarne ships were bedecked with gold chains. All the Viken court had turned out with their arms covered in arm rings and heavy gold chains about their necks until they looked far more like statues than real people. But Thyre knew she wanted something more. The pageant and parade counted for nothing when all Ivar did was glower and answer direct questions in monosyllables.

Thyre's wedding gown prevented her moving or even breathing properly. When she sat, it pinched her arms and when she stood, the weight dragged on her shoulders. However, the symbols were a combination of Ranriken and Viken, rather than Danish.

Whatever happened after the wedding feast, Thyre knew she would be able to have her own household, and would be in charge again. She would be the one to decide how wool was correctly spun, and the pattern that needed weaving. And she could decide whether to play the lyre or to play a game of *tafl*. All the arguments with Asa over the past weeks had worn her down. It seemed that at court, she did not have any friends or allies.

'Thyre, pay attention,' Asa snapped, tapping her on the shoulder. 'The king has toasted you.'

'I accepted it. I raised my horn to him and saluted him. It is the proper way.'

'Use the right words. Any child should know them. You are far from being stupid, Thyre. Your mother must have taught you,' Asa said in a furious undertone. 'You seek to dishonour your father through your ignorance.'

'I was not trying to.' Thyre tightened her grip on the eating knife.

Ivar's voice boomed out, accepting the toast with great formality.

Asa glowed triumphantly. 'There, see, Ivar has done it properly.'

A half-smile twitched on Ivar's face as he raised his horn towards Asa. 'I only repeated what Thyre had said, Asa. And do you not think the new saga that Thyre helped compose is charming? Thorkell appeared to enjoy it.'

Two spots of colour stood out on Asa's pale cheeks. 'I must have misheard, then. I do beg your pardon, Ivar.'

Thyre studied the intricate table covering as her mind reeled. Ivar was willing to stand up for her. Maybe she was not so alone.

After the series of formal toasts, the real business of eating began as platter after platter of heavily spiced meat appeared. However, Asa refrained from making any more spiteful remarks.

The headdress dug into Thyre's forehead, making it ache, and the absurd shoes that Asa had insisted on her wearing pinched her toes. She longed to leave, but how and when? No doubt there would be another ceremony that Asa had forgotten to tell her about. She crumbled a soft piece of bread into the sauce and pushed it about with her knife, thinking to come up with a suitable excuse.

'Do you wish to be abducted quietly or forcibly?' Ivar asked, laying his hand on her waist and sending a warm pulse through her body. Dressed in his soft leather trousers, fine wool tunic and scarlet cape with no less than three chains about his neck, Ivar was every inch a proud Viken warrior.

It took all of her will power not to lean her head against his chest. Standing close to him, she realised how much she had missed him and his conversation. In such a short span of time, he had become important, far more important to her than she had imagined possible.

'I have no wish to be abducted.' Thyre looked at him from under her lashes as she strove for a natural voice. 'But I should like to leave.'

'All Viken brides are abducted.' A dimple flashed in the corner of Ivar's mouth.

Thyre look around at the throng of people. 'I believe you are attempting to tease me. Asa would have said something. She spent the purification ritual telling me all the rules of marriage. What I should and should not do and how I must obey you in all things.'

'Did you take the lesson to heart?' His eyes sparkled with mischief.

'After the first ten admonitions, I allowed my mind to wander back to Ranrike,' Thyre admitted. 'Asa has a way of making the simplest thing appear complicated.'

'Then you missed the explanation.' His eyes danced with mischief. 'Forcible abduction will save the need for any response from you.'

His hands went about her waist, lifting her off the ground and putting her over his shoulder. The hated headdress began to slide further down her forehead, threatening to fall off. Thyre gave into temptation and helped it along its way.

'I take it the headdress did not meet with your approval.'

'The headdress was Asa's idea.'

'I prefer you with your hair down. Keep still.'

Ivar drew his sword and held it aloft. He started to advance as the crowd pressed inwards. Lots of ribald comments and helpful hints about how to pass the evening filled the air and Thyre knew her face flamed. Her hands gripped the red material of Ivar's cloak. Beneath her fingers, his back reverberated with laughter.

He was enjoying this! This spectacle!

He swung her about so her feet skimmed the goblets, causing a giddy sensation in her middle as Asa and her ladies gave gasps of horror.

'Mind the glass, Thyre. It comes from Byzantium.' Asa's voice resounded above the cheers.

Thyre shook her head. As if she was trying to do anything except to keep from falling. She repositioned her hands, grasping Ivar's cloak more firmly and tried to lift her legs higher.

'Ivar, put me down! This gown will rip! It took me hours and is supposed to be my court dress…' Thyre beat on his back with her fists, but he simply strode onwards towards the door.

'Perhaps you should have considered the consequences…more thoroughly.'

'You wanted it this way. You did not give me enough time.'

'One has to seize one's opportunities.' He gave a low rumble of laughter as he advanced towards the doorway. 'King Thorkell, I am taking your daughter.'

'I see you are prepared to fight!' Thorkell made a gesture with his hand and the guards unsheathed their swords.

'I can and I shall,' Ivar roared.

'Then have at it.' Thorkell lifted a finger and the guards advanced. 'You will only take her if you are man enough to defeat my men.'

Ivar deflected a half-hearted blow from one of the guards. He turned and clashed swords with another. 'Is this the best you can do? I had expected a fight.'

Amid the shrieking from some of Asa's ladies, the other Viken warriors leapt to their feet and began to fight. The air rang with sword meeting sword.

Ivar quickened his pace and with his sword fended off several feeble attempts to stop him. Thyre noted with amusement how much the Viken seemed to enjoy the sport. The warriors appeared to be lining up to aim a blow, making sure that Ivar's sword crossed at least once with theirs.

'Was this strictly necessary?'

'You had to be abducted properly. I will not have it said that my bride was improperly wed. Your father has insisted.'

'I was not party to that.'

'Some day, you will start taking responsibility for your actions, Thyre.' His eyes flashed blue fire, reminding her that this marriage had not been his idea. How much of this was to show Thorkell his independence? 'Stop wriggling now and allow me to fight. The sooner we are through this crowd, the sooner we can go.'

When they reached the courtyard, he dumped her on a horse with a golden mane. Then he mounted the horse behind her. One arm came about her waist and dragged her back against his chest. Her body reacted with little tongues of fire lapping at her. 'Hang on tight. We are not yet clear of the maddening crowd.'

Ivar pulled back sharply on the reins and the horse reared upwards. Thyre found her hands clinging to the red wool tunic. She forgot everything but the nearness of the man. The horse then pawed the ground and galloped away. The screams and shouts from the crowd echoed in her ears.

'You live for moments like that,' Thyre said as soon as her heart stopped beating in her ears.

'Yes, and you do as well! Your eyes are sparkling, Thyre.' Ivar gave a great laugh. 'A man who is unwilling to fight for his bride does not deserve to be called a warrior.'

'The customs are somewhat different than in the steading, but then it is not warriors who marry, but farmers and foresters. I have never seen the wedding of a warrior until today.'

'And did it meet with your expectations?' His warm breath tickled her ear, sending a cascade of pleasure radiating down her body.

Thyre shifted in his arms. Every time the horse took a step, she was aware of the shifting muscles of Ivar's thighs and body.

'Hopefully the dress will not be ruined,' she said primly, trying to keep the subject away from desire. 'Asa already gave me a lecture about the expense. The material was supposed to be for her new gown, but she felt I had the greater need. I was not sure whether I should be insulted or flattered. She conceded on the embroidery.'

'I am amazed you were able to change Asa's mind at

all. She can be very determined. My late wife and she were friends, but then Edda was Danish and never crossed her directly. Asa was very good to Edda.'

Thyre froze. There were so many questions she wanted to ask about his wife and their relationship. 'I had not realised.'

'Asa encouraged the match. She wanted her ladies to be happy and settled with Viken warriors.'

'And was she?'

'Edda said that she was happy.'

Thyre closed her eyes. She wanted to look back and see his expression. Was he remembering the other wedding day as well as this one? She hated feeling a stab of jealousy towards the dead woman. 'How did she die?'

'I was away on a voyage. She was on my estate and liked to go for a walk in the mornings. No one was around and she tumbled down a cliff. My steward found her after several hours, but already it was far too late.'

Thyre closed her eyes. The poor woman, and what a tragedy for Ivar to come home to. To lose someone you loved for no good reason.

'Do you think you could have saved her?' she asked, choosing her words with care.

'I do not know. She was six months pregnant and I was determined that our son would be born on the estate. I told her that she had to go and her fears were foolish. I over-ruled Asa as well. Edda went. She became convinced that walking was good for the baby she carried. Normally I think she would have been more agile. It was simply a terrible accident. They found her at the base of a cliff overlooking the bay.'

'And you came back to an empty house.' Thyre resisted the temptation to turn around and examine his face. The bleakness of his tone told her all she wanted to know. He did blame himself. Even if he had been there, there was no guarantee. And yet, the stab of jealousy inside her increased.

'It is one of the reasons I prefer being on the sea. The estate holds too many memories.'

'New ones can be made. Ones that do not replace the old ones, but ones you can hold in your heart alongside.' Thyre fought to keep her voice from trembling. 'It is a matter of how you drank at the well of Mirmir.'

His breath kissed her temple. 'The well of Mirmir. Do you believe in such things?'

'Sometimes. Believing the improbable means you can accomplish the impossible. My mother used to say that.'

'And is it true?'

'She thought so.' Thyre leaned forwards and twisted the horse's mane about her fingers. She had missed more than she had thought possible. 'It always made sense to me.'

'I find it is deeds that are rewarded and not sayings.'

He reined in the horse as they came around the bend, and a crystal blue lake appeared below them. The still waters seemed to reach up to her.

'I think it is time to wash away the feast.' He spurred the horse onwards until they reached the edge of the lake. Jumping down, he looped the reins of the horse about a pine tree.

'You have been here before.'

'Yes. After every feast. I find the smoke and the sweat makes my skin crawl.'

He divested his garments, laying them in a neat pile on the rock, and then dove into the crystal-blue water. For an instant, his body hung in the air, strong and masculine. Enticing.

'Come bathe with me,' he called, rising up out of the water. 'It will refresh your temper.'

'I cannot get out of this gown without assistance.'

Thyre regarded the lake with longing. After the noise and the crowds of the wedding feast, she wanted to wash away everything. She wanted it to go back to being just Ivar and her without any need for court protocol or other people. When they were alone, a current of energy ran between them.

'And…have you tried?'

She tried to ease her way out of the dress, but the sleeves did not permit movement. Thyre gave a loud exclamation that echoed across the lake, mocking her. 'Please…Ivar.'

'I take that as a plea for help,' he murmured, coming towards her. He came up out of the water, the droplets rolling off his muscular chest like glistening diamonds. Thyre wet her lips, remembering what his skin tasted like. 'Asking solves many problems.'

She nodded, unable to speak. She clasped her hands together, torn between the desire to touch and the desire to keep looking.

His hands reached out and tore the gown down the back seam. The heavy silk cascaded to the ground, making a pool of scarlet and silver. The late afternoon sun caressed her skin and a light breeze blew her shift against her legs. She stood savouring it.

'You are free to swim in the water, if you know how.' Ivar's breath tickled her ear, fanning the primitive heat that grew within her.

She pivoted and her breasts encountered his wet chest, turning the linen of her shift translucent. The peaks of her nipples showed dusky rose through the damp cloth. And under his hooded gaze, they hardened further.

He raised an eyebrow, but made no move to touch her. Steam rose from his body.

'I missed you. I want to feel your arms about me,' she said, putting her hands on his bare chest. Her finger trapped one of the droplets of water. She brought it to her lips and tasted it. The fresh water contrasted with the warm masculinity of his body. She leant forwards and captured another drop, this time with her tongue lapping his skin.

His response was to gather her in his arm and swoop down to steal a kiss. It was hard and fierce, creating a maelstrom of desire that called to her inner being. Their tongues met and warred, tangling and twisting, as the heat grew within her. He tightened his grip and pulled her firmly against him, leaving her in no doubt of his desire for her.

Her damp linen shift moved against her breasts, causing a tantalising friction over her nipples. And she knew as they stood there, feasting and devouring, that it was not the strictures of the Viken court that had caused her restlessness, but her desire to touch him and to be with him. The knowledge swamped her, scaring her with its intensity.

She breathed and tried to cling to her last ounce of common sense. Her hands cupped his face, holding his entrancing mouth away from her. Even the smallest distance made her body scream with frustration, but she knew she had to do something or she would be completely lost. 'Are we going for the swim? I am dressed for it now.'

'Later. There are other things that need to be attended to first.' His voice had become a husky rasp as he lowered his mouth to hers again. This time, the kiss was lazy, tantalising her senses, playing across her as his hand slowly drifted downwards, caressing her buttocks, holding her against him.

Her legs gave way, and she clung to his shoulders, trying to stay upright, but also seeking to keep their bodies joined. A moan escaped the back of her throat. He raised a hand and traced the line of her cheekbone. 'Patience.'

'Must we?'

His laugh echoed over the lake. Supreme, male and confident. 'Yes, wife, we must.'

He eased her backwards so that she was lying on the warm stone. She held out her arms, bringing him with her. His heavy weight covered her, moulding her curves against the hard muscle. Her hands ran down his sculpted back. At the base of his spine, a tiny pool of water had gathered. Her fingers dipped in and spread it out over his back, making his skin slick and supple.

His lips lazily moved down her throat and over the material to capture one erect nipple. His tongue lapped at it, making the fabric wet. He blew cold air on it, which contrasted with the heat. Her body arched up towards him, and the shift seemed to imprison her. Her hands tore at it until he lifted it over her and her body was revealed to him.

Thyre had thought that after their earlier encounters she must know everything about pleasure, but she realised that she had not even begun to dream.

Ivar's hands skimmed her body, barely touching but following the contours of her curves. Her body buckled, anticipating his next move, but he caught her foot and slowly pushed off her boot. He held the foot in his hand and with his knuckle traced her instep. Then he took each toe in turn into his mouth and suckled.

Her entire being quivered and the burgeoning heat within her demanded more. She wanted all of him, right here, right now. She reached up with her arms and drew him towards her. Little noises came from her throat. He appeared to understand. His masculine sigh of pleasure echoed out over the darkening lake.

He wedged open her thighs and settled between them, his arousal pushing at her innermost core. She wrapped her legs about him and pulled him in, and felt her body give way and welcome him. This was about more than the meeting of bodies; this was a melding, a true joining.

Together they rocked as the water lapped on the shore and the sun beat down on them.

Ivar eased his body from Thyre's. Their joining had been every bit as passionate as in his dreams of the last few nights. How he was going to be able to be away from her, he did not know, but it had to be done. There was no one else that he would trust to lead the *felag* to Ranrike. And when he had finished, the Ranrike would understand the folly of menacing Viken shipping and the necessity of providing hospitality according to custom.

'Time to go back to Kaupang. There is just time for a wash.' He pressed a kiss to Thyre's temple. 'The sun will be up soon. We have spent the entire night here.'

Her eyes opened, pools of blue mirroring the blueness of the lake. She stretched, thrusting her breasts up towards his chest. 'I can think of worse places. You, me and the fresh air.'

'But we need to go.'

'To your house? The bed is piled high with fur. I wonder—is it better to sleep out under the stars or to be enveloped in luxury?' Her eyes held a wicked glint, beckoning to him.

'No.' Ivar forced his body to ignore the blatant invitation and reached for his trousers. The responsibilities of the *felag* beckoned. A week ago it had seemed the perfect solution—marry and then leave. He would demonstrate that he was not to be manipulated. But now, after last night, he knew how hard it would be to leave Thyre. She would be safe and well cared for. Both Thorkell and Asa had given their word.

'Where, then?' Her eyes shone with passion's promise. Ivar felt his body respond. Despite what they had shared, he wanted her again, under him, and above him.

'You will return to court. The *felag* sails later this morning for Ranrike.'

'*Felag?* Why did no one tell me? I have been so worried. All Thorkell did was to pat my hand and change the subject.' Her brow knitted. She pushed her hair out of her eyes, the sleepy passion vanishing to be replaced by something hard and speculative. Ivar winced. 'Who is in the *felag?*'

'Haakon's brother Thrand and Erik the Black will captain the other ship, but Thorkell has given overall command of the *felag* to me.'

'You are going to Ranrike.' She drew her knees up to her chest and her hair hid her face. 'I will come with you. I will be part of the *felag.*'

'That is impossible. Women stay in Viken where they can be protected.' Ivar had told himself all throughout the preparations that this would be the best way. But now, having held her in his arms again, he knew that there would be a gaping hole in his heart until they were together again. But it had to be this way. 'Women do not take part in *felags.* Women stay where they can be safe. We protect our women. How can a man fight properly if he is worried about his woman?'

'It is my country you are going to. My family are in danger. I know the countryside. I can help you.'

'Ragnfast and your sister are my first priority.' Ivar moved away from Thyre and stared out at the lake. The sunrise cast faint pink-and-orange hues on to the surface of the lake. It would be tempting to give into Thyre's request, but what would happen if she did become hurt? How could he live then? This time, he would keep his wife safe. He would protect her. 'Trust me. I argued in the Storting to go to them first, before we confronted King Mysing. Peace will be possible if the king honours the *frithe* he made with King Thorkell, all those years ago.'

'And if he doesn't?'

'There will be war. Thorkell desires peace with Ranrike, but it must be an honourable peace.'

'If I can't go on the *felag*, I want to go to your estate.' She looked away, making it impossible for him to see her face. Had Thyre paid no attention to earlier words? Edda had died on the estate. He refused to risk Thyre in that way. She was his wife and her duty was to obey him without question.

'Thyre, Thorkell and Asa have agreed to house you. You will stay with them and take your proper position in court. You will enjoy yourself. You can teach the court skald all the Ranriken versions of the sagas.'

'Not the court.' She rolled her eyes heavenwards and shook her head. 'Surely I should be going to your estate and taking up my duties there. Winter will be here soon.'

'My steward looks after it well enough.' Ivar reached for his sword belt. 'Court is the best place for you. Thorkell agrees. He wants to see his daughter settled. He is enjoying having you there.'

'You might have consulted me. I find it difficult to breathe at court.'

'Why?' Ivar asked slowly. Surely Thyre had to understand that he could not afford to worry about her when he was leading the *felag*. The Viken court was the only place for her. Asa would look after her.

'Asa hates me.' Thyre stared out at the lake. 'Nothing I do is correct, no matter how hard I try. She finds fault with the way I spin, sew and even the way I hold my shoulders. I will never be part of her inner circle.'

Ivar hooked his thumbs in his belt buckle, resisting the urge to gather her in his arms. He had told Thyre about how Edda had died. He refused to risk it again. He could not fight battles while he was worrying about Thyre.

'Asa was a good friend to Edda. In time you will realise that Asa does have her heart in the right place. She wants you to succeed at court. You are the king's daughter.'

'She wants me to fail. Do you know what it is like to have everything criticised? I have been in charge of Ragnfast's estate since my mother died when I was eight. I know the proper way to spin and embroider.'

'Customs differ.' Ivar gave a shrug. Thyre might beg and plead, but she would go. It was the only place for her where he could be confident of her safety. He was responsible for her safety now. He refused to repeat his past mistakes.

'I will not be happy.'

'We must all do things we dislike.'

'Not you. You do whatever you please. You are only going to Ranrike because you want to. Thorkell could have easily chosen someone else. You desire this voyage. You want to leave me.'

Ivar froze. 'Why do you think I want to go on this *felag*? Your stepfather needs my help.'

'Yes, you want to go.' Her blue gaze pierced him and saw into his soul. 'You cannot wait to go or otherwise you would have told me about it before now. You kept it from me because you knew I would want to go.'

'It is far too pleasant a morning to be arguing. We have little time left.' Ivar dropped his voice into a caress.

'Then we had best return to Kaupang and our lives.' She stood up with her hair flowing over her shoulders. The sunrise gave her skin a rosy hue and Ivar used all his self-control not to pull her back into his arms.

'We could linger a little longer.'

She picked up her discarded gown with distaste and struggled back into it, pointedly not asking for his help. 'I should not like to be accused of delaying the *felag*. There are many more important things than us.'

She went over to the horse and stroked its nose, making crooning noises. Ivar tried to tell himself that it was for the best, but a huge weight had descended on his chest. Some-how, it was not how he had imagined the parting. 'Thyre, be sensible.'

'I am being sensible. You will do exactly as you please. And that is the end to it.'

'And you object to my going without you and you think by behaving in this fashion, I will agree to take you with me. You are exactly like Edda, Thyre. At least Edda only asked for new dresses and trinkets. I go to war, Thyre. Blood will be shed. And you blame me for wishing to keep you safe.'

'How do you expect me to respond to that?' Thyre asked with a great weariness in her voice. She drew her brows together and her mouth took on a mutinous expres-sion.

'You do not have to come to the waterfront and wish me goodbye then. I do not want you there. But you will stay in Kaupang. I will not come back to another empty house.'

'Some day, you will see me for who I am, instead of who you think I am.' Thyre held out her hand. 'We will say our goodbyes now.'

'It is not goodbye, Thyre.'

Chapter Fourteen

She had lied. And Ivar had to have seen through her. Thyre pressed her hands to her eyes, and sank down on the low bed in her chamber in the king's hall. She had known the lie before the words had spilled from her throat back at the lake. Bitter, ugly words about Asa and the court, instead of begging him to take her on the journey.

She wanted to be there and to know how Ragnfast and Dagmar were. She wanted to see her uncle's face when he realised that his scheme to terrorise the Viken had failed. Over the past few weeks, seeing how Thorkell worked, she found it impossible to think her uncle, the king of Ranrike, had not given his consent to Sigmund. Her uncle must have anticipated the consequences. But mostly she wanted to be with Ivar to make sure he survived. It no longer mattered that he might use her to challenge King Mysing for the Ranriken throne. He might worry about coming back to an empty house, but she worried about only having his shield returned to her.

Now, Ivar had left her at the door to her chamber in the hall, a prison more than a chamber, with little more than a perfunctory goodbye. They might never see each other again, and he did not even trust her enough to let her look after the estate. She was not his late wife. She had run Ragnfast's steading since she was eight. She knew how to work with the seasons, how to farm, to cook and to supervise. She knew the dangers.

She sank down beside the bed. Her mother would never have permitted this to happen. She would have demanded until she had her way. Or else she would have run away, a little nagging voice sounded in her head.

Thyre clenched her fists. She had no desire for war. There might be a way to get King Mysing to listen to Ragnfast's counsel now that Sigmund was dead. She was not running away from court, but towards her destiny. She refused to give up. Even now, there had to be a way of getting on the *felag* and going on the boat despite Ivar's refusal to consider it. He had forced her into subterfuge.

Asger. Thyre put her hands on her cheeks as her mind raced. He owed her a life-debt. All the men on the boat did. They had said so. She would use that life-debt and would reach Ranrike. To stay here would be worse than dying.

The more Thyre thought, the better the idea seemed.

She began to tick off the items she would require: a cloak, stout boots, her mother's dagger, some sort of disguise. A flicker of unease passed over her. If Ivar discovered her too quickly, he would force the *felag* to return, but she had to hope that by the time he realised they would be too far from Kaupang. All she knew was that she refused to remain here under Asa's thumb, worrying about him.

She threw open her trunk and started rummaging through, making a pile of things she might need.

'Daughter, what are you doing?'

Thyre jumped at Thorkell's voice and slammed the lid back down. The king stood silhouetted in the doorway. His deep purple cloak and the circlet he wore on his head showed that he was about to depart for the harbour.

'I am merely trying to find…to discover another Ranriken poem. The skald—'

'It is an odd way to discover anything, making stabbing gestures in the air over an open trunk.' He held out his hands. Thyre rose and greeted him with a kiss on her cheek. 'I am about to go down to the harbour and give the *felag* my blessing. Asa and her women are busy dressing. Asa is determined that the men will be given the correct send off.'

Thyre crossed her arms and refused to panic. 'I am not going. My gown will not be correct. My gown yesterday… Asa is quite firm about her ladies appearing in the proper attire.'

'Asa thought you would have taken that particular lesson to heart. She sent me to see you so that I could ease my mind.' Thorkell nodded, inviting her to continue.

'I have no wish to disgrace anyone.' Thyre hung her head and hoped she looked suitably humble. She kicked the dagger with her foot so that it went under her skirt. When she returned, triumphant, she would apologise.

'It can be hard the first time your man goes off on a *felag*. I have lost count of the number of women that Asa has had to comfort. It is why Asa invented her rules. They give women an excuse.' Thorkell put his hand on her shoulder; she put her hand over it and squeezed.

'The truth is best. Ivar only told me about the *felag* this morning.'

'I know, I know. He convinced Asa that if you knew, you would twist me around your finger and join it. As if I would permit such a thing. Women are to be protected. Asa has worked hard to keep you occupied.'

Thyre stared up at the ceiling. Here she had blamed Asa and it had been Ivar all along. 'How truly noble of her. The truth would have been better.'

'Ivar did what he thought best.'

'Undoubtedly.' Thyre hated the way her voice trembled. Suddenly everything was much harder with Thorkell standing next to her and she struggled to keep from blurting out the truth.

'For appearances' sake, it would be good if you could come to the harbour. I would have liked my daughter there to wave her husband off. But I can see that you agree with Asa about the seemliness of it.'

'Asa has the most experience with this, but I have no plans to challenge her authority.'

Thorkell touched her hair. 'You remind me of your mother. Full of fire and passion. Put it to good use.'

'I don't follow.' Thyre tilted her head and glanced up at Thorkell.

'You find court hard, but that is because you are working against it. People behave in different ways and have different customs. Asa does want to help. She will make a good ally.'

In the short time she had known Thorkell, she had come to respect him and to care for him. He was a father that she could be proud of. She would always be grateful to Ragnfast, but there was something about Thorkell and the way he thought that made sense to her. Her one regret about her scheme was that they would not have any more time together. 'I do find the ways very different. And I am trying.'

'In time, you will learn. The queen can be a hard

mistress, but she is loyal. She wants the best for you because you are my daughter and it was hard on her, thinking up excuses about why you could not see Ivar.' Thorkell gave a half-smile. 'Sometimes, I think she sees more than I do.'

'What would you suggest?'

Thorkell looked at her sharply and she wondered if he had guessed her plan. 'Follow your heart. It will lead you where you need to go. It is the same advice I gave your mother once.'

'Thank you.'

'My pleasure, daughter.' Thorkell kissed her forehead. 'You are a daughter to be proud of. You and Ivar will end your differences when he returns victorious.'

Thyre put a hand to her face. In many ways, Thorkell's revelation changed nothing. She knew Ivar did not want her there. He wanted to sail away and forget that she ever existed. With each breath she delayed, she risked missing Astrid and Asger. Whatever happened, Thyre knew she had to be on the ship. She had to go with the *felag*.

'Ah, before I forget. Asa has sent you a present.' Thorkell held out a little pot. 'She thought you might be able to use Annis's preparation for softening hands. Apparently your thread keeps breaking and Asa was worried that the problem might be caused by calluses on your hands from when you row.'

Thyre stared at the little pot. Rowing? The only time she had rowed was… She barely restrained from laughing out loud. The queen had guessed her intention and approved. Did her father guess as well? 'The queen has hidden depths.'

'Many have misjudged my wife.' Thorkell gave a

pleased smile. 'Her heart is in the right place. And now I must leave you. The purification ceremony needs to be completed before the tide turns. Ivar is determined that nothing will go wrong with this voyage. He intends to return to you.'

'Goodbye, Father, and thank Asa for me.' Thyre's fingers curled around the little pot. She would do it.

'You know, daughter, it is the first time you have called me Father.'

'It felt right.' Thyre hated the way her throat closed. She had just found him, but she had to leave. Her sense of honour demanded it. 'I am proud to call you that.'

'That is how it should be.' He pressed his lips to her forehead. 'Your mother and stepfather did well. You remind me so much of her.'

'Goodbye, Father,' she whispered after he had gone. 'You will be proud of me.'

Ivar turned his face towards the sea as the waves began to lap the boat. His hand lightly gripped the steering oar. Always previously this casting off had been his favourite part of the voyage, when all possibilities lay before him and the adventure beckoned. But this time, he wished Thyre had been in the crowd.

She had locked herself away ever since they'd returned, running off before he'd had the horse fully under control. Then when he sought to follow, she had disappeared into her chamber, slamming the door with a loud bang. He refused to be any woman's lapdog. She had to learn who the master was, and that he acted for her safety.

He grimaced. Thyre was nowhere to be seen amongst Asa's ladies. A large part of his heart hoped she would have regretted her harsh words and been there, but it was not to be.

Ivar had asked Astrid to convey his goodbyes when she brought his nephew to the harbour, but all his sister had done was to glare at him with fierce eyes and burst into copious tears. Asger had hung his head in embarrassment at his mother's behaviour. After gasping out that Asger should keep his cloak about him as the sea was bound to be rough at this time of year, Astrid had gone and the boy had silently taken his seat.

Ivar glanced up to where the boy sat hunched over his oar. Asger had obviously taken his mother's advice to heart as the cloak completely enveloped him.

Later when they had cleared the harbour shoals, he would relinquish the steering oar to Brami and have a quiet word with the lad about the proper rowing technique. He appeared to have forgotten everything from the last voyage.

The final horn sounded.

Ivar narrowed his eyes as the lad reached forwards to readjust the oar. The lad's back was far too shapely for Asger. Immediately he dismissed the thought. Thyre could not have been that foolhardy, nor could she have arranged things that quickly. He was imagining things.

When he returned, they would start again. But for now, he had to be content that she had obeyed him and was safe in Kaupang.

'Put your back into the oars, boys! Who do we sail for?'

'We sail for Viken's honour!' came the answer from all the throats.

'Viken! Viken! Viken!' The familiar chants rose and swelled around him. The other boats joined in and the chanting echoed backward over the water towards Kaupang and Thorkell's hall.

Ivar risked one backward glance. Had Thyre heard the noise? Did she even care? He had thought that leaving would make things easier, but he hated it. For the first time in his life he wanted to stay with her rather than fight the sea, and it frightened him.

Thyre rested her head against the oar. Sweat dripped down her face and into her mouth with each pull of the oar. Rowing was far harder than she had thought. It had seemed so easy when they had arrived in Kaupang, but now the tempo was far faster.

Her right palm burnt and she suspected her hand would be badly blistered long before nightfall. She hoped Asa's ointment would help.

'You have had your fun, Thyre, but now it is at an end.' Ivar's hand descended on her shoulder, pinning her to the trunk while his other hand flipped the hood back. Instantly the cool breeze fanned her face.

Silently Thyre cursed whatever little gesture she had made to alert him. She looked up at his unyielding face and shivered. 'What happens next?'

'I signal to the other boats. We turn around and head back to Kaupang. Once there, I tear my young nephew limb from limb for being party to such madness.'

'I forced him to do it because of the life-debt he owes me,' Thyre said before her courage failed her. 'If you must punish someone, then punish me.'

'We are in agreement on the true culprit, Thyre. Right now, I would happily tear you limb from limb.'

'I should like to see you try.'

Ivar looked away first. 'You have no idea what you

have done. How much trouble you could have caused, had my entire being not been alert to you. But in the end, the only thing you have done is to delay the *felag* and to delay the possibility of justice for your stepfather. You will have to live with that knowledge.' He raised his hand to give the signal to turn the boat around.

'No.' Thyre leapt up and grabbed his arm. 'No, you will not do that.'

Ivar's face contorted, making his scar stand out vividly from his cheek, but he stood absolutely rigid.

Quietly Thyre forced her fingers to release his arm. She took a half-step backwards. Her thighs met the edge of the boat.

'How dare you say no! You will do as I say!' he grounded out in a voice that struck her like a lash. 'You have no right to be here.'

'I earned the right to be on this *felag*!' Her heart thudded in her ears.

'And when did you earn this right?' His gaze raked her form. 'When did you become a man?'

'When I killed Sigmund Sigmundson, I earned that right. When I sacrificed my apron dress, so that the mast remained in one piece and the ship could sail safely back to Kaupang, again I earned the right!' Thyre made her voice carry to every part of the ship. With each word, she knew more men listened to her. If she could convince them, then Ivar would have to give way. She refused to allow him to travel without her. 'Every man on this boat owes me a life-debt, including you, Ivar Gunnarson. Would you deny that debt?'

All about her, she heard the men begin to murmur. It was like the ebb of a tide, first a trickle and then a flood. They supported her. She risked a breath. Triumph coursed through her.

'Thyre, you are my wife.' Ivar slammed his fist against the side of the ship. 'You must listen to reason.'

'Being your wife has nothing to do with it!' Thyre glared at him. 'Being your wife does not change my right.'

'It changes my responsibilities towards you.'

'I want to be on this *felag*, Ivar,' she said quietly. 'I deserve to be here. I deserve to see this through to the end. You are going to save my family.'

'Thyre should stay!' one of the men called out. 'She has brought good luck. The gods favour her.'

Others shouted agreement, but Ivar's scowl increased.

'You are asking them to do something that is improbable, Ivar—are you going to take away hope?' she asked in a low voice.

'I am giving you one last chance, Thyre.' His voice became chipped from ice. 'You stop this mutiny before it happens. We turn around and you return to Kaupang, quietly and obediently as a wife should. You stay at court until I return. You will be good and obedient to Asa and Thorkell. You will make me proud of you.'

'One last chance to slowly die?' Thyre said. 'Asa's court is stifling me, killing my spirit. I can never live there. Do you want to return to another dead wife?'

'That remark is beneath you.'

'But it is true.' Thyre crossed her arms and refused to look away. 'You speak of honour, but what about my honour? Women can have just as much honour as men.'

For a long moment their eyes warred. Then he looked away, up towards where the swell hit the boat. No one spoke or moved. Far away, the shouts from the other boats echoed across the water.

'Do you seek to challenge for the leadership? I have no wish to fight you with a sword, Thyre.'

'No, I only seek what is my right.' Thyre used all her energy and kept her head upright. 'I ask you on the life-debt you owe me and on your honour as a warrior.'

Ivar stood there, his hand clasped around the hilt of his sword, his face thunderous.

'Very well, you may stay. Far be it from me to deny a life-debt.' He inclined his head. 'You may join the *felag* as I will honour my life-debt.'

A ragged cry rang out across the ship. Thyre felt the tension ease from her shoulders. She had won. Then she stopped and stiffened her spine. It was too easy. Ivar had capitulated far too quickly.

'Thank you, Ivar. You will have no cause to regret me joining the *felag*.'

Ivar's smile became colder than a glacier. 'You did not let me finish. You may stay with the *felag* until Ragnfast's steading. There you stay, and Ragnfast will get the dubious honour of looking after you.'

'I had thought that I might be able to persuade my uncle King Mysing.'

'Persuade? Thyre, he banished your mother. Why would he listen to you?'

'He listened to my mother. I can remember the rune sticks he sent—'

'The affairs of state are no place for an untried woman.' Ivar's nostrils flared. 'You may go to Ragnfast's or not at all.'

Thyre pressed her lips together. It was better than nothing. She wanted Ivar to understand that she could help, but he didn't. To think she had even begun to hope that he might be the man of her dreams, a man ready to listen to her and to respect her. The dream tasted like ash in her mouth.

'And afterwards…when you return from seeing the

king?' Thyre whispered, her heart thudding loudly in her ears. Once, she had longed for this, but now she feared it.

'You show little desire to return to Kaupang. Far be it from me to force you to go against your *honour*.'

Thyre kept her head up as a great empty place welled up within her. Their brief marriage was over, but in many ways it had never begun. He was asking her to choose between her duty to her family and her feelings for him. 'Thank you for understanding, Ivar Gunnarson. You will have no cause to regret our bargain.'

Ivar turned away from her and then stopped. He swung back with a calculating smile. 'One more thing, Thyre, Thorkell's daughter, your actions have cost me an experienced oarsman.'

'It was necessary. Asger and I agreed.'

'You will have to take his place.'

'Take his place?' Thyre regarded the hated oar. Her right palm ached at the mere thought of more rowing.

Ivar's smile held a certain amount of smug satisfaction. 'I expect you to pull at the oars. Every member of a *felag* works. In fact, the newest members always work the hardest.'

'I…I…' Thyre reached forwards and grabbed the oar, wincing as pain shot up her arm. 'I understand.'

'This is no pleasure outing, Thyre. Neither is this a trading vessel with sails. This is a dragon ship and I intend to get to Ragnfast as quickly as possible.'

Thyre watched the gleam in his eye increase. He expected her to give in. She straightened her back, and ignored the ache in her arms and legs. 'I have no problems with rowing. I had expected to row. It is a price worth paying.'

'I wonder if you truly know the price you will have to pay.' He turned, calling on the oarsmen to redouble their efforts.

* * *

After two days of relentlessly pulling at the oars, Thyre had ceased to remember what it felt like not to have arms and legs screaming at her. After four days, her rhythm had improved and she began to enjoy the movement and the freedom of being outside. During her shifts, Ivar kept the sail tightly furled, forcing the ship to move through oar power alone. But she never complained and never allowed any of them to see her distress.

Each time her shift was over, she stumbled from the oar and lay down, using the cloak to cover her, and fell into a dreamless sleep. When she woke, the cloak was tucked tightly around her as if someone had made sure she was looked after. Ivar? She rejected the thought. He was determined not to lift one finger to help her. It had to have been someone else. However, her heart persisted in hoping.

Unexpectedly, she had cause to bless Asa. The ointment she had sent eased the ache in her hands, keeping the worst of the blisters at bay. As she rubbed it on her hands, she wondered if Asa knew how valuable the gift was. She found it impossible to rid her suspicion that both Asa and Thorkell had known about her plans and approved. And her respect for them grew.

Once they reached the steading and Ivar had departed, Thyre hoped the ache in her heart would ease as she became immersed in the normal routine of her work. In time, life would become easier and she might only remember Ivar in her dreams. But for now, every particle of her being was aware of him.

'Bay to the left. Pull hard on the oars!' Ivar's voice echoed throughout the boat.

Thyre braced her feet and pulled with all her might,

proud that she could keep a tempo with the others. Slowly the boat turned and she saw the familiar rocks and shoreline. Not just any bay, but *her* bay.

She redoubled her efforts, concentrating on pulling her shoulder blades together. Each stroke was closer to the time when she would see Ragnfast and Dagmar. Each stroke was closer to the time when she could pick up the threads of her old life. A great weight bore down on her, making it harder to pull the oar. Each stroke took her closer to goodbye.

A firm hand clasped her shoulder. Heat shot through her body. 'Thyre, whatever happens, remember you are a member of the *felag*. Until you are dismissed, you owe the *felag* your loyalty.'

'How could I forget?' Thyre frowned. There was something in Ivar's eyes and the way he held his body, shielding her from viewing the shoreline. 'I gave you my word. I have kept my word. How can you doubt me now?'

'And remember, you can count on our support. You have shown great courage with your rowing. You have done as much as any man. You have proved me wrong. A woman can have the heart of a man. However—'

'What are you saying, Ivar? What have you seen? Ragnfast will greet you with hospitality as long as your shields remain hung on the side.' Thyre's throat closed around a tight hard lump. Her insides knotted and re-knotted but he remained silent, blocking her vision. 'Tell me now. You must have seen something. What has happened? Are there dragon ships here? Tell me the worst! Show me!'

He turned so his face was in shadow. 'Look now!'

Thyre swivelled so she could see where Ivar was pointing. The gables of the main hall should have been clearly visible, but nothing was there. In the sky a faint black curl of smoke rose. She screwed up her eyes and opened them again, squinting against the sun. Perhaps she had made a mistake. Perhaps this was not the right place. She scanned the horizon, left, right, and back again. It couldn't be. The hall with its weatherbeaten gables had to be standing. She took a steadying breath. It had to be. But in front of her, only a blackened pile of ash and timber smouldered. 'Ivar…'

The ship erupted into pandemonium as Ivar bellowed across the water towards the other ships to prepare. Within a few breaths, shields had been raised and weapons drawn. Thyre froze, unable to remember if she pushed with her feet before she pulled back with her arms. She attempted to push it and the oar swung wildly, crashing into the one in front of her.

'Thyre, keep your hands on your oar and pull!' Ivar's bellow broke through her panic, calmed her.

'I am trying.'

'Don't try. Do! You are a member of my *felag*! I believe in you!'

'It is fine for you to say. Now!' Her hands were slippery and she found it impossible to grip the oar properly. She released it, wiped her hands on her trousers and tried again. Her heart soared. Ivar believed in her.

'Dagmar and Ragnfast might have survived. Such things do happen.'

'There is no need to honey coat your words, Ivar, you think they are dead.' She glanced up at him and his face showed grim compassion. 'You think they were punished because of what I did.'

'With you, Thyre, I would not dare. You must be prepared for their death, certainly.' His brow creased.

'There are some things that a lady should not see. As to the other, we do not know who did this or why. Wait before you worry.'

'I am prepared. The sooner, the better. Sometimes, a lady has no choice.' Thyre gripped the oar tighter, as the longing to have his arms about her swamped her. She concentrated on the oar rather than the horizon and regained control. She had forced the bargain. She would not be the one to change it. 'Now if you will excuse me, I must row. It is the only thing I can do.'

'As you wish… You are truly a warrior, Thyre.'

Thyre fancied she saw a gleam of respect in his eyes.

She reached forwards and brought the oar back, a simple motion but this time it gave her strength. She could do something. She did not need to depend on Ivar. But in her heart, she wanted to be enfolded in his arms and be a woman again.

The ship rounded the final bend and the great smouldering black lump of charred wood that had been the hall rose up before them.

Chapter Fifteen

Thyre pulled hard at the oars until the keel of the boat scraped along the bottom a few yards from the shore. Then unable to stand the torture of not knowing what had happened to Ragnfast and Dagmar any longer, she let go of the oar and stood. Her back was plastered with sweat and her palms ached, but the smouldering ruins rose before her and the shore was devoid of life.

How long had it been since she had first spied the burnt-out remains of her former home? More than enough time for anyone who remained to appear on shore. Surely they could not all be dead.

Without waiting for a signal, she jumped out of the boat and into the surf. The cold water soaked her trousers, but she pressed onwards, ignoring Ivar's strident command to get back in the boat.

When she reached the shore, all was unnaturally silent and deserted. A flock of seagulls rose up as one, twisting and turning in the air. The ash and blackened wood still gave off a faint heat. Thyre started. The hall had burnt only several days before.

'Ragnfast! Dagmar! Hilde! Sven the forester! Anyone!' Thyre called over and over again, hoping against hope that somehow her instinct was wrong and this was a terrible accident with a cooking fire rather than an attack.

The seagulls mocked her cries, but slowly a bedraggled cat came picking its way delicately through the wreckage. Its fur was partly singed. Seeing Thyre, it gave a pitiful yowl.

She ran to it, picking it up and exclaiming over and over. Beygul gave a loud purr. Somehow, it made everything better and worse at the same time. Beygul had obviously not eaten for days. The knowledge drove all the air out of her lungs. Dagmar would never have let the cat get into such a state. Even Ragnfast saw to the comfort of his animals.

'Thyre, you are endangering everyone by remaining here out in the open,' Ivar thundered. 'Come back here with the men, until it is safe. Do you know nothing of military strategy?'

'I found Beygul, my cat.' Thyre held the cat out. 'But there does not seem to be anyone here. There are no boats. Nothing.'

'Whoever did this may have come and gone.' Ivar pointed towards the shoreline. 'You can see where they burnt your stepfather's boat along with the trampled sand from the footsteps of the warriors. And reddened sand.'

'Reddened sand?'

'I am sorry, Thyre, someone died and since the last rainfall.'

Her eyes followed his hand and saw the blood-soaked sand. She forgot how to work her lungs and gasped for air.

A raid had caused this destruction. It could not have been anything else. Her insides ached. It had to have been Sigmund's men. But would they have acted without orders from the king against a jaarl? Her uncle had ordered the destruction of their home. Her mother might have forgiven her banishment, but she knew she would never forgive this.

'This is where my family lived. My home since I was born. I can even see Dagmar's weaving frame in the rubble.' She clutched the cat tighter. Her entire being trembled. To him, it was another burnt-out hall, but to her, it was her home. She knew every piece of charred wood. How many people had been killed? Where were the survivors? If she had been here, could she have prevented the deaths? Waves of helplessness and regret swept over her. She buried her face against Beygul's fur and willed the tears not to come.

'This should have been prevented. They should have been warned,' she said when she was certain her voice would be firm. 'We should have returned here, rather than going on to Kaupang. Do you think I was feasting when—?'

'Do not torture yourself, Thyre. It was my choice, not yours.' Ivar laid a heavy hand on her shoulder. 'And the past is carved in stone. We can only change the future.'

'I suppose you are right.' She resisted the urge to lean against his chest, instead forcing her legs to walk away from the ruin and towards where the bathing hut had stood.

'I know I am.' He put an arm about her waist and led her away from the smouldering ruin.

Somehow, it made it worse that Ivar was being kind. His anger and stubbornness were known quantities and she could have raged against him. But his kindness showed how much she had lost and how many mistakes she had made. How much she would miss him when he went. She wanted to believe in second chances, but their bargain was very clear. She had made her choice.

'Thyre? Lady, is that you?' A woman's voice called from the trees at the edge of the wood. 'I have been praying and praying, but the gods appeared to be deaf.'

Thyre peered into the gloomy forest and the outline of a shawl-draped woman appeared beside the large oak tree.

'Hilde, thank all the gods in Asgard that you are alive.' Shaking off Ivar's restraining hand, Thyre rushed towards the woman. Beygul squirmed slightly in her arms and she allowed the cat to escape. When Thyre reached the woman, she was dismayed to see that Hilde was on her own. 'Where is Dagmar? Ragnfast? Are they…?'

'I have no idea, my lady.' The woman dropped a nervous curtsy. Her face sported several bruises and she had burn marks on her wrists as if she had fought the flames.

'How can you not know?' Thyre looked at Hilde in amazement. The maid had been here all the time. She had to know what had happened. She had to know where they were, where everyone was. 'How many are left? Did anyone survive besides you?'

'A number of the household survived. But we hid when we saw your ships. We do not want any more warriors here. But then I remembered about your going with the Viken, and I volunteered to spy and to see if these warriors were friends or not.'

'But surely Ragnfast?'

'They left before the warriors came, the both of them for Ranhiem and the Storting. Ragnfast decided that the omens were better for going by the mountains rather than the sea. Dagmar was determined to rescue you. She kept on and on to Ragnfast about it until he agreed to go and to take her with him. She is going to plead with your uncle for your safe return.'

'But where are his men?'

'He took too many. He thought no one would attack us. A few days after they left, Sven spotted the ships, we went out to greet Sigmund's men as we have always done and…'

Thyre's knees went weak and relief rushed through her. Ragnfast and Dagmar had missed everything.

Ragnfast would never have left if he thought his hall or people were in danger. Three years ago when the barn burnt after a lamp was turned over, he had refused to go to the Storting as the omens were not correct. Dagmar had thought to rescue her from the Viken. Thyre had to smile at the irony. She had been so concerned about rescuing them that she had never considered Dagmar would attempt to do the same.

Her breath froze as Hilde's other words sunk in. This was no random attack. Dagmar and Ragnfast even now were walking into a trap. Somehow, there had to be a way of warning them.

'Did everyone else get to safety?' Ivar asked.

'Mostly.' Hilde swept into a curtsy. 'They knew what to do, thanks to Thyre. All these years, we joked about how you made us practise, my lady. How we knew how to go to our hiding places with our eyes shut. And how it would never happen.' Hilde's face crumpled and tears spilled over her dirty face. 'But it did.'

Thyre reached out a hand and Hilde's gripped hers. No words were necessary. For a long time, they stood there, looking at the ruins. 'The hall will be rebuilt. Better. Ragnfast always said that he wanted to replace that raven gable on the right.'

'If you say so, my lady.'

'Thyre,' Ivar rumbled in her ear. Thyre gave into temptation and laid her head against Ivar's broad chest, drawing comfort from the steady thump of his heart. It seemed incredible that after all they had been through together life seemed easier just because he was standing next to her, but she also knew that he must not guess her feelings. She took a deep breath and stepped away from him. His arms fell to his sides. 'Do you know where Ragnfast is?'

'Ragnfast and Dagmar are safe. Or at least as safe as they can be. They are not lying in that pyre. They are on their way to the Storting. Ragnfast wanted to go overland so they missed Sigmund's dragon boats. Dagmar is determined to rescue me. But, Ivar, they are heading into a trap.'

'Why did the hall burn? Has the woman told you that?'

'Warriors came…Sigmund's men.' Hilde stepped forwards. 'They told a story about Ragnfast being disloyal to the king and the Storting giving its permission. But Ragnfast is the king's brother-in-law. King Mysing knows he is loyal.'

'Did they burn the hall straight away?' Ivar asked. 'How many lost their lives because of this attack?'

'Some of us thought that they would go away, contenting themselves with a few pigs and sheep, a bit of grain.' Hilde paused and wiped her eyes with the corner of her dirty apron dress. 'But Sven the forester, he wanted to prove that Ragnfast was wrong to reject his suit. He wanted to show that he too could be a warrior. I expect he thought if he saved the steading, then Ragnfast would agree to let Dagmar marry him.'

Thyre closed her eyes, and braced her body for what must come next. Even now, she could clearly picture Dagmar's face when she first confided how wonderful Sven was and how much she longed for their life together.

Ivar's arm reached for her again. She was grateful that he was willing to offer his support but she hated her need for it. She shook off his arm and stood alone, trying to control the trembling in her stomach. 'What did Sven do?'

'He took Ragnfast's second sword from its hiding place. He defied the Ranriken captain. And he told him that he was dishonouring the house of an important jaarl, a jaarl who enjoyed the king's protection.'

'Where is Sven now?' Ivar asked, interrupting the woman's flow. 'What has happened to him?'

'In Valhalla. They made him into a blood eagle as a warning to the others who might protest. Then they torched the hall and killed all they could find…for sport.' Hilde spat on the ground. 'Ragnfast should not have left us without protection. Sven had no chance. He loved trees, not swords. All he wanted to do was marry Dagmar. His only crime was to fall in love with the wrong person.'

'Was a funeral pyre lit for him?' Thyre asked. 'Did anyone compose a funeral poem?'

'It has been done, my lady.' Hilde bowed her head. 'I made sure of it. The women and I made sure of it for all the men. After the warriors left. The dead need to be honoured.'

'He needs to be honoured. Dagmar… Dagmar would want it to be done.' Thyre regarded the smouldering hall. This was more than a simple raid; this was a lesson administered, retribution for her killing of Sigmund. How would her uncle greet Dagmar and Ragnfast? Would he be willing to accuse Ragnfast of disloyalty then?

'Will they come back, my lady?'

'I do not know,' Thyre replied slowly, dragging her thoughts away from the future. 'I sincerely hope not.'

'You will have protection now, Viken protection. No

matter what happens, you will not be left without warriors again,' Ivar declared. 'This bay is vital to both countries.'

'You are very good,' Hilde said, falling to her knees and kissing Ivar's outstretched hand.

Ivar lifted Hilde to standing and spoke to her in soothing tones about what would be done and where the survivors were.

'This steading belongs to Ragnfast the Steadfast. It is not mine or yours to give away.'

Ivar's lips thinned to a white line and the breeze blew his hair. He stared down at her for a long heartbeat, but Thyre stared back at him.

'Then he should have protected it better. It is far too valuable. It cannot fall into the wrong hands, men who would use it against the Viken. I claim it for Viken now. Who will fight me for it?'

Thyre glared up at him. When was her punishment going to end? Must everyone who was dear to her lose everything? 'It does not need a Viken to defend it. Ragnfast's arm has been strong…'

'And Ranrike has served it well? Ragnfast gave his allegiance to Ranrike and this is how King Mysing repaid him. Who will your uncle send next?' Ivar lifted a brow. He inclined his head towards where the other Viken warriors were landing. 'Thrand is in need of land. Such a place would suit him admirably. He can be the new jaarl of Eastern Viken.'

'This is what this *felag* is about—conquering Ranrike?' Thyre stared at Ivar in disbelief. 'It is no wonder that King Thorkell kept it from me. I thought you were supposed to be aiding my family.'

'Are you suggesting that we sail on and leave these people as prey to any wandering warship? Haven't they suffered enough?' His eyes glowed with blue flames. 'With you, Thyre, I am always the villain.'

'Not always,' Thyre admitted.

'It is good to hear.' He gestured towards the ruins. 'Thyre, the hall can be rebuilt, but things can never go back to the way they were before. Your life here is finished.'

'That remains to be seen. No one can predict the future.' Thyre tilted her chin upwards.

She dampened the sudden longing that sprang up within her. What was between them was over, strangled. They could never be friends and she knew that she wanted much more than friendship.

She had to be practical and think of others. Ragnfast would never be able to regain this land without help. 'Dagmar will inherit this land. Thrand is unmarried. It is possible that Ragnfast will agree to this solution...if we can find him...before...before... I want to avoid bloodshed, Ivar.'

'Matchmaking, wife?' Ivar's voice was laced with an irony. 'That is an occupation fraught with danger. It is rarely advisable to force a marriage.'

Thyre's heart soared at the word 'wife' and then plummeted. She picked up Beygul again and buried her nose into the soft fur to cover her confusion. 'Despite unpromising beginnings, some arranged matches thrive.'

'Never a truer word was spoken. But you cannot be sure which ones will. It takes two people to make a marriage.'

The words stabbed in her heart.

'It is best to allow these things to develop naturally then, but Dagmar always did have an eye for broad shoulders and a slender waist.'

Ivar gave a shout of laughter and she knew the danger had passed. 'It is wonderful to know that women are interested in such things even at times like these. But you need to stop organising lives. You will become worse than Asa.'

'If I consider the future, then I can forget about this.' She gestured towards the hall, ignoring the Asa comment. She would never be worse than that woman.

'Thyre, sometimes there is only so much we can do. A match between Thrand and Dagmar would solve a number of problems, but it must come from them…in time. Thrand will start rebuilding the hall in a few days. He will need your expertise to know where the seasoned wood is. When Ragnfast returns, then they can negotiate payment.'

'They did not sail here straight from the battle where I killed Sigmund,' Thyre said, looking up at the sky. He could not leave her here with Thrand, not with so much unsettled. She had to be with him.

'How do you know this?'

'Our encounter was weeks ago. The embers remain warm. The king had to have ordered this. No mere captain would have dared attack a jaarl's steading. Allow me to come to Ranhiem with you and explain the situation to Ragnfast. Jaarls in the Storting listen to him. My uncle has never dared move against him in the Storting.'

'What can you do there?' Ivar laced his fingers through hers. He brought them up to his mouth and her heart skipped a beat. 'You should stay here where you are safe.'

She disentangled her fingers. 'My safety is no longer your concern. We agreed that. You were to take me to Ragnfast. The bargain is not yet complete.'

Ivar's face drained of warmth. 'I remember my promise.'

'Then I will hold you to it.' Thyre took a step backwards. Hopefully he would think she was only concerned about Ragnfast, rather than the truth—she needed to be with him.

For a long time, Ivar was silent. 'I could hardly leave you here. The amount of trouble you could get into frightens me.'

'I will be good.' Thyre pressed her hands together. He had to take her with him. She could help.

'Trouble is something that follows you about, Thyre, like a lap-dog.'

'I have noticed that you are no stranger to it either.'

'I am a trained warrior. You are my wife.'

'And I believe that I have proved my worth to the *felag*,' Thyre said. 'I can row without complaining.'

A dimple flashed in his cheek and Thyre knew she had won. 'I believe you have done enough rowing. Thrand will be able to spare one of his warriors.'

'But you will take me. I must be there.' She hesitated. 'I will urge King Mysing to listen. We share a common blood.'

'You can come, but, Thyre, if there is any fighting, I want you to stay in the background. What happened between you and Sigmund could never happen again. And you must obey me in this.'

'Thank you, Ivar.' Thyre clasped his hand and was amazed at its icy coldness. 'I, too, keep my promises.'

'You may have cause to hate me, Thyre.' His eyes crinkled at the corners and Thyre's heart turned over. 'Most women would run from such a proposition.'

'I am not most women.'

'That is an understatement.'

Thyre took a bite of the lightly cooked trout. She had forgotten how good fish could taste. They had departed from the burnt-out steading a day ago and had pulled the boats up in a small deserted bay a short row from Ranhiem where Ivar and his men had stopped on their outward journey to Birka. Thyre tried to put the stench of the burning wood behind her and not to think about what lay ahead of her.

Thrand and his warriors had remained behind, but the others had sailed on. Ivar had been polite but distant.

'I am impressed with your cooking skills.'

'A man needs to know how to survive,' Ivar commented, giving a careless shrug, but Thyre could see the flash of pleasure flicker over his features. It seemed incredible that her emotions should be so attuned to his. She wanted him to be happy. And she could feel the moments slipping away from them. He rubbed his hands together and held them over the fire.

'It will be another day until we reach Ranhiem. Once we arrive, you must stay on the ship where you will be safe. Women have no place in war.'

'Ragnfast will trust you more if I am with you.' Thyre hugged her knees. 'He values my counsel. And it is not war yet. It is politics, and that is different.'

'It is a pity Thyre was not born a man,' Erik the Black said. 'What a king she would have made.'

'I am very grateful that Thyre is a woman,' Ivar replied.

The full force of his blue gaze slammed into Thyre. A warm curl wound around her insides and she wondered how she'd survive without him.

Erik the Black started to say something, but Ivar held up his hand, silencing him. 'Someone is coming. I can hear horses.'

The Viken stood up as one and drew their swords, forming an arc in front of the boats. Ivar kicked sand over the fire, plunging them into the dusky gloom.

Thyre's muscles became taut. To have come so far, and now this. Another battle.

'Do you think anyone lit the beacon, Thyre?' Ivar asked.

'No,' Thyre replied, stung that he could even think anyone at the steading would play him false. 'Who would want Sigmund's men to return? The anger towards him and the king is great. Ragnfast is well respected. All the foresters and farmers I met rained curses down on my uncle Mysing's head.'

'I will take your word for it. Forgive me for even asking, Thyre.'

'I do know my people.' Thyre's insides twisted. Against her will, she loved Ivar more now than when they had departed Kaupang. He was exactly the sort of warrior she had always dreamt of marrying. She had been wrong about him not respecting her. His actions showed that. They had both made mistakes.

A light voice floated on the breeze, laughing about something. 'It's Dagmar. She is alive and well and I am certain that I heard Ragnfast.'

Ivar lifted his hand and the shields were lowered. 'Are you certain?'

'She is my sister.' Thyre pressed her hand against her mouth. The time had come to part and she desperately hoped she would be strong. He must not guess her true desires. 'You have kept your word, Ivar. You brought me to Ragnfast before we reached my uncle's court. Our bargain has been fulfilled. I will leave the *felag* now.'

'Ragnfast will need to know about the destruction of his estate, and he will have to make a choice.' Ivar gave no sign that he had heard her. 'Does he stand with me and Viken or does he stand with a cowardly king who makes war against the people he swore to protect?'

'I will tell Ragnfast. If I explain about the steading, he will support you.' Thyre kept her back straight. She wanted to speak about them, and not Ragnfast, but their bargain stood between them.

'You would do that?'

'It is no more than needs to be done. This feud between the Ranriken and the Viken needs to end. Ranrike needs a strong leader, one who is willing to take to the seas and trade, instead of cowardly attacking passing ships.' Thyre blinked rapidly and cleared her throat before continuing. 'I have no idea who it could be. Ragnfast may have an idea. But it must be someone of the royal house of Ranrike.'

'Thyre…'

Thyre clenched her fingers around her thumbs. She had her pride. 'I have learned many lessons, Ivar, and I am grateful. I will keep to my part of the bargain. Our marriage is at an end, even though I deem it an honour and privilege to have been married to a man such as you.'

'In another time and place, we will speak about our marriage. But I need to see to our visitors.'

Thyre closed her mouth with a snap. The infuriating man would not even allow her to take her leave properly.

Ivar quickly wrapped some moss and grass around a branch and stuck it into the warm embers. A flare arose, illuminating the glade, showing strange elongated shadows.

'Who goes there?' Ragnfast's voice called out.

'Travellers with news,' Ivar answered. 'Important news for Ragnfast the Steadfast.'

'Is that you, Ivar Gunnarson? This is indeed a surprise.' The soft hiss of swords being withdrawn from hilts filled the air. 'What have you done with my stepdaughter?'

'Ragnfast, I am here with Ivar Gunnarson,' Thyre called out before Ivar could make a mess of his words. Ragnfast must be prevented from drawing his sword or blood would be shed. 'We come to save your life.'

'They come to bring war. It is the Viken way.' Ragnfast dismounted and drew his sword. In the starlight, his men-at-arms' swords gleamed. 'Once I was weak. I should have fought you, Viken, when you threatened Thyre. You dishonoured my stepdaughter.'

Behind her, Thyre knew the Viken would be longing to draw their weapons and what had started peacefully would end in destruction, unless she took charge.

'King Thorkell, my father, has no wish for war with the Ranrike,' Thyre said. 'He never has. He let you and my mother live in peace. He sends greetings to you, Ragnfast the Steadfast, and remembers the time you fought together.'

'You have met him? And lived?' Ragnfast lowered his sword.

'He acknowledged me without hesitation.' Thyre kept her words measured. 'You must listen before you act. Your life is in danger—'

'Ragnfast, your hall has been burnt,' Ivar said, interrupting her speech. 'Sigmund Sigmundson's men burnt it after they received permission from your king. Sven the forester died, defending it. The Ranriken made him a blood eagle. There were no warriors when we landed. No remains except blood, ash and charred timber.'

'You lie, Viken. My king would never do that to me.'

'If you will not believe Ivar, Ragnfast, you may believe me,' Thyre said, holding out her hands. 'Ivar left warriors, good warriors there to hold the land and to rebuild the hall. But everything is gone—the new barn, your bed with its furs and my mother's loom.'

Ragnfast staggered back, ageing before her eyes. 'I don't believe it. King Mysing would never have dared. I am his brother-in-law.'

'I speak the truth. My mother's burial mound was

wrecked. It has been put right and Sven's ashes lie in a fresh mound.'

'Sven is dead?' Dagmar asked. Her shoulders shook and great sobs filled the air.

Thyre rushed forwards and gathered Dagmar in her arms. 'I am so sorry, Dagmar. Sven died a hero, according to Hilde.' She touched Dagmar's cheek, wiping away the tears. 'I think he wanted to prove to you that he was worthy.'

'He was too good for me.' Dagmar buried her face into Thyre's shoulders. 'What was worse is that when I saw him again, I could only think about the sacrifice you had made for us and how you lost your freedom. And I knew that I could not rest until I had rescued you. Sven could not understand why I felt that way. We quarrelled before I departed. I shall never love again.'

'I am free now, Dagmar.' Thyre lifted Dagmar's face and looked her directly in the eyes. 'I have no regrets. And you should not wish away your future. Sven would want you to live.'

'What has happened to my land?' Ragnfast asked. 'Does it remain in danger?'

'Ivar has left a Viken jaarl to protect it, in case anyone else tries to take the bay, but the hall is gone. The men are dead.' Thyre kept her tone measured. 'My father, King Thorkell, will offer you sanctuary, if you desire it.'

'I want my land back. I want justice. King Mysing will pay if what you say is true.'

'For far too long our countries have warred,' Ivar said. 'I want peace. King Thorkell wants peace, but we want it on our terms. You gave us hospitality and now we shall return the favour. We will defeat the men who did this to you. You and your family are under my protection.'

'Do you think I will seriously answer that?' Ragnfast went red in the face and started to make a choking sound.

'Please, Ragnfast, listen to him,' Thyre said, grabbing both his hands and holding them between hers. 'For my sake, listen to my husband.'

'Husband?' Dagmar squeaked. 'You married your Viken?'

'Yes.'

Ragnfast bowed his head. 'I respect your counsel, Thyre. I will listen to your husband, but I reserve the right to make up my own mind. What are your plans, Viken?'

'Shall we speak a little away from the others?' Ivar motioned to Thyre to stay and to speak with Dagmar. Thyre's face was mutinous, but she obeyed him. He did not doubt her strength, but he wanted to keep her free from danger. 'Things need to be said between us. We need to plan our approach.'

They walked a little distance from the group. Ivar's gut tightened. He was about to make the hardest bargain of his life. The *felag* was far more important than his feelings and his desire to keep Thyre with him. He had given a promise to protect her. Thyre wanted to be with Ragnfast and her sister. It was why she had joined the *felag*. It had nothing to do with him. He might need her as much as he needed air to breathe, but she wanted to be with her family.

He clung to her use of the word 'husband' as a dying man might cling to a spar. Somehow, he would find a way to win her heart.

'King Thorkell insisted I marry Thyre once he discovered her parentage. He disliked the thought of his daughter being my concubine.'

'I begin to like him all over again. We raised our swords together once and I saved his life. He allowed Thyre's mother to go partly because of the life-debt he owed me.' Ragnfast gave a hoarse chuckle. 'I would have loved to have seen his face when he realised one of his jaarls had made his daughter into a concubine.'

'Thyre has no wish to remain in Kaupang. She stowed away on my boat and made the journey despite my displeasure. I fear Thorkell's queen aided and abetted Thyre. She does not want her at court and I did not see this until too late. Above all things I wish to keep Thyre safe.'

'She does have royal Ranriken blood.'

'I refuse to have my wife used by men to achieve their own ends. Thorkell knows my opinion. I would never have led this *felag* if I thought Thyre would join it.'

'But she did.'

'I underestimated her strength of purpose and her determination. But this *felag* is not about enlarging Viken's borders.'

Ragnfast stared. Ivar willed him to believe. 'Thorkell agreed. He cares about his daughter.'

'Thorkell has an unusual way of expressing his concern,' Ragnfast said. 'Sainsfrida wanted the best for her daughter. She had a long discussion with Thorkell's chamberlain and decided to keep Thyre with her. Thorkell had a new wife and she deserved to have some measure of happiness. What do you want me to do now?'

'Take Thyre back to the steading. Keep her safe. When it is over, I will come and claim her.'

'Wouldn't it be better if you allowed her to make a choice before? Have you ever given her a choice?'

'Thyre is my wife. That is the end of the matter.'

Thyre kept her arm about Dagmar as Dagmar's sobbing slowly ceased.

'I should have loved Sven more.' Dagmar wiped the tears from her eyes. 'I should have kissed him goodbye, instead of being excited about getting to meet our uncle. I was finally having my chance to be brave like you. I am even trying to learn my runes.'

'I suspect we all wronged Sven. He would have made an admirable husband.' Thyre looked out at the darkened bay. The water slapped against the boats and her heart ached. Too soon, Ivar would be gone. In his own way, Ivar had attempted to keep her safe.

'I wish I had told him one last time that I loved him. I even refused to renew my vow to Sven until you were back with us. I had to fight for you as you had sacrificed your future for me.'

Thyre went cold. Had she ever said anything to Ivar? Did he even guess how much she wanted to stay with him? About how much she loved him? She might have had the courage to go on the *felag*, but did she have the courage to fight for Ivar? Somehow, she needed to find a way for them to begin again, before it was too late. There was a difference between her and her mother. Her mother had insisted on having her way without compromise, and in the end had run away from her strong-willed Viken lover. Ivar needed to know that her love for him was unquenchable and that she respected him.

'Thyre!' Ivar called out. 'Plans have changed. You need to leave. Now!'

'Is there a problem?' Thyre hurried to where Ivar stood. A frown creased his forehead. 'Have the Ranriken discovered us?'

'Ragnfast and I have agreed that you are to be part of his party and will return overland to the steading.' His eyes held a determined look as if he expected a fight. 'This is where we must part company.'

'But why?' She stared blankly at him. After all that had passed between them, he was simply going to walk away.

He was not even going to give her the opportunity to change his mind.

'It is the best way to keep you safe. Keep to the hills and none will notice you.'

'But what will happen to you? You will return and let me know what passes between you and King Mysing.'

He laced his fingers through hers. 'I do not know what the future will bring, Thyre. You will know one way or another.'

'But you said…I was part of the *felag*. I should stay until the end.'

'The agreement was until we encountered your stepfather. You will go with him now. He will keep you free from harm.'

'What are you going to do?'

'Lead my *felag*. Fulfil my duty. Go to war if King Mysing will not renew the *frithe* that existed between the two countries.' His fingers flipped a tendril of hair back from her face. 'It is a dangerous occupation and not one for a lady.'

'I was once your concubine.' She forced a laugh when all she wanted to do was cling to him and kiss his lips.

Ivar's face did not soften, but his hand held her hard against his body for a long heartbeat before he put her away from him.

'You are now my wife and deserve a wife's respect.' He glared down at her. 'And you would drive most men to distraction. Is it any wonder that I want rid of you before I meet King Mysing? Argumentative. Unwilling to take no for an answer. Always wanting your own way. Putting everyone in danger with your headstrong ways.'

'We are better off parted. Thank you for seeing sense.' Thyre blinked back tears. She was grateful that she had not confessed her love. Ivar would simply crush it into the dust.

She kept her back as straight as a newly forged sword. 'I have no wish to cause any more danger to the men or to you.'

'I will fight better knowing you are safe, Thyre. But you must believe that I will come back to you.'

'Ivar,' Thyre called out as he started to turn away, 'may all your journeys be easy ones.'

He lifted his hand.

'I will wait,' she whispered, but he did not turn back. An empty place appeared where her heart had been.

Dagmar put an arm around her shoulders and attempted to lead her back towards Ragnfast and his men. Thyre resisted, but then gave in. 'It is better this way. Didn't I tell you that Far would get everything sorted? You will be with us now. For ever. Life will be just as it used to be.'

For ever. The words resounded within her, making that hollow place grow larger. She thought she could let him walk out of her life, but she saw that she had done nothing to hold on to him, nothing to tell him the way she felt. If he knew, he might return.

'Ivar,' she called out and rushed back to his side, hating her need to try, but knowing that she could not live with the thought that it might have been.

'What is it?' His voice was far from welcoming, but she forced her hand to reach out and touch his shoulder.

'I forgot to say that I love you. It changes everything.' She waited for him to sweep her into his arms and lower his mouth. He had to understand. 'I made a mistake. I should never have bargained with you. I should have done as you asked and gone back to Kaupang. But I wanted to be with you. Come back to me and we will begin again.'

'That is for the future, Thyre.' His hands put her away

from him. 'Love needs to be something more. Love is shown through deeds.'

'Will I see you again?'

A smile tugged at his features. 'If the gods will it. Offer your prayers if you wish.'

If the gods will it. Her stomach knotted. He did not believe in the gods' power. They were merely words to ease her mind. This was truly the end. She could feel it in her heart.

'Everyone thinks you are brave, Ivar. They all look up to you and believe in you. Are you brave enough to accept my love? Deeds, not words.' She took her mother's amulet from around her neck. 'You have this. It will keep you safe until we meet again.'

He raked his hand through his hair, but he made no move towards the amulet. She thrust it out again and their fingers touched briefly. He held the small figure in the palm of his hand. 'I will treasure it.'

'You are not giving me a choice. You have never given me a choice. It has always been about you. What about me? When are you going to stop running away and start living? There is more to life than cheating death.'

'What about you?' His face hardened and he plucked her restraining hand from his arm. 'Did you ever give me a choice? Have you ever thought about me as a man? Or am I only a warrior?'

'Yes,' Thyre whispered. 'I know you are a man as well as a warrior.'

'Then allow me to do a man's job.'

Chapter Sixteen

Thyre stood on the moonlit path. One way led towards the steading and safety and the other towards Ranhiem. Suddenly, in the distance she saw flickering beacons. Someone knew of the Viken, she realised, her heart plummeting. Ivar was about to sail into a trap. He would be killed along with everyone else in the *felag*. 'We turn down here.'

'You are going the wrong way,' Ragnfast protested. 'You want to go this way.'

'Ivar is sailing into a trap, Ragnfast. We have to do something to help him.'

'Why do you want to go to Ranhiem? To fight the king and regain your mother's honour?' Ragnfast asked. 'That is a pathway to destruction.'

'To make sure the people know the truth—the Viken have no quarrel with the Ranriken people. My uncle needs to hear the words from my throat. I know what Kaupang is like. I have seen that we can work together.' Thyre held up her hand as her heart whispered the true reason—she had to go to Ivar. She wanted to be beside him, no matter what happened. 'It may be that I am wrong and the king has nothing to do with the destruction that has happened over the past few years, but if he does, he must pay. I will not have my husband trapped.'

'Stop deceiving yourself. You are doing this because you want to save your Viken. Both of you are seeking to keep the other safe, but you never listen to each other. Your mother had to learn to listen to her heart.'

Thyre put her hand to her head, hating that she had been that transparent. 'Does it show that much? I fear King Mysing will welcome Ivar with open arms before putting a knife in his back. And I refuse to let that happen. Generation after generation will hate each other and all because my uncle was too weak to fight his battles openly. I know now that I must challenge my uncle to keep the peace.'

Dagmar came and stood beside Thyre. 'You are right, sister. We must go to Ranhiem and confront the king about what happened at the steading.'

'I have never sought a battle, but I have never run from one either,' Ragnfast said, sitting straighter on his horse. 'Your mother asked me to keep the peace. I failed you once. I will not now.'

'Will we arrive before the Viken?' Thyre asked.

'Our horses are strong. And this part of the journey goes far more quickly by land then by sea.'

Thyre breathed easier. She would find a way to settle this with her uncle, once and for all. Ivar needed to know the treachery her uncle had planned. 'Then our family goes into battle together.'

The grey light did little to enhance the ramshackle collection of huts and houses as Thyre turned her horse into the main street. There was no reason why it should not be every bit as prosperous as Kaupang, except that the king had chosen piracy rather than trade and hard work.

A seagull cried and she glanced down the muddy track towards the harbour. None of the ships in the harbour were Viken. Thyre gritted her teeth. Ragnfast spoke the truth. They had arrived before the Viken.

How would Ivar arrive? Did he suspect a trap?

King Mysing and his court had to understand the sequence of events. Once the Ranriken Storting realised about Sigmund's cowardice, she had little doubt that they would vote for Ragnfast's protection and to continue the *frithe* with the Viken. Ivar would meet with peace instead of war.

'There is the king!' Dagmar's voice rose with high-pitched excitement as she clutched Thyre's arm. 'King Mysing comes to greet us. Maybe he has decided that he was wrong and does want his nieces.'

'That remains to be seen. We must be cautious. Our uncle is the only man who could have ordered the attack.' Thyre looped her hair behind her ear with a trembling hand. This was far worse than when she had confronted King Thorkell. Then it had only been her future. Now it was Ivar's and indeed two nations' future that she bargained for. 'You have not seen the destruction he caused.'

She had not really noticed the people lining the route as they rode into Ranhiem and up to the king's hall. But they were there, waving banners, welcoming them. Had she been wrong? Had Sigmund's men acted on their own? Did King Mysing remain a friend to Ragnfast?

Ragnfast appeared quiet and subdued. His pallor was slightly green and he complained once or twice of pain in his left arm, but he refused to stop or to allow Thyre to do anything for him. Thyre gave him a nervous glance before she concentrated on the scene in front of the king's hall.

'Ah, Ragnfast, you have arrived before the Viken.' A tall man came out of the king's hall. His features resembled Dagmar's. Thyre froze. Her uncle. He stopped to brush a speck of dust from his cloak and his gaze, cold like a snake's, touched hers. His thin lips smiled. 'How convenient. The jaarl Sigmund is dead and you sent my niece to Viken to sue for peace, Ragnfast the not-so-Steadfast. Is this how you repay my generosity in allowing my sister Sainsfrida to live—by becoming an ally to the Viken king?'

'You lie,' Thyre cried out. 'You are the one who has ordered cowardly attacks while you sit here in your hall. No one else would have dared!'

'Who is this woman?'

'Thyre, Sainsfrida's daughter.' Ragnfast bowed low. 'Your niece. As you can see, she is not at the Viken court.'

'She is the elder? The Viken king's spawn? Has she returned because he would not have such an abomination in his court?'

'My *father* welcomed me. He has a great affection for all his children. He would have me live as a princess in his court,' Thyre said.

'Did he send you here? Maybe he thinks all will rise up when they see you. A new queen. The Ranriken need a strong king, not a weak woman.'

'There we agree, uncle. The Ranriken people deserve a strong and honourable man to lead them.'

'What are you saying?' Her uncle paused, and his eyes grew crafty. 'Are you saying that I am a coward?'

'I was on board ship when Sigmundson attacked a trading vessel. He hid until all danger had passed.' Thyre put a hand on her hip. 'A trick I believe he learnt from you, Uncle. He would never have dared to attack Viken ships without your expressed order. You and you alone broke the treaty.'

King Mysing paled. 'And you, niece, are too much like your mother. Your tongue is far too bold for my liking. What I should have done on the day of your birth, I will not hesitate to do now. The Ranriken royal blood will cease to carry the taint of the Viken king.'

'Do we make the sacrifices to the gods or do we simply depart for Ranhiem?' Erik the Black's voice brought Ivar back to the darkened bay.

Ivar had stood watching Thyre leave until her figure was no more than a memory. His hand tightened around the amulet. 'Yes. Make the sacrifices.'

'I thought you did not believe in them.'

'In times like these, men need all the help they can get. They need to believe someone else is willing to fight for them.'

'Where do you think she has gone?'

'To Ranhiem. I know my wife. She will do as she wants and not as I ask, but we will get there before her.' Ivar shook his head as the amulet dug into his palm. 'I am getting worse than Astrid for getting premonitions. I keep thinking if she goes there then she will meet her doom. Dreams have never plagued me before. But lately my dreams have been troubled.'

'Did you tell her your fears? Or did you simply tell her what to do?'

'All I wanted to do was to protect her.' Ivar slipped the amulet over his head, so it lay next to his heart. 'I have been afraid that she would feel it her duty to challenge for the crown. I want her for my wife, Erik.'

'You can't protect her if you are not with her, Ivar. Neither can you keep her from her destiny.'

'When I need your advice, Erik, I will ask for it.'

'Then can you tell me how we go into Ranhiem— shields up or hanging from the side?'

'We go to rescue a member of the *felag*.' Ivar lifted his shield. 'What scares me, Erik, is that I want to believe in the impossible. I want to believe that she loves me.'

'Bind me? Bind a woman?' Thyre stared at her uncle King Mysing. 'Why do you fear a mere woman, Uncle?'

There was no way her stepfather could fight him. And the rest of the jaarls appeared spineless or simply unwilling to risk his wrath. Ivar and the rest of the Vikens should be here. She wished that her life had not come down to this. It would have been far easier if she had died with her mother. But she hadn't and she refused to be intimidated by King Mysing. She knew what a real warrior could do.

'Do what you like to me, but leave my stepdaughter alone. She is innocent,' Ragnfast said. 'I welcomed the Viken and offered them hospitality. I obeyed your sister's wishes and the *frithe*.'

'Not so innocent. Viken blood runs in her veins. She is a member of the Viken court.'

'It only runs because my wife, your sister, was sent as a hostage. A woman, a beautiful woman, sent to the court of a virile young king. What did you expect when you told your father to send her?' Ragnfast thundered back.

'Are you questioning my judgement? My sister should have died rather than being dishonoured. Once you spoke against me the Storting believed you over me.' King Mysing jabbed at Ragnfast with his forefinger. 'But this time, this time, I will punish you for consorting with the Viken.'

Ragnfast made another choking noise. His complexion

was more of a sickly yellow than mottled red. She watched in horror as Ragnfast's throat worked, but no sound came out.

'Does anyone wish to challenge my right to punish this jaarl?'

Thyre glanced over at Ragnfast, who half-put his hand out in a pitying gesture. They were dead, all of them. They should have gone back to the steading and safety. She could not expect Ivar to arrive in time. But she knew that she would do what he would have done.

'Yes,' she said. 'I will challenge you, Uncle. You are wrong about the Viken and wrong about their intentions. Ragnfast did nothing except extend hospitality, a custom that the gods bless. Ranriken are not pirates, and yet that is what you have turned them into. It is why the gods have turned their backs on this town and this kingdom. I challenge you.'

Nobody said anything. Nobody responded. Thyre's shoulders sagged. She had failed before she had even begun. King Mysing whispered something to one of his men, but he seemed content to ignore the challenge.

Thyre tried again. 'In the name of my mother whom you banished and all whom you have murdered, I challenge you! By the royal blood that runs in my veins, I challenge you for the right to wear the crown. I will regain the Ranriken honour that you have lost.'

'A woman!' King Mysing laughed and the remainder of the company echoed the laughter. A crowd began to gather at the edges of the square, coming in ones and twos, but coming to see what was happening amongst the nobles. 'A woman challenge me? A woman rule? Women cannot do any such thing.'

'I killed Sigmund Sigmundson when he threatened me. If I can fight a jaarl, I can fight you.' Thyre squared her shoulders and tried to be as positive as Ivar had been with Sigmund. If King Mysing were shown to be a coward, the crowd might turn against him and his followers.

'And how will you fight me?' He gave another laugh and his eyes glittered with the coldness of a snake. 'Shall we use weaving shuttles? Or maybe spindles? What shall we fight with?'

'Swords,' Thyre replied quickly. Somewhere she would find the strength. Her arm muscles were strong from rowing. She could fight. It was the only way of preventing the tragedy she saw unfolding. She drew another breath and wished Ivar was there. 'The challenge is serious, Uncle. Surely you are not afraid of a mere woman? Or do you always avoid challenges? Sigmund did as well. Perhaps he learnt from you? Trading vessels make for easy prey, but they do not bring lasting prosperity to this country. I have been to Kaupang and I have seen what trade can do. We are losing because of you and your ways, not because of Viken aggression. Think on that and answer my challenge.'

'Thyre, have you lost all your senses? You will be killed,' Dagmar's hoarse whisper rang out. 'The king will not take the insult lightly.'

The growing crowd murmured behind King Mysing, but it was impossible to tell whose side they were on.

Thyre forced her head to stay erect. She was dead. She had accepted that, but she would have died anyway. And if she was going to die, she was going to go defiantly. She would die free.

'You have not answered my challenge, King Mysing. Are you afraid?'

'I do not fight women, even one as bold as you, Niece. No warrior with any honour would. There is no sport in it. Do you have a champion?' A queer smile played on his lips as Thyre slowly shook her head. 'I thought not. They have all deserted you. Those Viken you put your faith in. Untrustworthy. They have probably all sailed for home.'

'Thyre does have a champion—me.' Ivar's voice boomed out. 'I will fight you, Mysing, for the crown. It should adorn a more honest head.'

'You have tricked me, Niece.' King Mysing shook his head. 'I will not be tricked into fighting.'

'I have challenged you, Mysing.' Ivar drew his sword and moved to the centre of the yard. 'Answer my challenge.'

'And what is the challenge of a Viken jaarl who comes without an army?'

Thyre glanced at the hostile faces of the crowd. Surely they were not so lacking in honour that they would follow King Mysing now. He had refused a direct challenge. Would he now order his guards to kill Ivar? And she was powerless to do anything but to stand and watch.

'What is it that you want, Mysing? An army bringing death and destruction on us all?' Ragnfast thundered. 'When did you become such a craven coward?'

'You said something, Ragnfast?'

'Ivar,' Thyre breathed. 'He has given you an opening. Ragnfast is telling the Storting to stand with you.'

Ivar nodded.

'Fight, Mysing, or for ever let it be proclaimed you are a coward. I challenge you in the name of Ragnfast the Steadfast and his family. I come to avenge your cowardly attack on his lands.'

'Very well, Viken, if you want a fight, you shall have one. I have fought many times and I have never lost. No man calls me a coward and lives,' Mysing proclaimed as he drew his shining sword.

Ivar advanced forwards and his sword hissed from its sheath. Before Thyre could breathe, steel met steel.

Immediately it was apparent that her uncle had not lied. He was a highly skilled swordsman. And the two opponents were evenly matched.

The clang of the swords rang in Thyre's ear as the men circled. Each probed for the other's weakness. Ivar lunged forwards, missed, leaving his body open.

Her uncle instantly reacted, realising his opportunity. The back of his sword sent Ivar sprawling to the ground.

Thyre groaned, but could not look away. Silently she implored him to stand up.

Mysing put his foot on Ivar's chest and pointed the sword at Ivar's throat. 'You see, Viken. I am the victor. Know that your woman will soon join you in Hel's embrace.'

He lifted his sword slightly, preparing for the final blow.

Ivar thrust his sword upwards and the Ranriken king's expression changed.

'My wife will live free.' He withdrew his sword and thrust again. This time King Mysing fell forwards, impaled on the sword.

'You have bested me, Viken,' Mysing said with a gurgle before he lay still.

'The king is dead in an honourable fight. Ranriken honour demands we support the new king.' Ragnfast staggered a few steps and fell down, clutching his heart. Thyre rushed to him, but she could find no breath of life. Silently she cursed. She should have seen how ill he was, and what he had tried to do. She had been so wrapped up in her own world that she had failed to notice. She should have gone to the steading, instead of forcing him here. Tears streamed down her face. For Ragnfast. For this situation. She raised him up a little.

The guards holding Dagmar let her go and she stumbled over to Thyre.

'He suspected he was dying,' Dagmar said, tears streaming down her face. 'But I insisted Thyre needed rescuing. Far believed he had caused the situation through his greed.'

'You will be protected, Dagmar. I promise.' Thyre held out her hand and Dagmar curled her fingers around it.

'Thyre.' Ivar's voice resounded throughout the court yard. 'I thought we agreed that you would go to the steading, but I see you have disobeyed me once again.'

'No, Ivar, you are wrong. I thought to save you.' Thyre stood up and faced her husband. 'My place was here, waiting to warn you. We discovered that King Mysing planned to ambush you. I could not let you die. It was the only thing I could think of.'

'You challenged the king to save me?' he asked in amazement.

'I would give my life for you. It is the only reason I am here. My challenge was to save you, not to gain the crown. You must believe that, Ivar.'

'Ah, yes, the crown.' Very deliberately Ivar walked over to Mysing's prone body and plucked the circlet from his head.

'You will need your crown, Thyre,' he said, placing it on her head as the crowd began to cheer. 'It belongs to you by right. I was your champion. I won this crown for you. But it is *your* destiny. The Ranriken people need a strong ruler. Accept it.'

'I never asked for it,' she said, backing away. 'My one desire is to be a good wife.'

'This country must have a ruler. Who better than you?'

'You have won the crown, not I,' Thyre said. 'This

country needs a strong and wise ruler. You have proved your worth, Ivar.'

The crowd murmured its agreement. Thyre kept her gaze focused on the faces in the crowd, honest hardworking faces, people who deserved a better king than they had had. It had to come from him. He had to want to stay. But he simply looked at her. 'I am a Viken jaarl, Thyre. Take the crown.'

'You are my heart's desire, and I want nothing more than to be your wife,' she said, ignoring the intake of breath and the hum of the crowd. 'My heart belongs to you. We will go where you say.'

He did not move, but stood rigid, the circlet clasped lightly in his hands. 'If that is what you truly want…then who am I to disagree? But you will wear this crown, Thyre, if it is the last thing you ever do.'

Thyre resisted the temptation to step into his outstretched arms. 'Will you rule with me? A queen must have a consort.'

'I love you, Thyre, and I intend to tell you those words every day of our life together. And if it means being king, then I will accept it as a burden I must carry. But do you love me enough to share your life with me? All of it?'

'Yes.' Thyre forgot to breathe. He had said the words she thought impossible. She took the circlet from his hands. 'You will need this. A king needs a crown. We will rule together. Equal.'

'Together. I would not have it any other way.' He bent his head and brushed her lips as the crowd cheered their new king and queen.

Epilogue

~~~~~~~~~~

One year later

'I believe the name-giving ceremony went well,' Thyre said, taking off her circlet and setting it on top of the iron-bound trunk. She shook out her hair so it flowed loose over her shoulders, the way Ivar preferred it.

Immediately Beygul jumped down from her perch on the bed and wound her body about Thyre's legs, purring, before going off to welcome Ivar back into the chamber. Ivar obligingly bent down and scratched the cat under her chin.

Their chamber in the king's hall was a safe haven away from the noise and bustle of ruling the kingdom. And the crowds had been especially numerous today as everyone had wanted to see the name-giving ceremony of their future king.

'Young Ragnfast has loud enough lungs. He nearly deafened the soothsayers.' Ivar took their newborn son from the nurse, dismissed her and laid him down in the cradle. The tiny baby gave a contented sigh, but otherwise kept his eyes closed. The soft sound of his snores filled the chamber. 'And he tried to grab the sword from the sooth-sayer's hands. He will be a great warrior.'

Thyre looked at her baby's long lashes and the way his bottom lip moved. Ragnfast had been Ivar's suggestion for the name rather than his own father's, and she thoroughly approved. It seemed right to honour her stepfather in this way. Over the past year, in their dealings with the Ranriken Storting, she had learnt about the respect he had com-manded, respect she had not truly appreciated before. 'I begin to understand why Astrid is always worried about Asger. Let Ragnfast be a baby. It is far too soon to think about the time when he will become a warrior and fight.'

'He is my son and one day he will rule.' Ivar came over and put his arms about her waist. 'But I am certain he takes after you—ready to argue and inclined to want his own way.'

'I am not that bad.' Thyre leant her head back against his chest. 'I let you have your way last night…eventually.'

'Eventually, we found a solution that suits us both.' Ivar nuzzled her neck and his arms encircled her waist, re-minding her exactly how good the solution could be. 'I would not have it any other way.'

'We make a good team.' Thyre put her hands over his, holding them against her waist. 'It was wonderful that Dagmar arrived in time for the name-giving ceremony. Your name choice meant a lot to her.'

'It was good that Thrand came as well. He is full of plans for the timber from your stepfather's old estate.'

'But I worry about Dagmar and him. Things seem to be unsettled between them. Dagmar thinks—'

'He came here because he does not want to risk losing her for a moment. He worships her, even if she does not see it.' Ivar pulled her closer as he laid his circlet next hers. 'I know how stubborn these Ranriken women can be, refusing to see what is before their eyes. Let them settle it in their own way.'

'You are the master of my heart, my love. How could I refuse you anything?' Thyre touched his cheek.

Ivar put his finger against her lips. 'No, I am the partner of your heart. Surely you know the difference by now.'

Thyre linked her arm with his. She knew he was right and she had found everything she could desire in a man with her Viken jaarl. 'Yes, I do.'

They stood together, hands intertwined, listening to the gentle sounds of their baby, and Thyre knew that sometimes words or actions were not needed. It was being with each other and listening to their hearts beating as one that mattered most.

Author's Note

The tale of how Richard I of Normandy met and wooed his wife Gunnor in the early eleventh century as related in *Queen Emma and the Vikings* by Harriet O'Brien helped to inspire this story. Basically, in order to save her sister Sainsfrida's virtue, Gunnor took her place in Richard's bed when he visited the family home on a hunting expedition. Although the incidents in my story happen during the late eighth century rather than during the eleventh, there is plenty of evidence from the sagas that providing physical comfort to visiting males of a higher status was a widespread practice during the Viking age. For example, the saga of Bosi and Herraud as well as the saga of King Gautrek feature this sort of sleeping arrangement.

The sunstone that Ivar used to navigate was a piece of iolite. It has the nickname of the Viking's compass and is a natural polarising filter.

The name Thyre is the modern Danish equivalent of Thorvi, but I happen to prefer the spelling. Also once again I have used the modern 'Storting' to describe the assembly rather than the more probable Thing or Ting. I used moose as the American moose is the same species (*alces alces*) as the Scandinavian Elk and in North America elk refers to *cervus canadensis*. Hopefully the reader will understand and forgive the anachronisms.

Books I found useful include:

Jesch, Judith, *Women in the Viking Age* (1991, The Boydell Press, Woodbridge Suffolk)

Larrington, Carolyne (trans.), *The Poetic Edda* (1996, Oxford University Press, Oxford)

O'Brien, Harriet, *Queen Emma and the Vikings—The Woman Who Shaped the Events of 1066* (2005, Bloomsbury, London)

Magnusson, Magnus KBE, *The Vikings* (2003, Tempus Publishing Stroud, Gloucestershire)

Palsson Hermann and Paul Edwards (trans.), *Seven Viking Romances* (1985, Penguin Books, London)

Rosedahl, Else, *The Vikings* revised edition, translated by Susan Margeson and Kirsten Williams (1998, Penguin Books, London)

Sturluson, Sorri, *The Prose Edda*, translated by Jesse L. Byock (2005, Penguin Classics, London)

Woods, Michael, *In Search of the Dark Ages* second edition (2005, BBC Books, London)

'THIS EVENING I'm flying to New York for two weeks,' Jasim imparted with a casualness that made her heart sink like a stone. 'That's why I had you brought here. I own this apartment and you'll be comfortable here while I'm abroad.'

'I can afford my own accommodation although I may not need it for long. I'll have another job by the time you get back—'

Jasim released a slightly harsh laugh. 'There's no need for you to look for another position. How would I ever see you? Don't you understand what I'm offering you?'

Elinor stood very still. 'No, I must be incredibly thick because I haven't quite worked out yet what you're offering me.…'

His charismatic smile slashed his lean dark visage. 'Naturally, I want to take care of you.…'

HPEX0110A

'No, thanks.' Elinor forced a smile and mentally willed him not to demean her with some sordid proposition. 'The only man who will ever take *care* of me with my agreement will be my husband. I'm willing to wait for you to come back but I'm not willing to be kept by you. I'm a very independent woman and what I give, I give freely.'

Jasim frowned. 'You make it all sound so serious.'

'What happened between us last night left pure chaos in its wake. Right now, I don't know whether I'm on my head or my heels. I'll stay for a while because I have nowhere else to go in the short term. So maybe it's good that you'll be away for a while.'

Jasim pulled out his wallet to extract a card. 'My private number,' he told her, presenting her with it as though it was a precious gift, which indeed it was. Many women would have done just about anything to gain access to that direct hotline to him, but his staff guarded his privacy with scrupulous care.

Before he could close the wallet, his blood ran cold in his veins. How could he have made such a serious oversight? What if he had got her pregnant? He knew that an unplanned pregnancy would engulf his life like an avalanche, crush his freedom and suffocate him. He barely stilled a shudder at the threat of such an outcome and thought how ironic it was that what his older brother had longed and prayed for to secure the line to the throne should strike Jasim as an absolute disaster....

* * *

What will proud Prince Jasim do if Elinor is expecting his royal baby? Perhaps an arranged marriage is the only solution! But will Elinor agree? Find out in DESERT PRINCE, BRIDE OF INNOCENCE by Lynne Graham [#2884], available from Harlequin Presents® in January 2010.

New Year, New Man!

*For the perfect New Year's punch,
blend the following:*

• *One woman determined to find her inner vixen*
• *A notorious—and notoriously hot!—playboy*
• *A provocative New Year's Eve bash*
• *An impulsive kiss that leads to a night of
explosive passion!*

When the clock hits midnight Claire Daniels
kisses the guy standing closest to her, but
the kiss doesn't end after the bells stop ringing....

Look for

Moonstruck

by *USA TODAY* bestselling author

JULIE KENNER

Available January

---

red-hot reads

www.eHarlequin.com

HB79518

REQUEST YOUR FREE BOOKS!

Harlequin® Historical
Historical Romantic Adventure!

2 FREE NOVELS PLUS 2 **FREE GIFTS!**

YES! Please send me 2 FREE Harlequin® Historical novels and my 2 FREE gifts (gifts are worth about $10). After receiving them, if I don't wish to receive any more books, I can return the shipping statement marked "cancel." If I don't cancel, I will receive 6 brand-new novels every month and be billed just $4.94 per book in the U.S. or $5.49 per book in Canada. That's a savings of 20% off the cover price! It's quite a bargain! Shipping and handling is just 50¢ per book.* I understand that accepting the 2 free books and gifts places me under no obligation to buy anything. I can always return a shipment and cancel at any time. Even if I never buy another book, the two free books and gifts are mine to keep forever.

246 HDN EYS3 349 HDN EYTF

Name _____ (PLEASE PRINT) _____

Address _____ Apt. # _____

City _____ State/Prov. _____ Zip/Postal Code _____

Signature (if under 18, a parent or guardian must sign) _____

Mail to the **Harlequin Reader Service:**
IN U.S.A.: P.O. Box 1867, Buffalo, NY 14240-1867
IN CANADA: P.O. Box 609, Fort Erie, Ontario L2A 5X3

Not valid to current subscribers of Harlequin Historical books.

Want to try two free books from another line?
Call 1-800-873-8635 or visit www.morefreebooks.com.

* Terms and prices subject to change without notice. Prices do not include applicable taxes. Sales tax applicable in N.Y. Canadian residents will be charged applicable provincial taxes and GST. Offer not valid in Quebec. This offer is limited to one order per household. All orders subject to approval. Credit or debit balances in a customer's account(s) may be offset by any other outstanding balance owed by or to the customer. Please allow 4 to 6 weeks for delivery. Offer available while quantities last.

Your Privacy: Harlequin Books is committed to protecting your privacy. Our Privacy Policy is available online at www.eHarlequin.com or upon request from the Reader Service. From time to time we make our lists of customers available to reputable third parties who may have a product or service of interest to you. If you would prefer we not share your name and address, please check here. ☐

HH09R